DEVIL'S DEMOCRACY

DEVIL'S DEMOCRACY

An Ulrik Torp Thriller

Niels Krause-Kjær

Translated from Danish
by David Young

Podium

DEVIL'S DEMOCRACY

CHAPTER 1

No one who knew Otto Brathenberg would have considered him to be the sentimental type.

Nor did he have any illusions about himself. Sentimentality was a weakness, a luxury one could only afford oneself in the most private moments, and even then, one shouldn't play around with such folly. He was heavy with grief when his golden retriever, Schmidt—named after the 1970s German Chancellor Helmut Schmidt—had to be put down, long overdue. To his great annoyance, he was caught with watery eyes by the press photographers when he had to resign from his position as Minister of Justice many years ago.

That was all.

Otto Brathenberg had lived a binary life in rationality. Power was there to be used, and if he didn't use it, others would.

Despite all this, he lay in his bed this Sunday afternoon with a view of the flat screen on the wall, knowing that his little sentimental spot would soon be growing—not much, not out of control, but just enough so that it would tickle just a little in his stomach. It always happened when there was an international football match at Parken and 40,000 souls ungracefully united the force of their throats with the national anthem.

Lise was on a long weekend in Jutland with her women's network group. This year's theme was sustainability, and it probably made a lot of sense. Otto had assured her that, despite a little fever and a sore throat, he could easily be alone in the Hellerup villa until Monday morning. The minor stroke of the winter was several months back, and he just needed lots of rest—and for goodness' sake, he wasn't even eighty yet. A private care service would come by this weekend with food, clean the house, and make sure he got the proper dosage from his arsenal of pills.

Off you go! He had actually been looking forward to being alone for a while.

The players came on the pitch.

Otto turned up the sound, which was already at a high volume. He wanted to capture the full atmosphere. In the kitchen at the other end of the villa, the woman from the care service was bustling about. Actually, it should be a social services task, he had argued to himself. But the welfare state he had fought for, and with, as a politician most of his long life was getting rather constipated. There were too many old people, too many expectations, and, not least, too many wealthy people, including himself, who weren't going to be satisfied with a middle-of-the-road service. Hence the private service company—the food was excellent, the cleaning top-notch, and the smiles broad. Today, it was a youngish, dark-haired woman he hadn't met before. Indeterminately Eastern European like most of the others, and just as sincerely service-minded as the woman who usually came. What had happened to the Danes?

The national anthem began.

Otto turned it up a notch more.

"There is a lovely country,

Covered with broad beeches."

The camera glided past the Danish national team players, who with varying degrees of enthusiasm and ability either pretended to sing along or actually did. Far from all of them were born in Denmark, as he knew from the recent debate. You could also guess which ones when you ran your eyes over the team. UEFA, the Union of European Football Associations, was considering introducing new rules for how many non-national-born players there could be on a national team. Otto thought it was a stupid idea. The crucial factors should be their citizenship and their ability to play football. All eleven were red and white, no matter how brown they might also be.

"Our old Denmark shall survive
As long as the crown of the beech
Is reflected in the waves so blue,
In the waves so blue."
Finally.

He once again confused the two buttons on the elevation bed.

Red was down. Green was up. Up. Now he was sitting right.

The service woman came in with the evening's tray—beautifully prepared open sandwiches, a jug of cold water, a thermos of coffee, and the box of pills.

"Oh, football!" she exclaimed, placing the tray on the trolley next to the mobile bed.

"Very important game."

Otto gave the irony exactly the right dosage so that he could confirm that it was an important match, but at the same time that it was only football. They smiled in agreement at each other.

"Have a nice day, Mr. Brathenberg. Don't forget your pills."

"You, too," he replied, nodding to her as she left the living room.

Alone at last. He put two red pills in his mouth, reached for the glass of water, and swallowed it all with a tilt of his head. Back to the match. Brathenberg felt a small jab in his chest; it was as if it was being squeezed a little.

Denmark had the honour of kicking off.

CHAPTER 2

A Volvo behind them gave a loud blast with its horn. Did he think they had stopped for fun? Ulrik Torp waved despondently with his left arm, signalling to those behind that they should drive past him, while he again turned the key in the ignition. Absolutely nothing happened. Karen gave him a sidelong glance. It had been her idea that they should take advantage of spring, his better mood, and their unexpected upturn to buy an old car. It had also been her idea to have an extended weekend in Berlin in their son-in-law's investment flat, before Torp had to start his new life in earnest as a freelance journalist with an office and fairly fixed working hours. *It's been so long since we've been anywhere,* she had reasoned. He turned the key in the ignition again with the same result.

The Volvo now swung out around them. The idiot jammed his hand on the horn again and stared angrily while demonstratively revving up. The other cars in the queue slowly followed suit, so that suddenly, they were the last car on the deck. Two of the shipping line's people came running over. In a few minutes, the ferry was to be filled with cars that were booked on the return trip to Rostock—there was absolutely no time for this. Ulrik rolled down the window.

"It's an old car. If you can give us a little push, it'll start."

"*Weg. Sie müssen weg gehen, schnell,*" commanded one of them.

What the hell was "push" in German?

"Künnen du nur ein bisschen . . . pushen? Push, push," he tried, thinking his arm movements were supporting his German instructions.

Karen stuck her head over towards them from the passenger seat.

"Können Sie dem Auto einen kleinen Schubs geben, bitte?" she said in friendly school German.

They nodded. Ulrik released the handbrake, put it in second gear, pushed the clutch on the seventeen-year-old Polo to the floor, and let the three men push them less than ten metres; clutch up, a small jerk, and the engine started straightaway. He trod on the clutch, gave it some gas so that it didn't stall, put it in first gear, and stuttered out of the ferry. Karen tried to wave a thank-you through the rear window, but the three men had already moved on. The cars going towards Rostock were about to board on the other side of the ferry.

Their few days in Berlin had actually been lovely. Spring arrived a little earlier in the German capital; the trees had just blossomed, and they had sat in several pavement cafés and only frozen a little under heat-lamps with their *weissbiers*. In Denmark, there was rain and wind as usual.

The flat was newly built, functional, and just as tasteless as its owner, thought Ulrik. Their son-in-law had given them to understand that he intended to sell it again with the prospect of a quick profit. Ulrik had argued that they could find some cheap accommodations themselves, as he didn't want to be in his debt, but Karen had insisted for the sake of family peace. It was already going to be an expensive long weekend, so Torp had quickly conceded. Some objections should be taken seriously, not literally.

They had agreed over a *Flammkuchen mit Speck und Käse* down by the River Spree that it had been a crappy winter in all respects. The threats of libel and his subsequent retreat and humiliation—all that now lay behind them, reasoned Karen. Now that she was going full time and he had established a base for himself with his obituaries and a freelancer office with colleagues. Ulrik didn't think he had depressive tendencies anymore, even though it might look like that to outsiders. The doctor's happy pills and the fourteen winter days spent on the west coast had set something in motion.

It was only after hard work from Karen that he had been able to get away in the first place.

"He's been a member for more than thirty years now and never received anything but your fucking magazine," he had heard her arguing on the phone.

To their surprise, the Danish Union of Journalists had got back to them the very next day. The *Daily News* had private health insurance and wanted to help. Torp could go on a fourteen-day therapy course in West Jutland starting as early as Monday. Mindfulness-Based Stress Reduction, MBSR, with certified coach Dion Hansen, the association's employee proudly explained. It was expensive, but she didn't have to think about that.

The therapy in West Jutland had—despite Torp's scepticism—not been without effect. He especially looked forward to the morning walks on the beach, where they had to walk in pairs for an hour *while the morning light slowly spread*, as it said in the programme, even though it was the beginning of December and never really got bright. Torp tried to take the walk with Vivi whenever possible, which he usually could. She was easy to talk to and tried with partial success to explain to Torp how it was possible as a social educator in a kindergarten to go down with stress. One never felt the job had been complete and always had a sense of guilt. He also felt that he was gradually getting to know her ex-husband really well. She did most of the talking. That suited Torp just fine.

He didn't have the energy to tell her about the humiliating calls to several Members of Parliament about fraud in the recent parliamentary elections, about useless calls to the Prime Minister's Office, and about his "insulting" debate post with a detailed description of a European lodge of former top politicians and top officials who were trying to maintain a liberal world order by illegal means. It had all gone totally wrong when he had tried to involve the chairman of the board at the *Daily News*, former minister Otto Brathenberg. He denied being able to confirm anything. The editor-in-chief at the *Daily News* was able to confirm that Ulrik

Torp, after several years outside the job market, had been in a munici-pally sponsored work-activation programme at the newspaper for a short period in the autumn and that, to be honest, it was a rather sad story and it was best to let sleeping dogs lie, not least for Torp's sake. In the end, the *Daily News*'s lawyer had to inform Torp and the community that there were limits to what both the newspaper and its board could accept in terms of lies and slander, even though for compassionate reasons they were willing to stretch things further than required.

The few times Vivi politely asked Torp, he simply explained that *something had happened* that he didn't have the energy to get into right now.

She accepted that without a hint of criticism.

"What about you when we're done here?"

Vivi hesitated. They had to speak extra loudly to be heard over the waves. "I'm on indefinite sick leave. Even if I got married to Dion Hansen, I don't actually think I would ever come back."

They had walked farther along the beach.

"And you?"

"My New Year's resolution will be to find a freelancer office in the city, turn up for work whether there is something to do or not, and then finish with communications and stick to journalism."

Torp hadn't thought the sentence out to the end when he had begun it, but it sounded right when it was finished. That was how it was going to be.

"You don't belong here at all, Ulrik," said Vivi, almost having to shout it.

"I did at one point."

She couldn't hear what he said, just laughed, shook her head, took his arm, and gave it a friendly squeeze. Maybe it would have happened anyway without the North Sea, Dion, and Vivi, but slowly—after com-ing home—he had lifted himself up and forced himself to get out of the flat when Karen was at school. He would go for walks, look people in the eye again, read the news on the Web, have an opinion on Prime Minister Palle Enevoldsen, go to a debate event at the Danish Union of Journalists, greet old colleagues, and ignore the talk in the corners. Slowly, he had crawled out of the cocoon and no longer wanted to feel he owed anyone an explanation, and anyone who wanted one could go to hell. The New Year's resolution to find a freelancer office had also been achieved. And that was how, in a fit of optimism, he gave free rein to Karen's hopes for the spring and found the Polo online. The argument of being able to get 3,000 kroner back in scrap value at any time made the investment, and thereby the risk, modest. Now they were on their way.

"A great match by the Danish national team. We've just taken a big step towards the finals." Ulrik turned off the car radio. Finally, they were the very last to arrive at passport control, which Sofie had warned them about when they had driven to Klampenborg to pick up the keys to the apartment. It had been several years since he and Karen had last been abroad, and it was hard to believe that the so fiercely discussed passport control in the once so border-free Europe was really literal. But it was, at least coming into Denmark. Ulrik glanced to the right at the old railway yards and the iconic Danish Rail tower from the affectionately remembered Olsen Gang film, *The Olsen Gang on the Track*; after fans raised enough money, the tower had been moved from destruction in Copenhagen to preservation in Gedser. Here, the construction of the new and—one came to gradually understand—permanent border control was in full swing. The buildings for customs officers, border guards, and police officers were progressing according to plan. Even though it was Sunday, work was continuing. The broad agreement on a "security package and expansion of temporary border controls" had an unspoken premise that everything was to be ready for the inauguration on Constitution Day, June 5th.

The Prime Minister, who had previously been the most ardent advocate for the Schengen Agreement and a border-free Europe, was now assuring everyone that he had, in fact, always been in favour of a border.

Ulrik stuck their passports out of the side window to the police officer, who flipped through them and looked at the owners to check if the pictures matched the people. Other than a Polish van, which was being ransacked by some police officers in the next lane, the entire stream of vehicles from the ferry had been checked through without any human traffickers, ordinary smugglers, or Muslim terrorists being detected, assuming that was the kind of people they were looking for. The Pole and Torp were their last chance under the temporary tent that was giving them all shelter from the downpour hammering against the tarpaulin above them.

The border uniform looked up.

"Switch off the engine."

The officer was fairly young, with forced authority in his voice. Why wasn't he on patrol in the Northwest district of Copenhagen?

"It won't be able to start again if I switch it off."

"Switch off the engine," repeated the officer, maintaining his gaze at Torp.

"The battery is dead. I can't restart it," Torp repeated back.

"Didn't you hear what I said? Switch it off!" ordered the policeman.

Torp switched it off. Maybe the car would be able to start again anyway.

"Your passport expired six months ago," said the officer, trying to hide the triumph in his voice.

He showed the page of the passport to Torp. It was right enough. The passport had expired in October. Torp was having a hard time taking it seriously. He was more concerned about whether the car would start when they were released.

"And what should we do about that?"

"Your passport has expired," the officer repeated. He was clearly expecting some form of remorse or submissiveness.

"And what do you want to do about it?" repeated Torp, now determined not to submit, but without any alternative plan.

It was Karen who rescued the situation for both of them.

"We really, truly apologise very much. It's my fault completely. It's been a long time since we've been out travelling. We'll order a new passport as soon as we get home," she explained, her head leaning over both the driver's seat and the culprit.

The officer was hesitating between the repentant wife and the fool.

"Okay. We'll let it go this time. But remember to get it renewed right away. This won't work next time."

"Thank you, Officer," said Karen before her husband could protest at his smarmy tone of voice.

Ulrik closed his eyes in equal parts distaste over the scene and in prayer that the car would start. He turned the key, and of course nothing happened, but it was actually a small triumph when the officer and one of his colleagues had to give the Polo the little push that sent them back to Copenhagen.

So, despite everything, the manpower mobilised at the border still had a function.

CHAPTER 3

"Well, now, what have we here—it's the plague from Lübeck. Good morning, Torp."

"Actually, it was Berlin."

Ulrik Torp forced himself to chuckle at Bertel's Monday welcome. He was happy with the shared office community—a former mansion flat with uneven floors in a side street to Strøget, the main Copenhagen shopping street—and had decided to accept the friendly but overly persistent teasing about his main journalistic occupation. It would stop at some point but was apparently going to continue into a fourth week.

Torp sat down at his desk in the corridor, which separated what had once been the fine living room from a smaller room that opened onto a bay window. For the last five office sharers to arrive, the corridor was also their office. It was narrow, and served not only as a passage for the proprietor of the bay window office, but was also the way to both the toilet and the kitchen.

"Anyone die over the weekend?"

Axel stood with the coffee-pot in his hand and asked in a friendly tone without a hint of sarcasm. He was the only one who didn't come with small snide remarks. He didn't even probe into the autumn fuss about Torp's expulsion from the *Daily News*. Torp would have to tell that tale himself if and when he felt like it.

"Three," said Torp, who had just read this weekend's harvest in an email on his computer.

He nodded his acceptance of the offer of coffee and pulled out his dirty cup from last week. He told them he hadn't seen the international match, but he agreed that it was nice that Denmark had won 3–1. Had it been an important match? He liked Axel Boas, who was a retired journalist but used the office to get away from home for a while with the fantasy that he was still working on a book project. The 2,500-kroner monthly cost of a desk in the co-working community, including internet, on-account heating and electricity, coffee arrangement, stair washing, and cleaning once a week, was his luxury as a pensioner. Others were welcome to go south or indulge their grandchildren.

Bertel placed a package from PostNord on Torp's desk. Like a child on Christmas Eve who couldn't get into the gift quickly enough, Torp ripped off the paper and opened one of the two boxes, even though he knew in advance what was in it:

Ulrik Torp—everything in journalism

The font was extra bold and in italics. Underneath was the address of the office, his mobile number, and his email address in normal text; no logo, no frills—just name, address, and phone number. No reverse-side text in English—which for that matter would also be the same, except for a pretentious +45 in front of the phone number. Who in all the world would need that? He had a choice of white or grey background when ordering, and had ticked grey. That would have to be enough. He opened the second box, which was slightly larger. Two hundred grey-and-white pens with *Ulrik Torp—everything in journalism* on the side and in the same font as the business cards. He didn't really know why the pens were supposed to be such a good idea, but he had been surprised at how cheap they were when ordering extra business cards.

Ulrik Torp, journalist, he said to himself. It sounded right. Obituaries were also journalism. He put the torn wrapping paper in the bin, put the boxes with now 199 pens and 1,000 business cards on the shelf opposite and turned to his computer, thinking about the obituaries:

Thorvald Vesterman, 82 years old, Kerteminde. Relative to be contacted: Hans Vesterman, son. Small obit for a weekly newspaper.

Bente Knudsen, 69 years old, Svendborg. Relative to be contacted: Michael Knudsen, spouse. Medium obit, Funen County News.

Karl Johan Kastrup-Davidsen, 9 years old, Dronninglund. Relative to be contacted: Peter Kastrup-Davidsen, uncle. Medium obit, North Jutland Times.

The last one would be a little awkward. Torp was grateful that one of the boy's uncles had taken on the task. It made things a little easier. The idea—conceived by Erik, an old classmate of Torp's from the Danish School of Journalism, now an involuntarily retired editor from the *Funen Times*—wasn't actually all that crazy. When people died and the undertaker presented the catalogue of services to the relatives, people rarely haggled over the price. It just wasn't done. *Should there be a bouquet of roses on the coffin when it is driven away?* Check. *Should it be the very small death notice or one with room for an extra line? It looks so nice . . . medium size, yes.* Check. It was like buying a summer cottage or choosing the serving size for popcorn and cola in the cinema. No one goes for the small one, very few the big one—the medium size suits the Danish mentality. It is just a matter of inventing a small service below and a large one above to sell what you want to sell, Erik explained when he brought Torp into his small corps of obituary writers.

The old editor had enticed Torp with the line that obituaries were a distinguished British tradition.

"They have the world's best obituaries, Torp, and when it comes to ordinary people, that shit can't be googled."

At first, he had said no, but Karen especially encouraged him to call back. It was a start. It was a base to build on. It was the reason for the office, the business cards, the weekend in Berlin, and the crumb of optimism. The fee of 300 kroner for a small obituary and 1,000 kroner for a medium was okay, without being showy. A large one, one of the sort Torp hadn't yet had, would have to be agreed upon from case to case. Erik promised to be able to get five or six medium obituaries a week, and he had delivered so far.

Torp pulled himself together and was about to call Hans Vesterman to offer his condolences for the loss of his father—it was hardly that big a loss, considering the size of the obituary—when the office community resounded with the cry of "buns and cakes all round."

Ghita Fussing came in with her arms raised high.

"I got it!"

"It" was a modest position in a social educators' union, where she only had to write some of the time.

"I will miss you all," she said with her mouth full of cinnamon swirl and without any fierce conviction in her voice, when they were all gathered around her desk a little later.

"You could just write some press releases instead of your fine French feelings. That kind of thing always has money in it," said Bertel, sounding more critical than intended.

Ghita Fussing rarely got annoyed by anything—and certainly not by Bertel, with whom she had a motherly indulgent relationship, despite his penchant for conversations that were predominantly about himself.

"Is it just because of the money?" Herman Krabbe—everyone called him Crabby—looked at the new employee in the social educators' union. She was going to start as early as next week.

Ghita Fussing swallowed the last piece of pastry and cleared her throat. "I'm sure you'll find it easier to earn a nice income. You're young and have contacts," she assured him.

If Ghita had been honest and known Crabby better, she would have continued with: *That's what you are forced to do after you were fired six months ago and are the main breadwinner for the villa in Vanløse and three children.* They all liked Crabby but also shared a concern about whether it was still possible to earn a reasonable salary by doing proper journalism as a freelancer.

"And it's also because of my age," continued Ghita in an attempt to comfort him. "When you're fifty-seven years old, you have to take what you can get."

She smiled apologetically at Torp. They were the same age. He smiled back awkwardly.

In a rare state of satisfaction, Ulrik took the last steps up the stairs to their two-room flat. Renting the flat they had originally bought as a parental purchase for Sofie, and which was now owned by their son-in-law, had begun as an emergency solution, but now Torp thought it symbolised a life on a low budget that made sense and hung together. He slid his tongue out into the right side of his mouth down by his jaw, to what still felt like a hole after the winter removal of a harmless lump. Torp noticed he was humming. Things were beginning to pick up; not hugely, not to great heights, but bit by bit in the right direction. One small and two medium obituaries. They had all picked up the phone right away. Maybe he could also find a second-hand battery for the car online. Then it would have been a good day in every way.

He had earned a day's wages. He had colleagues. Spring was about to set in properly—April was an underestimated month. Everything was getting brighter.

That was also why he was pleasantly surprised that Sofie and Jonathan were sitting in the living room when he entered the flat. It had been a long time since he had last seen them. They rarely came in from Klampenborg, and the invitations the other way weren't overwhelming, which suited both Torp and his son-in-law just fine. Karen had found ways to create mother-daughter time. It was a little harder with father-daughter time, Torp thought without being able to explain why, neither to Karen nor himself.

"Are you staying and eating with us?" exclaimed Torp expectantly.

Karen shook her head. "I've offered, but they have to go somewhere else."

Only now did he notice that neither of them looked happy as they sat there in the living room, each with their own coffee mug and raspberry slices from the baker. There was also one for him, he could see.

"Has something happened?" Ulrik suddenly had an icy feeling in his body. "Is it something with Jesper?"

Their son worked in Brussels, and they rarely heard from him. That was just how he was.

"No, no," exclaimed Karen. "Jesper's fine, or so we assume. No, it's not Jesper."

Torp looked around at all three of them. Jonathan cleared his throat.

"Yes, well . . . the thing is, Ulrik," said Jonathan, writhing in his chair, "the company isn't doing so well."

"Yes? Or . . . no, I mean."

Jonathan looked at his wife.

"Jonathan's been fired. Several months ago. He has had to sell your flat," said Sofie getting straight to the point. "Maybe we will also lose our house in Klampenborg."

"Several months?"

"He couldn't be bothered to tell the rest of us until now," said Sofie bitingly, staring down the former IT manager she was married to and had trusted. "Jonathan has spent the last two months leaving for work in the morning, to a job he no longer had, and has been returning home in the evening after being busy with absolutely nothing."

"What have you been doing?" Ulrik looked first at his daughter, then at his son-in-law.

"Networking, you know," he mumbled. "Trying to save the situation."

"But you get paid during the notice period, don't you?"

"No, he doesn't," came the sharp reply from Sofie. "As you can probably guess, Dad, it hasn't been a completely normal termination."

He could indeed. He looked at Karen, who was sitting bent over on the sofa beside Sofie.

"This flat has been taken over by some company or other. You have to be out in three weeks," said Sofie meekly. "I'm just so sorry, Dad." She started crying quietly.

The only thing Ulrik could think of was that it was good that she wasn't pregnant, and that this might mean that they would divorce. It had to be the happy pills. You never got completely up, but you were also never completely down.

CHAPTER 4

It wasn't until early Monday evening that Otto Brathenberg's death was announced.

His wife, Lise, had returned around noon from her networking weekend about sustainability in Jutland. The first thing she noticed as she unlocked the door to the villa was the television running at full volume inside the bedroom with an ancient American sitcom as the channel's cheap weekday filler. Her husband was lying in bed with a blanket over him, the elevation bed raised and his neck bent back. His mouth and his eyes were both exaggeratedly open—the old politician resembled a plausible version of *The Scream* by Edvard Munch.

The police and the ambulance arrived unusually quickly, but without sirens. There was no reason for that, Lise had assured the emergency services when she called them. Her husband was icy cold; rigor mortis had long since set in, and, as a politician's wife for fifty years, she knew instinctively that it was important to be in control of the story. Because it was, of course, a story that the country's former Minister of Justice and Foreign Secretary had died after a long life in the service of the nation.

No, she had been away all weekend and hadn't been in contact with her husband since she left on Friday. No, there was nothing unusual about that. They had been married for almost sixty years and both of them travelled a lot separately and had got out of the habit of feeling responsible for each other when they weren't at the same address. Yes, he had been ailing since his stroke—even more than he dared to admit. Yes, she had been worried, but not enough. Yes, they had entered into an agreement with a private service, which according to the plan had placed a carer in the villa both Saturday and Sunday; now she would have to find the number. No, she didn't need anyone to stay with her. She would like some peace in which to contact their children. The ambulance rolled away with her husband. The police followed suit—they had been given what they needed in what looked like a purely routine task. And suddenly, Lise Brathenberg was left standing alone in her living room looking around. There, in the corner, lay the blue V-neck cashmere sweater she had given him for Christmas—stretched over one of the armrests in a way he knew irritated her. She took out her mobile. First, she had to call their children. Then she had to contact the chairman of the Labour Party and leader of the opposition, Pernille Hjort. The party would have to take care of announcing his death.

The Labour Party's press service, on behalf of the party chairman, posted a message on their website and linked to it via postings on Twitter and Facebook soon after 7:00 p.m. By that time, rumours had already materialised as fact at Christiansborg—the Danish Parliament building known colloquially as Borgen—but weren't yet on social media.

Otto Brathenberg has died. It is with great sadness that I have been informed this afternoon that former Member of Parliament, Minister of Justice, and Foreign Secretary Otto Brathenberg has died in his home at the age of seventy-nine. Otto Brathenberg served the Labour Party and Denmark through a long and active life in politics, and we will miss him. My thoughts go to his wife, Professor Emeritus Lise Brathenberg, their two children, and the rest of the family. Further details regarding the funeral will follow at a later date.
Pernille Hjort

Torp was called up an hour later.

"Torp! It's Lindskov. Can you help an old friend?"

Torp immediately recognised the voice. The ageing society editor at the *Daily News* had miraculously survived all the austerity rounds, lay-offs, and structural changes at the newspaper. His method was simple—always be 100 per cent loyal to whoever happened to be the management, no dirty gossip in the corners, no demands for salary increases, always deliver on time, and finally, a working week far beyond the reasonable. That included staying on a Monday evening after 8:00. In addition, he wrote most of the lead stories. The editor-in-chief was neither a great writer nor did he have any special opinions.

"Have you seen that Brathenberg is dead?"

Torp had. It was out on all the news sites on the Net.

"What can I do for you?"

Torp suppressed his surprise at the call. Lindskov was clearly squirming.

"You know, all the cutbacks—I haven't had permanent employees attached to my editorial office for several years."

Torp knew that.

"I'm sitting with a lead story to be written and three pages to be edited and ready in an hour, and I only have one intern to draw on."

Torp had no idea what Lindskov was leading up to.

"I thought . . ." The society editor hesitated. "I was wondering if I could get you to write a quick obituary about Brathenberg?"

Lindskov clearly felt he had to fill the pause that followed his question.

"It's something you can bash out in half an hour with your eyes closed. Better than anyone else. Two hundred lines—I have a whole page."

He also sat on the newspaper's board. The society editor's arguments were stumbling over each other, making it all sound like an apology.

"Have you completely forgotten that I was dismissed six months ago?"

"Without a by-line, of course. Just to help an old friend. I can't pay you for it—it'll be noticed. But I can arrange twelve bottles of unusually good red wine. Torp, please. I need it in less than an hour. It's right up your street."

Lindskov was right about the last bit, thought Torp. He could write a portrait of Brathenberg pretty much without looking anything up. Should he also mention the private intelligence service the man had been a part of since his youth? Should he mention the pact he had made with former top politicians and top officials in several European countries, where they played at being freedom fighters and resistance fighters and made themselves lords and masters over life and death? A story that was never published because no one had had the guts and because Torp couldn't document it. Should he write the whole truth about a powerful gentleman and not just the slick version of a skilled and conscientious politician—a version that wasn't wrong, but not right either? Should he get personal and mention the warnings from the man's lawyers? Warnings that could only be perceived as a threat to Torp himself and his family—threats that, at Karen's earnest pleading, had made him back down, apologise, and go into winter hibernation on happy pills? Should he write the whole story or only half?

"Torp. Please. I'll have to defend this obituary at the editorial meeting tomorrow. Just write it free-hand and I'll correct it. Within the hour. Twelve bottles."

"This is for you, Lindskov. Not the twelve bottles," Torp heard himself say as he switched on the computer. Karen wasn't home; he might as well use the time for something.

With the death of Otto Brathenberg, one of the great politicians not only of the Labour Party but also of Denmark has passed away. The long-standing Minister of Justice and Foreign Secretary continued to the end to be an avid public debater and valued member of, among other things, the board of the Daily News. *Not many people could have foreseen this future when Brathenberg was born in a three-room flat in Vesterbro seventy-nine years ago as the fourth child of brewery worker Jens Peter Brathenberg and his wife . . .*

Torp wrote easily, quickly, and fluently. It wasn't at all difficult to be a hypocrite. Twenty-five minutes later he sent 200 lines to Lindskov—not even a comma needed to be corrected.

* * *

It happened less and less often, but on Tuesday morning, Torp bought a newspaper printed on paper. The *Daily News* cost thirty-nine kroner, the cinnamon swirl twenty-two. Torp was in doubt about which price was the most insane when he put his sixty-one kroner down, and the surly girl behind the counter in the bakery slid them into her hand, presumably miffed that he hadn't paid by card or MobilePay like everyone else. He searched in vain for a seat in the Metro, but the rain had made the morning rush hour even more chaotic. Both the newspaper and the pastry had become a little damp during the trip from the bakery to the station. At Nørreport, he stuffed both of them into the inside pocket of his too-thin jacket and ran the 400 metres to the office. He was drenched as he stepped into the office, said hello to Bertel, nodded to Ghita, Axel, and Crabby, and sat down at his desk in the corridor.

He yawned and felt the tiredness in his body. After he had finished his obituary of Brathenberg, Karen had returned home from some meetings at the school. They had sat for a long time talking about where they were going to live in three weeks' time. In a way, it was fine that they had been snatched out of Jonathan's claws. It was untenable having to rent from a son-in-law whom neither of them—and especially not Ulrik—could endure. But three weeks to find a new home in Copenhagen, when into the bargain you had no money, was a challenge, to use the language of modern management. In ordinary Danish, it was a massive problem. They had neither a solution nor a plan.

Torp's thoughts went to his morning shopping. The far-too-small inner pocket of his jacket had compressed the damp cinnamon swirl into a lump; he stuffed it into his mouth and rinsed it down with Axel's coffee. The *Daily News* wasn't entirely crisp enough to thumb through either, but he managed to get to the page with Brathenberg's obituary without destroying the newspaper.

Enevoldsen: "He was one of the greats," preached the headline. The obituary filled the entire page except for the column furthest right, which was devoted to comments from several political leaders, both current and former, with the Liberal Prime Minister, Palle Enevoldsen, as the most prominent. Lindskov had done a great job. Torp lingered a bit over the sentences he had written the evening before. There was of course no by-line on the obituary. A small *dn* at the end of the article showed that it was one of the *Daily News*'s anonymous heroes who had been sitting at the keyboard. Lindskov would probably be criticised, thought Torp, for not having put his own name on the obituary as the editor responsible, or for not having had one of the paper's heavyweight correspondents write it in advance. Torp quickly lost interest in his own article and flipped with a little difficulty through the damp pages to an article containing an interview with Kirsten Rolighed, the Liberals' political spokesperson. She used her angelic formulations to sharpen the tone not only in relation to the opposition but also in relation to her party chairman, the Prime Minister, and government policy. Torp noted that the article had been written by Simon Vestergaard, the talented intern he had worked with for a short period in the autumn. So, he had saved his skin at the *Daily News* after all.

"There's no timidity about her."

Axel poured more coffee for Torp and nodded down at the article and the large picture of Rolighed, an archive picture from the previous summer, where she was standing in the garden of her summer house in Hornbæk, in the process of hoisting Dannebrog, the Danish national flag.

Rolighed: "I fight for Denmark," the headline guaranteed. This explained the Dannebrog image from the archive. It was only possible to take such an idyllic summer photo at this latitude a few days each year.

"When she says she fights for Denmark, she must be of the opinion that some people don't. Otherwise, it makes no sense," remarked Axel, going out into the kitchen with the empty coffee-pot to brew more. It had become an unspoken rule that it was his job when he was in the office.

Torp skimmed through the article.

"As a politician, one has one and only one task—to fight for your homeland, especially when it is under pressure, as we experience it currently. I am more than willing to give overseas aid, but only when we have our own house in order. And we don't at the moment," stated Kirsten Rolighed.

The outer two columns to the right were devoted to an analysis by the *Daily News*'s political editor, Malene Astrup. Here was what the political spokesperson was saying "in reality" in the interview: that it was—yet another—warning to party chairman Palle Enevoldsen to either get himself together as Prime Minister or throw away the keys. No one believed he would sit out the entire period anyway.

"Who isn't fighting for Denmark, in her opinion?"

Crabby was reading over Torp's shoulder. It wasn't every day they had a print newspaper in the office. Torp looked up at Crabby's red eyes. The fired family father from Vanløse suffered from insomnia. It was presumably a combination of small children and big financial problems. Just that morning, his fellow office sharers had heard him almost begging on the phone. Crabby himself thought he had a good story, but the newspapers' previously swelling freelance budgets had been reset to almost zero.

"It's a kick in the teeth for Palle Enevoldsen. He is becoming increasingly alone in his parliamentary group—his authority is weakening bit by bit," explained Torp.

"Why's that?"

"He was once a modern politician."

"What happened?"

"I guess he couldn't keep it up. It happens to most top politicians, you know. They die ugly."

"Apart from Brathenberg," said Axel, joining the group in the passage and self-medicating with coffee.

"Yes," said Torp, "apart from Brathenberg."

They looked knowingly at each other.

"And what about her?" said Axel, pointing at the picture of Kirsten Rolighed with Dannebrog and looking down at Torp.

"She's likeable. Don't you think so?"

Both Axel and Crabby nodded.

"She hasn't been in Parliament very long," continued Torp, "she has a business career, she's quick-witted. She doesn't sound like a politician."

"And that's an advantage?"

"You know that as well as I do, Axel. That's what it's come down to."

Both were aware of the rumours that Kirsten Rolighed had rejected a minor ministry when Enevoldsen had formed a new government in the autumn. Instead, she had become her party's political spokesperson and for the past six months had used the platform to give her input in several of the areas that were actually a party leader's and prime minister's prerogative—namely, the right to independently determine the party's strategy and parliamentary wishes. She was always so well prepared that it was difficult to criticise her precisely for violating the line she was clearly violating. She could do it because she was good at it, and because a majority in the Liberal parliamentary group was alternately tired of and concerned about Palle Enevoldsen's lack of political results.

A little ping from Torp's computer announced that an email had come in. It was Erik, the obituary pusher, who thanked him for the two medium obituaries and the small stingy one. All was well. And now there was a special order for a large obituary for a man who hadn't even died yet, but had just been admitted to a hospice. Erling Jensen, long-time Member of Parliament for the Liberals, one of the grey, second-rank politicians that the people's government couldn't do without, a water carrier who had never become a minister but who could handle any negotiations until late at night in the Ministry of Labour without making mistakes and always keeping a sure eye on the issues and the party's interests. Erling Jensen was eighty-eight years old and wouldn't turn eighty-nine. His mind was still sharp, but he only had a few weeks left to live. It was a wish, both from the man himself and his family, that Torp should write an obituary so that it was ready. Torp felt the warmth spreading through his body. Erling Jensen was one of the first politicians he had had a confidential relationship with when he had started at the *Daily News*'s Christiansborg editorial office thirty years ago. Erling Jensen rarely spoke badly about anyone from the other parties and, even more remarkably, never spoke badly about his own party colleagues. Nevertheless, he became an invaluable source for Torp to ensure that he didn't write anything incorrect. With warm West Zealand understatement, he was able to give Torp warnings without revealing too much.

"What you say there, Torp, isn't necessarily completely true," Jensen would say.

Then Torp would know he had completely misunderstood the issue. Never, as in never, had Erling Jensen abused Torp's trust. The wish that he should write the obituary was, for Torp, proof that the trust hadn't been abused or misunderstood in the other direction, either.

Torp was to visit Erling Jensen at the hospice as soon as possible, as his son had put it without sentimentality. It was crucial and an express wish of his father. Torp could then contact the family afterwards.

Torp replied immediately that he would do what was requested. He was, in fact, looking forward to it.

CHAPTER 5

Tuesday was Ulrik Torp's long day—the day he and Karen went to couples' badminton in Østerbro. It was Karen's idea, an attempt to drag him out of isolation after he had come back from his course of therapy with Dion Hansen on the west coast. If possible, Torp loved her even more when she took on battles he didn't fancy but knew very well should be faced up to. She had done this many times over the years and on many levels—all the way from family dinners, boyfriend/girlfriend maintenance, their children, and the retention of friends to the need for vacations. He tended to let things slide until she reacted.

Karen's friend Tine was a happy woman, a little younger than Torp and Karen. To Torp's great surprise, Tine's husband Torben, an accountant, was astonishingly agile on a badminton court. He also—unlike Torp—had an intense desire to win matches.

"Out! Eight to four," called Torben in triumph from down on the back line at Karen's usually accurate clear.

Torp had him under suspicion of judging in his own favour when there was the slightest doubt. His thin legs swung delightedly forward to the serve line. The man served high and long. Torp tried to straighten his body and shift his weight so that he could move to the back line, where, under the arched ceiling of the badminton hall, the shuttlecock had now ended its journey upwards and initiated the vertical fall. Torp was too late with his shot and therefore had to bend his arm, so his racket came too far down. He hit the ball crookedly and saw it take an uneven and soft arc into the net on his and Karen's side.

"Nine to four!"

Karen and Tine looked forward to their badminton nights and, without discussing the agreement with anyone else, had planned a dinner for the two couples when the season ended in a few weeks. Torp didn't get the impression that Torben was enjoying either him or the game—but he clearly liked winning so much that it overshadowed both the activity and the company he was in. Torben and Tine's children had certainly never been allowed to come away with a victory in anything.

"You can deduct a hell of a lot when you have an office in the city and are self-employed. A hell of a lot," declared the accountant in the changing room. Torp mumbled something about probably being able to figure it out, but that didn't deter his badminton opponent. "Give me your accounts, and I'll certainly be able to take care of it so that your finances will be tolerable."

Argh, Karen told Tine everything. Tine told her husband everything. Everyone has someone they confide in. *If more than one person knows a secret, then it isn't a secret.* Torp remembered this from his teacher at the Danish School of Journalism when they had been taught about protecting their sources. Not even your spouse may know. *Protection of sources cannot be flexible. When you promise not to divulge anything to anyone, that is quite literal—only if the editor-in-chief is so tactless as to ask may you pass the information on, but not otherwise.* Torp had never had the experience of an editor-in-chief asking for the name of a source.

Karen had, of course, involved Tine over the years in their economic collapse—Torp's journey from unemployment benefits to the crumbs of social security, and onwards to the thin sliver of hope that the obituaries had aroused. She was probably sitting right now in the ladies' changing room telling her that their son-in-law had been fired and had had to sell the flat, that they would be homeless in three weeks. As if finding a car that could start wasn't a big enough challenge. Torp wasn't particularly embarrassed by his situation. He just thought it was private.

But it wasn't, as he now understood as they sat stark naked on the bench after a shower, Torben unconcerned about his bulging, hairy belly and thin legs. Torp looked down at himself. It wasn't impressive, but neither was it the opposite. Unlike his agile badminton opponent, he could hardly be said to weigh too much. On the other hand, muscles were few and far between, and those that existed weren't being used very much; he could feel that after he had begun challenging them every Tuesday night. Maybe it had been a good idea anyway for Karen to have forced him out of his cave, even though he was hurting and the company in the changing room was tiresome.

Yes, thank you. He would certainly come by with some accounts for the tax return if it became necessary, he replied. The accountant picked up on the measured enthusiasm.

"It won't cost you anything. And believe me, I can save you a lot of money. We always can. Always."

They said their goodbyes outside the badminton hall. The rain had stopped and there was a touch of spring in the air, even though it was both dark and slightly windy. Tine and Torben were going on to their flat north of Copenhagen and rolled off in their—his—Mercedes. Torp stood there in his worn jeans and pre-washed T-shirt, and each time was amazed by the enormous transformation that took place in those few metres—from the hairy naked man of the changing room to the well-dressed businessman in the parking lot, whose belly was elegantly hidden inside a 15,000-kroner Italian suit. He felt outside everything. No, they weren't in the car tonight; they had taken the Metro. So much hassle and humiliation every Tuesday just to lose to a winner.

We only sell Danish meat, it said in the butcher's window Torp walked by on his way to the office. He was carrying his left leg a little after the badminton battle the evening before. It was nothing serious, just a muscle being slightly surprised at having to be available after so many years of hibernation. The guarantee about the Danish meat should of course be perceived as a sales pitch; whatever was wrong with leg of lamb from New Zealand or rib-eye from South Schleswig? The sign was new, but similar signs, pitches, and advertisements were becoming more and more common. It had to give extra turn-over, he thought, trying to remember the name of the politician who, during the election campaign, had happened to promise tax deductions to companies that only served Danish open sandwiches in the canteen, provided that the ingredients were Danish and they were prepared by Danes. The problem wasn't so much the proposal—that kind of thing can always be found in a political supermarket with many shelves, perpetual sales, and a permanent department for spot goods. The problem was that Torp couldn't remember which party had proposed it, and that there could actually have been several.

Just before he turned down the side street where the office was located, he saw the society editor, Lindskov, coming towards him, struggling with two boxes. Their eyes met.

"Torp," he exclaimed, continuing until they stood face to face with each other. Slightly red in the face from the effort, he put the boxes down on the pavement.

"Twelve bottles of red wine. The finest French bottling. It may be that newspapers are on their way down, but we drink damn good red wine as we go," he puffed.

"And personal delivery. What could be better?" Torp nodded appreciatively, even though it was less than 500 metres from the *Daily News* building to his new shared office.

Lindskov writhed a little. "I'm responsible for managing the red wine stock at the newspaper—a lot goes in gifts, anniversaries, and the like, but I would prefer it if your name isn't in the books." He hesitated. "You know."

Torp knew very well.

"You could just put the office address down as the recipient," Torp said. "There's only five of us sitting up there, so all of them would know it was for me."

Lindskov nodded. "I'll do that next time." He paused, obviously a little uneasy about the situation.

"Next time?"

Lindskov hesitated and looked behind him. No one would notice two middle-aged men with a couple of boxes of red wine on a Wednesday morning in the middle of Copenhagen. More than that would be needed to cause a stir, let alone mere attention.

"You know my wife, Bente."

Torp knew her very well. She suffered from sclerosis but hadn't been severely afflicted by it for many years.

"Sometimes I have to go home early."

"I'm sorry to hear she's got worse," Torp heard himself say.

He was wondering where this conversation was leading. Apart from a couple of chance meetings, a little nod to each other and a hello, he had had nothing to do with Lindskov for many years.

"I was really glad it was you who wrote that Brathenberg obituary. It was ready to be put straight in the newspaper."

"Yes?"

"The thing is, I don't always have time to do my job when I suddenly have to go home to Bente. It's especially the leaders—the editorials—that I have trouble getting finished, because the subject matter is decided so late in the day."

Torp stared at him.

"Maybe, once in a while, we could agree that you write the leader for me. I tell you what it's about and what angle it should have, and you write it and send it to me. Then I can send it from home to the *Daily News*."

He was beginning to sound quite eager about his proposal.

"No one will discover that it's you. And then I can send a box of good red wine up to your office every time. And I mean *really* good red wine."

Torp turned his gaze to the two boxes that stood at his feet. Then he looked in disbelief at Lindskov.

"You want me to secretly write leaders for the *Daily News*?"

"It's just some text taking a position on something. It doesn't mean a thing. No one needs to know."

Torp fully understood why Lindskov thought no one needed to know. It would be an immediate firing for the loyal society editor if it emerged that Torp—of all people—was writing some of the newspaper's leaders.

"It won't be every day. Far from it. Maybe once or twice a week from now on. At the most. Maybe Bente will get better, and then it won't be necessary any longer. It's a little difficult right now."

Lindskov was almost begging for help. Torp bent down and took the two boxes of red wine in his arms. Why not?

"It has to be full-bodied wine. Preferably Italian. Otherwise, I can't be bothered."

They smiled at each other—Lindskov relieved, Torp diabolically. Then they said goodbye and promised each other they wouldn't reveal it to anyone. Fuck them.

Lindskov called the same afternoon from the car on the way home to his sclerosis stricken wife.

"A hundred fifty lines about Palle Enevoldsen. We're supporting the Prime Minister, but only just. Now he has to get his act together and show that he is actually concerned about Denmark."

Torp immediately guessed the reason. In recent weeks, instead of international trade, the EU, the threat from Russia, labour market reforms, schools, and the lack of craftsmen, politicians had been discussing the introduction of a National Day. It had begun as an article in a church magazine, picked up by a television programme in which the Liberals' political spokesperson, Kirsten Rolighed, had called it a brilliant idea, until everyone—as in everyone—was discussing it. The Prime Minister had initially chosen to ignore the debate but was forced to address it at a press conference the day before in the Prime Minister's Office together with the President of the European Commission.

Palle Enevoldsen had tried to parry with the fact that Denmark already had Constitution Day. There were very few who went along with that argument. Why was it so dangerous to celebrate a country with a history of more than 1,000 years? What was the Prime Minister afraid of? He had tried to argue that a day off would probably cost the state 2 to 3 billion kroner. So money meant more than national values? Yes . . .

or . . . no, damn it, it couldn't be presented in that way at all; he had an overall responsibility as Prime Minister. Was Kirsten Rolighed a threat to his leadership of the Liberals? What did he think about the National Day being 15 June—the day that Dannebrog had fallen from the sky in the Estonian capital of Tallinn in 1219? The Prime Minister emphasised that that was a myth, while the President of the European Commission received the translation in his ear in astonishment. Were there no questions about Russia and the ailing EU cooperation?

"Does the *Daily News* support a National Day on the fifteenth of June?" asked Torp.

"Not directly—or not yet," replied Lindskov from his car. "But we think Enevoldsen is displaying a strange resistance. He doesn't have to be in favour. But why is he against it? The leader is welcome to express this. More about Denmark, less about other countries. Something like that. He is abroad too much. Why isn't Denmark nice enough for him when it is for the rest of us?"

Lindskov tried to parody the attacks on social media until Torp interrupted him. He had heard plenty to find the melody in 150 lines.

During his seven years as Prime Minister, Palle Enevoldsen has always defended Denmark and the Danes. Certainly, it took a bit of persuasion and a European refugee crisis before it dawned on him that a country without a fixed border is not a country but just an area that others can intrude on. Better late than never. It is remarkable, however, that the country's Prime Minister is apparently—while a number of other political issues are pressing—spending time, energy, and political capital on being against something as innocent and unifying as a National Day to celebrate the Denmark and the flag that have been under so much pressure these past years.

Torp's fingers danced over the keyboard. The leader wrote itself once he caught the tone and the slightly muddy message.

At some point, Prime Minister Palle Enevoldsen has to decide for himself whether he wants to be the Danish Prime Minister. That point could very well rest on this case.

Full stop, full stop, comma, dash. The *Daily News* hadn't taken a position on the National Day. That was what a prime minister and a government were for. But the price of being against had now risen considerably. Palle Enevoldsen was hard-pressed on all fronts, and how much political equity did he actually have left?

The Facebook group Friends of Denmark had convened a demonstration and party on Friday "for Denmark." That only made it worse. Torp sent the 150 lines as an email to Lindskov. It had taken him less than thirty minutes. The wine probably cost 100–150 kroner a bottle. That was a nice hourly rate. Tax-free.

CHAPTER 6

The undertaker's shiny Volvo was well known on the quiet residential street in Frederiksberg. The average time for a stay at the hospice was less than three weeks, many lasting only two or three days before it was over. The nice version was that Treatment Denmark was able to skilfully sense when the end was approaching; the less nice version was that they overmedicated so that patients didn't get a dignified end in the peace and quiet that a hospice was meant to provide.

In any case, there was an almost daily flow of slow ambulances with terminal patients or quiet hearses with already deceased people at the newly built and state-of-the-art hospice with space for sixteen, run by the Deaconess Foundation.

The young, dark-haired woman smiled and nodded as she slid through the narrow entrance door that was open for the sake of the undertaker who was rolling a coffin in. The car was parked with the hatch open, routinely backed up all the way to the entrance. The undertaker smiled back with a professional smile that was neither too wide nor too reserved.

She accompanied the undertaker the first ten metres along the wide, curving corridor. Then he slid to the left behind his load and she to the right towards her goal. All the rooms were single occupancy, and Erling Jensen was quite perky this morning, despite his eighty-eight years and his death sentence. He had slept well, been given a small shot of morphine for the pain, but had otherwise stopped treatment in a mutual agreement with medical science, his family, and himself that it was coming to an end. He wasn't hungry, and his lean body lost, if possible, even more flesh, but he wouldn't say no to some water and especially a little beer.

All the rooms had windows that went down to the floor, and his room was at an angle out to the residential street, so that by stretching his dying body he could just about watch people walking dogs and children being accompanied to and from the little school that lay farther down the road. Erling Jensen had raised the headboard of the elevation bed a little so that he could observe, drink water, and read today's newspaper a little. The leader was harsh on the Prime Minister. Did he care about Denmark? When was one in tune with the times? When was one ahead? And when had time just run out? It was so indefinable in politics, but clear—especially when it was no longer working. Erling Jensen came to think of Bismarck's words about the statesman's task being the ability to hear God's footsteps marching through history and then trying to catch hold of His coat-tails as He marches past. It could be confused with opportunism, but that wasn't the German's intention. Opportunism was about methods—not direction. Such was politics at its best—even in a small country and a small party. It was no longer working for Palle Enevoldsen; he was no longer catching hold of anyone's coat-tails. His agenda was exhausted. He could no longer reinvent himself. The Prime Minister was also dying. Erling Jensen reached out carefully for the water, which was standing on a small table. It had already become lukewarm. He let a few drops roll around in his oral cavity to compensate for the saliva he almost couldn't produce any more, and swallowed with difficulty. He was tired, had come to terms with his situation while finding some things irritating, but wasn't quite finished with politics. One last move.

The door opened and a dark-haired woman entered—hadn't they just said that he would now be left in peace?

Ulrik Torp came to the hospice somewhat later than planned. It would have been easier to go directly from the flat to Erling Jensen as the first port of call, but Torp forced himself to go into the office every morning at the same time. It was slightly neurotic, he admitted, but it had now become—in addition to the morning pill—his way of re-establishing structure in his life. He had an office; ergo, he also had a job. And you went into work in the morning. He, therefore, took the Metro to Nørreport and walked over to the office, before he headed out to the Deaconess Foundation's hospice to fulfil his agreement and conduct his research for Erling Jensen's own obituary. Bizarrely, he looked forward to meeting the old politician again after so many years.

Several things had delayed him at the office. First and foremost, he was pleased with his first editorial in the *Daily News*—he had again spent thirty-nine kroner on a pile of paper but refrained from the cinnamon swirl. The case with the six bottles of Italian red wine had just been delivered. Now he had eighteen bottles. *Does Enevoldsen care about Denmark?* Lindskov had really stepped on the gas with the headline. There was no reason for that—not even with the question mark that could be perceived as conciliatory but in reality gave the appearance of being the opposite. It was a cheeky question. The man had fought for his country most of his life, sacrificing his leisure time, marriage, friends, and health on that account.

A small article stated that Brathenberg would be buried a week from Saturday; that would be a full thirteen days after his death, but very natural as it required quite a bit of preparation. Torp noted the date in his diary; he had never been to a gawp funeral before. It was to take place in Gentofte and would undoubtedly be a society crowd-puller.

A little unusually, everyone in the office community was present that morning. Crabby sat with his red-rimmed eyes but had picked up sugary pastries to mark the fact that—following up on a tip from a source—he had managed to sell a big story to the *Express*.

"We haven't agreed on a price, but the chief news editor acknowledged that it was a damn good story and they would take a look at it."

It was the first time in all the weeks that Torp had known him that there was the hint of a satisfied smile on Crabby's face.

"Now the story just has to be written. I can do it in two or three days," he said, almost to himself, as he invited everyone to sample the morning cakes.

Ghita announced that there would be farewell beers the next day. That meant that Torp would advance to a desk in the main room as early as Monday. They then had to find another person for the corridor. He had someone in mind for that and had already emailed her.

"I saw on Facebook that you're a member of Friends of Denmark," said Ghita, addressing Bertel. "It says that five thousand have signed up for the demonstration tomorrow. *Party for Denmark*, they're calling it."

"Signed up! That doesn't necessarily mean they're going," interjected Torp.

"The weather forecast is good for tomorrow. It's Friday. It's for Denmark. They'll be there," said Axel drily.

"Is it going to be held outside Christiansborg?" Torp asked.

Ghita shook her head. "It's all happening at the Liberty Memorial."

"What's that got to do with anything? The Liberty Memorial was raised for the abolition of serfdom and the agrarian reform two hundred fifty years ago," said Axel in obvious surprise.

"That's what they've written here." Ghita had brought up the Friends of Denmark page on Facebook. She adjusted her reading glasses. "The four statues by the obelisk symbolise the same virtues that Friends of Denmark pay homage to: fidelity, peasant diligence, bravery, and civic virtue," she read out loud. "The march will begin at the Little Mermaid on Langelinie at three p.m. People can join in en route. Bring a Dannebrog national flag if possible. The idea is to reach the Liberty Memorial by five p.m."

"The Liberty Memorial!" continued Axel. "Liberty from what?"

"Are you going along to clap, Bertel?"

Ghita was teasing, but it wasn't just good-natured.

"Nah, I'm going to our summer cottage this weekend. But would it be so wrong to participate?"

"I don't really know," said Axel.

Torp's mobile phone emitted the sound of two bamboo sticks colliding, signalling an email. It was a quick response to his offer.

"I've found someone who wants to move into the office," Torp said. "She can start right away."

"Hold on, now," laughed Bertel. "The body needs to be cold first."

"Her name's Emma. She's been an intern journalist at the *Daily News* but has dropped out of her course for the time being. She's a bit of a character, but she's smart with computers and the internet."

No one else had anything better to offer right away, so everyone agreed that she should just stop by and that it would take a real effort by her not to be admitted to the office community. The offer to be able to start—and pay—immediately was especially inviting.

By the time Torp rang the bell at the entrance to the hospice, it was past noon. The hearse in the square in front of the entrance made it a little difficult to squeeze past. Erling Jensen had passed away several hours earlier. His sudden death had surprised the staff, but it had been peaceful, it was emphasised. Torp thought that the coffin that had just been rolled past him was Erling Jensen's, but it wasn't. It was just a little busy today, explained the woman, who Torp could see from her nametag was called Susanne. The family had been informed and would be coming by later. He gave his new business card to Susanne and asked her to give it to the family when they arrived, with the message that he had been for a visit and that Erling's son was welcome to contact him. It was actually something he had himself expressed a wish for, so it would be completely uncontroversial, he assured her.

CHAPTER 7

There was a single new obituary for Torp on Friday morning. *Edith Pedersen, 82 years old, Ejby*. The contact person was her son. As it was a small one, Torp decided to write it straight away. If the fee were to make any sense at all, it shouldn't take more than an hour. The son picked up the phone right away and was fully prepared. Edith Pedersen got peace, and Ulrik Torp got 300 kroner. It was a nice exchange, and it wasn't even 10:00 in the morning.

Ghita was packing her last things next door. She was going to buy beers at 4:00 p.m. Torp made a quick check of the few things he had gathered around his desk during his mere four weeks in the office. He could handle the move in less than ten minutes. The eighteen bottles of red wine could be transported home when he had found a cheap battery for the car. For the time being, he had parked it on a private road on the outskirts of Frederiksberg, where there was free parking and a small hill and thus the possibility of rolling it out on his own. There were virtually no hills in Copenhagen. He wasn't going to look for a new battery today. He looked at his watch. He had promised to be with Erling Jensen's family at around 1:00 p.m. They lived on the outskirts of Holbæk, so public transport wasn't really an option. He would take the bus to the private road and the small hill, start the car, and then take the chance that there was also a hill close to the family's home in Holbæk. What did a new battery cost, he wondered? Probably a thousand kroner. It was almost half the value of the car, a little less if the tank was full. It didn't add up.

Torp gathered his notepad, pen, mobile phone, and travel card. He thought he could certainly manage to be back for Ghita's beers at 4:00 p.m.

Erling Jensen's son and daughter-in-law welcomed him with coffee and home baking. It was an anonymous yellow brick detached house with no special features; in that, the house resembled the occupants. Bjarne Jensen had acquired a pleasant plumpness after many years as a dutiful civil servant in local government. He had just gone on early retirement pay, which his slightly older wife, Ulla, had been on for a few years after all her years as a teacher at the local elementary school.

"Please eat," she said, offering a plate of buns with thickly spread butter to Torp, who hadn't had lunch.

"I'm really sorry I didn't get to have a chat with Erling," he repeated, taking half of the bun in a single bite.

"Don't be," said his son reassuringly. "It happened so fast for all of us. He was actually very perky the day before yesterday, when you take his condition into account. Who could have known he was only going to be in that hospice for less than a day?" He glanced at his wife.

"We should have kept him here at home," she said, nodding in the direction of the sickbed that was at the other end of the living room, which the local authority hadn't picked up yet. "The thought that he died alone isn't very nice, but the staff say he passed away quietly," she continued.

"That's what they always say, whether it's true or not," sighed the son.

They had been talking about it. Torp gulped down the other half of the bun. He didn't give a second thought to the abundantly thick layer of butter.

"It was very important to my father that you have a chat with him."

Bjarne again offered the plate of buns to Torp, who took one more. There was no reproach in the voice that Torp hadn't made it in time, more an emphasis on the old man being stubborn and used to getting his own way.

"It's also important for us that you write his obituary. Both because Dad wanted it, but also because he always talked nicely of you."

He paused.

"Which newspaper are you actually working for these days? I'm not up to date on that."

Torp could feel that the question was simple and completely without any ulterior motive. How wonderful it was to get outside the narrow and crowded circles of the capital, where his paranoia actually made sense.

"Sorry?"

"Which newspaper do you work for today? Is it the *Daily News*?"

Torp finished chewing.

"I'm a freelance journalist nowadays. That way I can deliver to all the newspapers," he said, making it sound like an advantage.

"We'd like to have the obituary in our own newspaper," interjected Ulla.

"And it will certainly be there, too," Torp assured her. "But that's all something the undertaker arranges. You don't have to give it a thought."

They nodded. Another bun? Yes, please—they're really good. Torp glanced at the plate with the homemade pretzel cakes. He could just allow himself one more bun before he went on to cake.

"Yes, it was a bit strange that Dad died just a few days after Otto Brathenberg."

Torp nodded to show interest, without being able to see what was so strange.

"Them having started to talk to each other just before they both died is a bit funny . . . or rather, not funny in that way," said Bjarne, correcting himself.

There was a way in which he seemed almost proud that his father had had contact with one of the great personalities of Danish politics.

"Your father was from the Liberals, Brathenberg from the Labour Party. There was almost ten years' difference between the two. Did they have anything at all to do with each other?"

"No, well . . ." Ulla took over. "We didn't know that, either."

"Dad didn't like Communists. Nor did Brathenberg."

"There were probably many people who didn't back then," said Torp with a smile.

"Dad really didn't like them. He was jubilant when the Berlin Wall fell in '89."

"But so were most people, Bjarne," his wife interjected.

"Brathenberg suddenly started calling. A week ago."

"They spoke to each other several times," continued Ulla.

They eagerly completed each other's sentences, but without interrupting each other. Like an old, experienced couple, they intertwined their sentences into an unbroken chain.

"And they talked about Communists."

"Communists?"

Torp looked up, fascinated by the marital manner of conversation as well as what came out of the two mouths in unison.

"What did Brathenberg want?"

The couple both shook their heads. They didn't know.

"There was also someone else that your father called several times about this," Ulla said. "That lady."

"That's right," said Bjarne, nodding. "Koch something-or-other. Maybe you should talk to her, too?"

Torp nodded, without intending to research the obituary further than the main person. If the fee were to make sense, the trip to Holbæk would have to be enough.

"At any rate, they agreed that they wanted to talk to you. I actually think it was Brathenberg's suggestion that it should be you."

Torp had his mouth full of the third bun and the thickly spread butter was clinging to his palate, so he tried to loosen it with a sip of lukewarm coffee. He succeeded.

"Because I should write their obituaries?"

Now they both laughed.

"No, not at all! They only knew that Dad was going to die. No, it was something you had to write about. That's why I thought you were at the *Daily News*. That that was the reason they wanted to get hold of you."

Bjarne got up, ambled over to the municipal sickbed, and took hold of a plastic bag, which he then handed to their guest. The bag was from the Coop, but with a logo and a font from many years ago. There was a small pile of papers in it—forty to fifty sheets was Torp's estimate. Most of them were yellowed and curled. Some yellowed sheets were sticking out through a hole in the bottom left-hand side.

"At one point, Dad was writing something that was going to end up as a biography or something along those lines. He was working on this to the last. Maybe it can be used as inspiration for a fairly long article about his life," explained the son, sitting down. "Maybe even a book?"

Bjarne looked hopefully up at the journalist from the capital city.

"Help yourself to cake. And more coffee."

Ulla sensed the pause in the conversation had lasted a little too long and pushed both the coffee-pot and the plate over to Torp. He gratefully availed himself of both offers.

"What did they want me to write about?"

Bjarne shrugged. He had just filled his mouth with a bite of pretzel, which he was eager to swallow so he could answer right away.

"I have no idea," he said, spitting a little cake into the air.

He looked at his wife.

"I don't know either. But they were up to something."

Her husband had finished swallowing.

"Incredible with those politicians, isn't it?"

He sounded both baffled and proud at the same time. His father and Otto Brathenberg—still at it to the last.

Once again, there was a long pause in the living room. Torp was puzzled about the Brathenberg-Jensen partnership. He couldn't make any sense of it. There was absolutely no common denominator between the two; two different parties, two different lives. One of them a stolid product of the yellow brick detached house they were sitting in, the other a self-proclaimed aristocrat. One of them a political craftsman and proud of it, the other slightly bitter about not becoming Prime Minister.

Torp didn't have the perception that they had so much as glanced at each other in their common time as Members of Parliament, Jensen busy with committee work and compromises, Brathenberg preoccupied with ministerial work and power struggles. He looked down at the plastic bag with what was obviously intended to be the first fifty A4 sheets of Erling Jensen's political memoirs.

"What had you imagined should be most prominent in the obituary?" he heard himself ask as he took out his notepad.

Bjarne and Ulla Jensen were both kind enough to help him by giving the Polo a push when it was time to drive back to the capital.

He parked at the flat, so Karen would have to help with a push the next time. He should also get hold of a cheap battery. That was the first priority as soon as the Erling Jensen obituary had been delivered. He took the Coop bag with Erling Jensen's poorly timed memoirs under his arm. It was almost 4:00 p.m. by the time he jumped on the Metro. He should just make it to Ghita's farewell beers.

"We love *Den*mark. We love *Den*mark. We love *Den*mark."

The battle cry spread up Strøget and down through the side streets, rolling back and forth. Bertel had opened the window and stuck his head out to both see and hear the demonstrators.

"There's a hell of a lot," he exclaimed, having a hard time concealing his enthusiasm.

"We love *Den*mark. We love *Den*mark. We love *Den*mark."

"Do you think they also love fish cakes?" asked Axel, taking an angry gulp of Ghita's farewell beer.

"That's so bloody cheap, Axel," came the battle-ready response from Bertel.

"Why is it cheap?"

"Because there are lots of people who don't give a damn about Denmark. That's why. All that fish cake crap is unworthy."

"Who doesn't give a damn?"

"Let's just start with the Prime Minister. He doesn't fucking love Denmark."

"You simply cannot be serious," replied Axel, his cheeks flushing.

"You can bet I am. Enevoldsen only thinks about his own power and his friends down in the Union. That's what he's thinking about—Brussels and fine dining. He couldn't give a fuck about his own country unless he benefits from it. Just like all the others."

"So what's your answer to all this, Bertel?" Ghita was trying to shift the mood at her farewell drinks by meeting him halfway.

Bertel didn't give it a moment's hesitation. "A border and a politician who can stop this madness."

"But you're getting the border," she objected in her efforts to reconcile the group around the table.

"It's a start, but it was only at the last minute."

"We love *Den*mark. We love *Den*mark. We love *Den*mark."

The noise from the demonstrators increased in strength, as they wound their way up towards Rådhuspladsen—the square in front of Copenhagen City Hall—and the Liberty Memorial. They sounded like Brøndby football fans, who couldn't really decide whether they were hooligans or cooligans on their way to the derby against FCK at Parken Stadium. Torp wanted to close the window, and yet he didn't.

Axel fell like a dishcloth back to his reclining self and spread his arms.

"It's amazing. Totally incredible," he said, almost to himself, while shaking his head. "Sorry, Ghita. It's your farewell drinks. Yes please, I would like one more." He looked at Bertel. "Cheers, Bertel. I come in peace."

Bertel hesitated for a moment. "Cheers, Axel, you old traitor. I hate fish cakes."

CHAPTER 8

We love *Den*mark . . . We love *Den*mark . . . We love *Den*mark."
The cries resounded around the twenty-metre-high obelisk on
Vesterbrogade up the road from Rådhuspladsen and down along the side
streets of Bernstorffsgade, Reventlowsgade, and—a little further down
and somewhat less prestigious—Colbjørnsensgade, all streets named
after some of the main forces behind the abolition of serfdom. Now their
brave and epoch-making struggle for the peasants' freedom was being
used as a backdrop for a new and magnificent freedom struggle—the
struggle for a Danish National Day on 15 June.

Ulrik Torp made a quick decision after saying farewell to Ghita and the
Friday beers; he ditched Nørreport and followed the sound and the demonstrators up to Rådhuspladsen and on towards the Liberty Memorial.

The Dannebrog national flags were fluttering in the April wind, which
couldn't quite make up its mind whether it should be the last twist of
winter or the first of spring. Torp found it a bit chilly, but it seemed as if
the demonstrators were fine. The mood was high among the Friends, who
comprised a cross-section of the population from children to pensioners.
Torp noticed a handful of shaven-headed young men with tattoos and
black boots. The media had previously described Friends of Denmark as
being like a magnet for the far right, but apart from the shaven heads, it

was now difficult to see any extremism in the flock. They looked like the common run of people. Ethnic Danes, mind you, but there was hardly anything strange about that.

Torp noticed an uncomfortable feeling in his body. He didn't like slogans and shouting, even if they had nothing to do with him. The discomfort was more due to the fact that he didn't like demonstrations. Except in a professional capacity as a journalist, he had never participated in one, not even once. They offended him somehow. There were probably several causes he could support if it came to it. But being one of a flock, shouting a unified slogan against some others, made him feel nauseous.

Maybe if he had lived in a different time. Maybe he would have become part of the masses if there really had been something to fight for. American independence. The French Revolution. The abolition of the absolute monarch. The abolition of serfdom, for that matter, he thought, as they approached the Liberty Memorial on Vesterbrogade and the thousands of people who were gathering there. If it was like that, then he could, at a pinch, see himself shouting against the powers that be— maybe he would let the others do the shouting—but at least he could see himself there. However, the conflicts that led to demonstrations in Denmark didn't seem to live up to that level, he thought.

"We love *Den*mark. We love *Den*mark. We love *Den*mark."

Torp noticed a group of youngish men in light shirts, each draped in their own Dannebrog flag and leading the singing, or however you would describe the trumpeting of the battle cry. He looked around and regretted that he hadn't taken the Metro home from the office. The atmosphere was otherwise good; people weren't angry, as they were at most demonstrations. Here people were *in favour* of something. Officially, at least. The biggest task for the police was to block off the streets and redirect the traffic in the Friday rush hour. Torp was surprised that the Friends had been given permission for the demonstration at all—both the time and the place were atypical. They must have good friends in the fight for their National Day.

A small stage had been built at the foot of the Liberty Memorial with the front facing Rådhuspladsen. Powerful loudspeakers were turned in all directions. Now the unofficial spokeswoman for Friends of Denmark took the stage.

"We love *Den*mark. We love *Den*mark. We love *Den*mark."

The spokeswoman, a fairly young, blonde parish priest, smiled broadly as she used her arms to gesture that the time had come to listen. It was only partially successful. Mona Kongsted, as she was called, had been interviewed and featured in several media outlets in recent weeks when it dawned on editors and politicians that Friends of Denmark was developing into more than just another group on Facebook. Mona Kongsted was not a member of any political party.

"I am a Dane" was her disarming explanation of the question of where she stood in the political picture, "and first and foremost worried about the future of Denmark and Europe. But as a Dane, it is Denmark that I relate to," she emphasised. She was quoted in several interviews as saying that "Europe is lost; now it's Denmark that matters." All the time with a friendly, disarming smile. No words that were violent in themselves, but the context was violent, the message harsh.

"How wonderful to see so many patriots," she said. There was a bit of howling in the microphone. She tapped it lightly. "Can you hear me?" she continued. The howling had stopped.

"The Great Replacement is on its way if we don't stop it," said the parish priest. She was known as a fierce debater who took resistance personally. Mona Kongsted didn't shout her message; her arms hung down by her side, and her voice was closest to what it would be if you were sitting next to her in confirmation class. "Ladies and gentlemen, I hereby give the floor to our first speaker, the Labour Party's Henning Vipper Hansen."

"Vipper," as he was simply called, was, as the British put it, a proper back-bencher. He had sat in Parliament for several decades without making a big impression. He had never been near a ministerial post, but he was an integral part of the no-nonsense trade union movement in Aalborg with its roots in the abandoned shipyard which reelected him time and again. Vipper was no great speaker. Torp watched the crazy scene of 20,000 people cheering at the sight of him. He was obviously not used to such a reception. Torp recognised several of his old journalist colleagues here on the outskirts of the demonstration. Simon, his intern partner from the autumn he spent at the *Daily News*, was also there—for a brief moment, they made eye contact from a long distance by mistake, before they both competed over who could look away the fastest, a competition which, by its very nature, neither of them could know who had won. Both TV stations were present with several cameras and live outside broadcast vans. This was bigger than Torp had imagined it would be.

Vipper wasn't unfamiliar with standing on a beer crate and talking to a bunch of factory workers, so he could do it even though the stage and scale were different.

"This," he began, sounding as if he were at a workers' fight in the '70s, "this, comrades, this is not about the Labour Party or the Liberals. It's not about what's going to happen down there in the Union. It's not about Moscow or Washington. This, my friends, this is about our own country. It's about Denmark's survival." Vipper raised his voice and his arms. Torp was impressed by the old man, until today a marginalised parliamentary politician.

The young men in the pale shirts began immediately, and within the space of a few sentences, most of the demonstrators were underway.

"We love *Den*mark. We love *Den*mark. We love *Den*mark."

Intoxicated by the mood, Vipper's voice rose an octave as he continued. Perhaps the words were also escaping in a single unguarded moment.

"If we're going to prevent the Great Replacement, the time is right now, my friends. This is our last chance."

"We love *Den*mark. We love *Den*mark. We love *Den*mark."

Or at the very least they loved Vipper, thought Torp, as his phone vibrated in his back pocket. He tried to get even farther away from the gathering and the noise and found shelter near Axel Towers in the direction of the Circus Building and the Palads Cinema. The sound coming out of the speakers from Vipper's big moment couldn't reach there, and the number of demonstrators was therefore also more limited. He could both smell and see that the area was being used as a urinal.

"Torp speaking," he shouted into the phone. He had seen the number before, without quite being able to place it.

"It's Bjarne."

"Hallo. This is Ulrik Torp!"

"It's Bjarne. From Holbæk. Erling Jensen's Bjarne. Am I disturbing you?"

Bjarne Jensen retaliated against the decibels. Torp had now come right in between two of the towers at Axel Towers, followed only by a single protester who didn't have time to completely prepare himself to pee before it started running, without it apparently bothering him. Torp tried to move a few metres away from the man.

"Hi, Bjarne. Thanks for your hospitality," he replied, now in a more normal tone.

"Not at all, thank you," came the response from Holbæk. "I've been thinking . . . yes, I don't really know what I've been thinking, but then . . ."

Torp routinely let the silence hang in the conversation. It wasn't only to get even more of a distance from the peeing protester, who in his state was spraying around a bit randomly, but also a journalistic habit. People don't like silence in conversations and typically continue if the other party doesn't say anything, even though they would actually prefer to hold back. And there—right there—is when there sometimes comes the sentence around which a whole interview can be built.

"Yes, well, Dad and Brathenberg didn't have very much in common, as we agreed."

"No?"

"But Dad did mention a committee in several of his phone calls. It was something Ulla remembered after you had left. Something they obviously had in common. Does that mean anything to you?"

"Nothing at all," replied Torp, a little impatiently.

Now the demonstrator had finished peeing. He zipped up, wiped the piss off his hands on his trousers, staggered past Torp, and tried without success after a few metres to fall into the rhythm of the battle cry. It just became a slightly delayed "Denmark" until Torp couldn't hear him any more.

"I was also thinking," continued Bjarne.

New pause, which Torp again allowed to expand.

"Dad's obituary, when do you think you'll have it done?"

"Tomorrow at the latest. Your local newspaper has set aside plenty of space for it on Monday."

"I was wondering if I could see it first. Just so . . ."

Ah, so that's why he's called, thought Torp. He could have just said that from the beginning. That he wanted to look through the obituary—and maybe make small corrections. Goodness me.

"No problem. I'll email it to you before twelve tomorrow. Just drop me your email address in a text message and it's a deal."

A clearly relieved Bjarne Jensen thanked him profusely, promised not to disturb him anymore, and explained how happy he was that it was precisely Ulrik Torp who was writing the obituary. They both hung up, and Torp went back to the demonstration.

The leader of the Nationalists was on her way down from the podium. She was being hailed, as he could sense and hear, as a saviour. This was her home ground. On her way down, Annegrethe Hulsig was embraced by an older man, Per Frost, the retired anti-Communist author who, in the 1980s, had been a liberal voice with both the spirit of the times and the print-run figures against him. On the other hand, he had hit the trend in his older days, thought Torp, not surprised to see him right here in a passionate embrace with the Nationalist Party's young leader.

"We love *Den*mark. We love *Den*mark. We love *Den*mark."

"We love *Den*mark. We love *Den*mark. We love *Den*mark."

Mona Kongsted, the parish priest and face of Friends of Denmark to the outside world, reappeared on stage.

"Our thanks to Annegrethe Hulsig." She paused, intending to build some expectation in her audience. "We have one more speaker. A speaker who is further proof of how cross-political the Friends of Denmark are, how broadly we embrace, and how important our struggle is. Please give a big welcome to the Liberal Party's political spokesperson, Kirsten Rolighed."

Mona Kongsted went up two octaves this time when she uttered the name. This was supposed to be big. And it was, thought Torp at once. Vipper was on the back benches of a large party. Hulsig was a front-bencher in a small party that had Muslims as the only real item on their agenda. Kirsten Rolighed was a scoop. Political spokesperson for a governing party, mentioned by some as a possible successor to Palle Enevoldsen, perhaps even in the middle of their period of government. Maybe Denmark's next Prime Minister. Torp saw several of his journalist colleagues from the written press and a few TV reporters doing live stand-ups. It was obvious that none of them had known about this in advance.

"Hi, everyone!"

Kirsten Rolighed waved to the gathering from the small stage at the Liberty Memorial. She turned her body and tried to conceal a powerful coughing fit, while waving backwards, as best she could, to the thousands standing on the other side. There was a roar of enthusiasm. It was as if all 20,000 Friends of Denmark had collectively realised that they had just been promoted from the second division to the Super League. Now, it wasn't just a Facebook group that had got lucky with a demonstration. Now it was suddenly a political force on a whole different level.

"I also love Denmark!" she began.

Another roar of enthusiasm.

"I've just been in China with a delegation of Members of Parliament." The gathering booed for fun. She acknowledged them immediately. "I know what you mean. I feel that way, too. The further you get away from Denmark, the more you love Denmark. Isn't that right?"

She was flirting with the audience and Torp could see that it was working. They loved her.

"I am a patriot," continued Kirsten Rolighed. "I am a national. And . . ." She held a rhetorical pause, then turned her head demonstratively towards the gathering so that everyone got the impression that she saw each one of them. "And I am a nationalist!" The gathering cheered, and many missed hearing her amused afterthought: "What else should one be?"

"For far too long, we have believed that things just happened of their own accord. That progress was a force of nature that we shouldn't worry about. That our welfare state was a one-time invention and not a daily struggle. That the contract we have with each other—I take care of you, you take care of me—was unbreakable."

Kirsten Rolighed was a confident speaker, thought Torp. Not great, but confident. She saw the whole gathering, she was incisive, she made contact. You didn't need any more.

"For far too long, we have believed that this small speck of land, from Skagen in the north to Gedser in the south, was probably looked upon with envy all over the world, but it was still our small speck. A small speck that our parents, grandparents, and many others before them had looked after and cared for so we could have a good life. And which we look after and care for so that our children and grandchildren can have a good life. For far too long . . ." repeated Kirsten Rolighed, raising her voice, pausing, and looking out over her audience again. For right now, it was hers. Her voice cut through clearly; for the first time, there was almost calm among the demonstrators. Everyone looked up towards the Liberty Memorial and the Liberals' political spokesperson.

"For far too long," she continued, "we have taken it all for granted. That is a luxury we can no longer afford, and I would like to thank you all for that, Friends of Denmark. You are our national conscience. Of course, we must have a national day to celebrate the fatherland. Of course, it has to be June the fifteenth. Of course, we have to look after Denmark. Of course, it's our country. Thank you for reminding me and many others of that. Thank you, friends!"

The roar of jubilation rose to new heights when Kirsten Rolighed acknowledged that she had finished her speech. She raised her arms and clapped in an attempt to show that it was them she was clapping for, not herself. Per Frost, Annegrethe Hulsig, Mona Kongsted, Vipper—all of them received a warm and close embrace from the Liberals' political spokesperson.

"We love *Den*mark. We love *Den*mark. We love *Den*mark."

"We love *Den*mark. We love *Den*mark. We love *Den*mark."

"We love *Den*mark. We love *Den*mark. We love *Den*mark."

Torp pressed himself through the Friends of Denmark in the direction of Halmtorvet. He wanted to find the Metro and get home to Karen. He had to get that obituary written, and they had to find somewhere to live.

CHAPTER 9

Ulrik Torp pressed "Send."

It was a good obituary. Clear and simple with a common thread about a political craftsman who thought first of his country, then his party, and finally himself. Maybe a bit of an exaggeration—things had a tendency to flow together—but if anyone deserved such an exaggeration, it was Erling Jensen. He had flipped through the Coop bag with Jensen's own notes and old papers but quickly put it to one side. It wasn't relevant for the obituary and would have to wait for another time.

Torp leaned back contentedly. He was enjoying the Saturday silence in the office and remembering the weekends at the *Daily News*. It had been a long time since he had felt such satisfaction at a piece of journalistic work as with this obituary, a long life condensed into a few lines, knowing full well that nothing is meant to come after that. Full stop.

For twenty-seven years, Erling Jensen was a faithful and unerring voice in the Danish Parliament. As business spokesman for more than a decade, he was involved in promoting the conditions for small and medium-sized enterprises. He was also, as a long-standing member of the Committee on the Intelligence Services—better known as the Parliamentary Control Committee—from its formation in 1988, and as a member of the Foreign Policy Board, deeply involved in Denmark's security and foreign policy.

Right up until his death, Erling Jensen maintained a close relationship with . . .

If it had been a British obituary, and if Torp had dared to do it, he would have added a section on the man's reputation for running after young secretaries at Christiansborg—even at quite a mature age and sometimes with the result desired by him. It was Erling Jensen's luck that the #MeToo wave had waited fifteen years to hit the coast. Even a British obituary would probably have danced around his wife's suicide and would also be above suggesting a connection between the young secretaries and the tragedy. Torp had liked Erling Jensen a lot despite his mistakes and shortcomings. Now the son was given an hour to nitpick the memory of his father and make sure none of the above was written about or implied. Then Torp would send it to his obituary pusher, who would arrange for further distribution and remuneration. Torp glanced at the small note on which he kept track of his tasks and his income. Erik had actually kept to the prospects he had offered. He had invoiced for obituaries for almost 20,000 kroner the past month. Twelve medium, five small, and now the big one with Erling Jensen. It was an acceptable income if one was an assistant in a Netto discount supermarket. As a journalist, it was lousy, but he knew many freelance journalists who weren't earning much more and never would. In Torp's time, the profession had gone from the upper middle class to the proletariat. The stars still got an unreasonable amount, but the broad base was just that—a base.

Torp felt he was slowly making his way up out of the quicksand. Not in a quick surge, but it would be all right. Maybe he could even make a living from it again. Maybe it was time to drop the happy pills. For the first time in a long time, he allowed himself a bit of optimism at the thought of his coming—final—ten to twelve years in the job market.

He looked around at his new freelance office. It was cosy, even on a Saturday morning. And he even had eighteen bottles of the *Daily News*'s really good wine. Several more were probably on their way if Lindskov's Bente wanted it that way. Could they live here? Just temporarily? Torp pushed the thought away. It was not just illegal and impossible. Karen wouldn't accept it, either. Had it just been him, he could have managed with a sofa. They would be without a home in less than three weeks.

The newspapers' websites were full of the demonstration at the Liberty Memorial the day before, especially Kirsten Rolighed's unreserved support for a National Day on 15 June. Several commentators were asking whether she was speaking on behalf of the government. And, of course, she wasn't. She was the political spokesperson for the Liberals' parliamentary group. Ministers—and ultimately the Prime Minister—spoke on behalf of the government. No one else. And no one from the government, not even Palle Enevoldsen, had commented on her unequivocal promise to Friends of Denmark that they—and Denmark—should of course have their wish for a National Day fulfilled. On the other hand, there were plenty of people eager to comment on her speech. The leader in the *Daily News*—Torp recognised Lindskov's pen—was overwhelmingly positive.

Rolighed shows that she can cut through all the political chatter . . . of course Denmark must have a National Day on 15 June . . . where is Palle Enevoldsen . . . is he even bothering to be the Danes' Prime Minister? . . . Rolighed has made a convincing bid to be his replacement.

The other newspapers expressed the same opinion to varying degrees, and social media was overflowing with more enthusiastic support for Rolighed and criticism of Enevoldsen.

An opinion poll from one of the major institutes showed that the bottom was about to fall out from under the Liberals; the party had lost eight percentage points in just two months. Torp could, with seismographic certainty, predict the upcoming opinion polls—they would set Enevoldsen up against Rolighed. Who do you prefer? And will you vote for the Liberals if: a) Palle Enevoldsen is the party's leader, or b) Kirsten Rolighed is the party's leader? The worst thing wasn't the answers. The worst thing was the questions. The moment they were asked, the erosion and the downturn became fact. In the space of just a few days, it would be decided whether Palle Enevoldsen was politically dying. Torp flipped through the comments on the news pages and social media to see if leading Liberals were offering their names in support of their Prime Minister. He didn't find a single one. The prayer mats were already being moved.

Torp closed his computer, locked the door behind him, and decided to use what looked like the first real spring day to stroll home from the Inner City to the flat in Frederiksberg. He was really looking forward to it, and grabbed one—no, two—of Lindskov's bottles to take with him in a bag.

The story came in the middle of the afternoon and spread over the course of half an hour to an extent that social media advisers later used in their lectures as an example of the power of the internet and of how bad it can go if one doesn't react immediately.

The light wasn't perfect—it was unclear whether Palle Enevoldsen was sitting in a meeting room at his official country residence at Marienborg, in the Prime Minister's Office, or in a separate place entirely. Several people suggested that it was Marienborg. The original sender was an anonymous and newly created Twitter profile who called himself, or herself, monkeybusiness. It wasn't clear whether the clip was recorded before or after Kirsten Rolighed's speech at the Liberty Memorial. It could, in principle, have been recorded many days earlier. On the other hand, it was clear that the Prime Minister was speaking to more than one person because his face and eyes were moving. The sound, unlike the pictures, was clear and distinct. Even on a mediocre smartphone, Prime Minister Palle Enevoldsen could be heard declaring his unreserved opinion about Friends of Denmark, the desire for a National Day, and the politicians who were promoting it:

"I can't be bloody bothered to hear any more about those idiots in Friends of Denmark. I don't want to waste my time on such a bunch of provincial fascists. They can piss off with their fucking National Day—do they think I'm raving mad? A dog they can just push around? A little fucking puppy? I don't give a damn about those politicians who don't dare to speak out against them. Christ Almighty, what a bunch of sissies."

Torp was sitting at home in the flat. Two hours had now gone by. More than 1,000 retweets on Twitter and even more comments. More than 4,000 people had shared the clip on Facebook, and it had now been played 200,000 times—in two hours. *Provincial fascists* and *fucking National Day* were the words that were most often echoed in the comments. These were also the words that the journalists could pull up into the headlines of their online articles this late Saturday afternoon. Enevoldsen was nowhere to be found. Kirsten Rolighed had "no comment," which of course, given the situation, was also a kind of comment. On the other hand, there were a lot of remarks from politicians from all the other parties. The clip had also caused a handful of Liberal MPs to sense the wind direction and go from being anonymous scumbags to putting their names to the criticism. *Shocking, lavatorial* and *un-Danish* were common terms for the statements by the country's Prime Minister.

"What an idiot."

Karen and Ulrik were sitting on the sofa for once watching the news on TV. They had talked about getting rid of the little subscription package but kept it anyway. They agreed that if anyone was going to stick to ordinary TV for a few more years, it was probably going to be their generation.

Politicians were queueing up to repudiate the Prime Minister. All of them stressed what warm supporters they were of the introduction of a National Day on 15 June, even those who until now hadn't taken a stand on it or, behind closed doors, thought the same as the Prime Minister, albeit in slightly different terminology. Two commentators—one alleged to be on the left and the other alleged to be on the right, so the channel had covered both sides—talked about Palle Enevoldsen having committed character suicide. Now it was at least certain that Denmark would get a National Day, they both said and nodded eagerly to each other, the host, and the viewers.

"But he's right," objected Karen, pouring more of the *Daily News* red wine for both of them.

It was of a quality they were only used to at the son-in-law's in Klampenborg, where they would be served some of the really good stuff from Piedmont.

"For a people who don't believe in anything at all, we have plenty of special days off," she continued.

Ulrik agreed completely, but like so many others who watched television, his thoughts were elsewhere. Bjarne Jensen had called back early in the afternoon. He was very happy about the obituary. So was his wife, he assured Torp. That was the end point they had wanted. During the conversation, Torp had again been reminded of the strange partnership between Brathenberg and Jensen, who had absolutely nothing in common, apart from the fact that they had both died at an extremely mature age within the space of a few days. Why on earth had they been lying in their beds ringing each other back and forth? And Erling Jensen on his deathbed, to boot. Torp couldn't get his son's remark out of his head. Bjarne Jensen had almost enthusiastically said that, in reading his father's obituary, he had remembered the name of the committee that Brathenberg and his father had talked about several times over the phone.

"*. . . just as he, as a long-standing member of the Committee on the Intelligence Services, better known as the Parliamentary Control Committee, from its formation in 1988 . . .*" Bjarne Jensen read aloud from Torp's obituary. "That was the committee we couldn't remember. Ulla is quite certain. The Control Committee. What does such a committee do?"

Torp owed the son an answer and subsequently had to look it up, even though he could only vaguely remember why the committee had been set up. It was in the last days of the Cold War and was based on several cases involving the intelligence services which had been running their own programme. Changing oppositions talked about a state within the state and demanded parliamentary control of both the Police Intelligence Service and the Military Intelligence Service. The Control Committee was the political compromise—five Members of Parliament from the five largest parties could here be provided with deeply confidential information from the Ministers of Justice and Defence and top officials. The price was that the information couldn't be passed on or used for anything. Torp had never quite understood what the actual point of the committee was.

"The Prime Minister is right," repeated Karen and got her husband back to reality in front of the television.

"Maybe it's not a bad idea at all, having that National Day," exclaimed Ulrik, not really thinking about what he was saying.

"You don't mean that."

"If we all said yes now, then it would be over. No more Friends of Denmark." Ulrik spread his arms. "Then we all agree. No one is an enemy."

Karen rolled her eyes. "You don't even believe that yourself."

He shrugged. No, he probably didn't.

"But what are we going to do, Karen? Tell me that. And moreover, tell Palle Enevoldsen." He pointed in the direction of the television, where they were showing archival images of the Prime Minister who wasn't available for comment.

"But he's right." Karen pushed herself up on the sofa.

"Not with those words, Karen. Not with those words."

CHAPTER 10

Ulrik Torp was taken aback by how happy he was to see Emma when she entered the office apartment carrying a hefty Apple laptop and wearing an overly thin jacket and tight jeans so full of fashionable holes that, at one point, he feared that the pieces of fabric would fall apart.

He gave her a hug, the awkwardness of which they were both to blame for, and introduced her to Bertel and Crabby. Axel hadn't arrived yet, but he rarely came in on Mondays and, should the occasion arise, not before noon.

"Bertel is our communications and all-purpose journalist, when he isn't just celebrating National Days or off in his summer cottage," explained Torp, making it sound as if he had been in the office for years and knew Bertel from school days. "And Crabby is our real journalist. The only one, in fact," he said with a weak laugh.

Emma silently held out her hand to shake theirs. She wasn't good at such things and didn't even try to be.

"When did you graduate from the School of Journalism?" began Crabby at the sight of the slender girl.

"I didn't," she said with a shake of her head.

"Are you even a journalist?" exclaimed Bertel, looking at Torp.

"Since when has it become a protected title?" replied Emma. "I dropped out of my internship at the *Daily News* last autumn. When they chucked that one there out," she said, nodding in the direction of Torp.

"Okay, so what we have here is a lady with principles," said Bertel, with feigned fright in his voice.

"I can also clear off if it's a problem," came the whiplash response.

"No, no," said Bertel, defusing the situation. "Principles are all very well, provided you aren't too rigid with them."

"Then they're not principles, are they?"

Bertel stared in fascination at the ring in her nose and chose, wisely for once, to back off. Crabby suppressed a rare laugh.

Torp intervened. "Now I'll show you to your desk—it's over here in the passage. It's very central."

"Did you really leave the *Daily News* because of me?"

Torp had made coffee in Axel's absence and handed Emma a cup. She had settled into his old spot and had apparently already begun to work on whatever it was she was doing. She looked up with a rare smile.

"I didn't want to be in a place where doing the right thing means so little. It wasn't because of you—I was thinking about myself."

"What about your education?" he asked, suppressing a slight disappointment.

"That doesn't matter so much." Now she laughed. Genuinely. "You're all so funny."

"Us?"

"Yes, you boomers. What good is an education if I'm better than most people who have completed their education—and if I can't learn anything at school that I can learn better on my own?"

"Then you have papers to prove it," tried Torp. He only had a vague sense of what boomer really meant, but that was enough.

"Papers!" She smiled—almost to herself. "You and your papers."

Torp smiled back. There it was again, the chasm, which alternately frightened and fascinated him.

"I'm glad you're here," he said, settling for that.

"So am I," replied Emma. "Really."

Torp looked around.

"Don't you have anything else with you?"

"What do you mean?"

"Other than that thing," he said, pointing at her laptop.

"What would that be?"

Torp hesitated. "A poster. A blotting-pad. Some books. Notepads, pens, a plant, a framed picture. Anything."

"What for?"

Emma had turned all the way around on the office chair and was looking inquisitively up at Torp with the coffee cup in her hand.

"Nah, I just thought that . . ." Torp spread his arms self-deprecatingly. "I guess I wasn't really thinking about anything. It's just great that you're here, Emma." He was interrupted by his mobile.

"Torp speaking."

There was a buzzing at the other end. It sounded like a bad connection.

"Hello! This is Ulrik Torp."

He could hear a faint sound of breathing and still the hiss that, on second thought, didn't really sound like a bad connection. It was a background sound he didn't recognise.

"Hello!"

The line went dead. Emma had turned to her computer when the phone rang as a sign that their conversation was over. Torp went into the fine living room and sat down at Ghita's old desk. Crabby was working on his article for the *Express*—this was going to secure his monthly salary and some of his next mortgage payment. Torp hadn't really been listening when he had told them what it was about—something to do with a confidential source, some documents, and millions.

"Have you agreed a price with the Express?"

Crabby looked up, shook his head, and registered a mild reproach from Torp.

"We'll sort something out. I went to the School of Journalism with the chief news editor."

Torp gave him a neutral smile.

There were a couple of new dead people from Erik. One small and one medium. Torp had to pull himself together to get started. Then his phone rang again. It was probably the call from before.

"Torp speaking."

"Good day; you're talking to Emil. Are you the person responsible for purchasing electricity at Torp Communication?"

"Am I what?"

"I'm calling because I have a good offer. Your company can save up to twenty per cent on your electricity bill if you switch to North Energy. And then you have a guarantee that over half of the power comes from sustainable sources."

"It is already."

"Sorry?"

"It is already from sustainable sources. Half, that is."

"That's exactly what I'm saying. If you . . ."

Torp hung up and blocked the first four digits of Emil's number. That way, maybe half of the call centre staff could no longer call him. It didn't stop the offers from coming, but he had learned from experience that being systematic with it limited them to a tolerable level. Torp looked at the number from the call with the hissing background. It didn't look like part of a number from a call centre that had been making a nuisance of itself. Hmm.

"What's the password for the Wi-Fi?" called Emma from the middle office.

Bertel shouted back that it was on the router next to his desk. She would have to come in herself and write it down.

"It's a long one," she said, squatting down.

"That's what she said," replied Bertel and waited for the applause from his audience.

"I have an uncle like you," Emma snapped as she got up.

"Well, now—you're certainly a cheerful lady."

Emma ignored her office co-worker, who unusually had a slight blush arising around his throat.

Torp googled the number. Unsuccessfully. He spread his arms.

"Do you have a problem?" Emma was standing by his desk looking down. Torp showed her the phone number. She took out her mobile and pressed a few keys.

"Benedikte Koch."

"What?"

"Benedikte Koch. The subscriber at the number who called you and hung up."

"How did you do that?"

"You don't mean that."

She must have been able to tell from his face that he did.

"The oldest trick in the modern era. Go in on MobilePay, enter the number, and, for example, write one krone as the amount—nine times out of ten there's a response. Even prime ministers use MobilePay."

She held out her mobile and showed him the name that had appeared just below the amount and phone number.

Torp was impressed—mostly because that he had never heard of it or thought that it could be that simple.

What was it that Bjarne Jensen had said? That there was a Koch that both Brathenberg and Erling Jensen had talked to on the phone in the days leading up to their deaths. And it was a woman. It had to be the same one, of course. So why had she happened to call him? By mistake?

"Have you sent her a kroner?"

"No, of course not. You stop as soon as the name appears. So now you've learned that. Without having had to go to journalist school." Emma laughed.

Torp called and let it ring. The answering machine was anonymous; the telephone company's voice simply repeated the number and informed him that he could record a message. Torp refrained from doing so. He didn't quite know what he would talk to her about—apart from why she had called his number a few days after he had written obituaries of two elderly men she had been in contact with. About what? He hesitated and wrote a text message instead: *Dear Benedikte Koch, I would like to speak to you. It's probably nothing important and will only take a few minutes. Call when you have a couple of minutes. Kind regards, Ulrik Torp, journalist.* He found a Benedikte Koch on the University of Copenhagen's website. The picture showed a good-looking woman in her mid-fifties. The mobile number under the department's telephone number wasn't the same as the one Torp had. She must have two mobiles—one private and one for work. That wasn't particularly normal anymore, thought Torp. He called what had to be her work number. Here she had herself recorded a message on the answering machine—in both Danish and English. He tried the department.

"Ulrik Torp, journalist. Can I speak to Benedikte Koch?"

"What's it about?"

It dawned on Torp that he didn't actually know.

"It's about some research I'm doing . . . in the initial phase. She isn't answering her mobile."

"One moment." The voice returned after less than half a minute. "She sits in the Centre for Elections and Parties. Benedikte Koch is off sick."

"Just today?"

"I really don't know," replied the voice, now beginning to sound irritated.

"Do you have a private address for her?"

"If I did, I wouldn't be allowed to pass it on. Is there anything else I can help you with?"

There wasn't. Torp googled Benedikte Koch's name to find her address, and that was much more successful. She lived in the Kartoffel-rækker, the "Potato Rows," in the Østerbro quarter of Copenhagen. These rows of terraced houses had originally been built for shipyard workers, but had since been gentrified into an exclusive district just a few hundred metres from the office of her department. He googled her name. Bene-dikte Koch's husband was an architect; pretty much all of them were in the Kartoffelrækker, thought Torp, feeling a hint of envy about the privi-leged lifestyle he imagined the narrow townhouses had to offer. It was a long time since he had last felt that way. No children, apparently. Worked for the Parliament at Christiansborg before she came to the University of Copenhagen in the mid-'90s. Pigs could be fed on that CV, it was so anodyne, thought Torp. He went over to his old desk and to Emma, who had now found an internet connection and was doing whatever it was she was now doing.

"Are you busy?"

Emma looked up. Not particularly, she seemed to signal with her body language.

"Otto Brathenberg and Erling Jensen—do you know who they are?" He continued without waiting for her answer; of course she knew Brathenberg. "Erling Jensen was a Member of Parliament. They've both just died and had little to do with each other until their deaths."

"What do you need to know?"

"They've obviously had something going on. Something or other ties them together. Erling Jensen's son and daughter-in-law say that they were talking about the Parliamentary Control Committee. Maybe it's that."

Emma looked at him in such a way that Torp understood he should continue.

"The Parliamentary Control Committee is a relic of the Cold War and is about political control of the intelligence services. Its proper name is the Committee on the Intelligence Services. I didn't think it actually existed any more. No one really talks about it nowadays."

"Exciting," said Emma, with a tone of voice that suggested the opposite.

"And if we can connect this Benedikte Koch to them, then it's in the bag."

"And we—that's me, right?"

"As quickly as possible," said Torp, laughing uncertainly. He didn't quite know if Emma was happy or irritated, but had a feeling that she would get started right away.

"I have Monday cakes with me."

Axel's voice tore Torp out of the conversation with Emma. He had to get going on those obituaries. One small and one medium. He started with the small one. Maybe he could finish it before the cinnamon swirl was served. The relative to the dead person picked up the phone immediately, he offered his condolences, and yes, she had been waiting for a call and even written some notes; now she just had to find the piece of paper. Twenty-two minutes later, Else Pedersen, seventy-nine, of Nyborg had been ticked off the list, just in time for Axel's announcement that coffee and cakes were ready. Torp would sort out the medium obituary afterwards.

It was beginning to resemble a proper job.

Torp decided to take a detour and then take the Metro home from Øster-port. He convinced himself that it was to get some fresh air, now that it wasn't raining for once but almost blue sky. In reality, he was fooling himself—he wanted to take the route past the Kartoffelrækker and look up Benedikte Koch. He was curious about what she had had going with Otto Brathenberg and Erling Jensen. An experienced editor had explained many years ago that the most important thing for a journalist was a hunch, and the ability to follow a hunch when something gave you misgivings. This matter gave Torp misgivings.

On the way there, he saw today's placard from the *Express*. Even though the newspaper was now selling fewer print newspapers than a medium-sized local newspaper, its placards and front pages continued to live on as if it came out in 200,000 copies and could overthrow politicians. The *Express* could still do that—just not on its own.

Prime Minister Palle Enevoldsen was still in post but was taking a battering for the secret recording where he had spoken his mind about the National Day. Now there was a minister who was disassociating himself. *Minister pulls rug out from under Enevoldsen*, the placard promised. It wasn't correct. Firstly, a minister couldn't do that, and if you read the quote inside the newspaper by the Industry Secretary Hans-Erik Kolt, you would find that the front page was of course a condensed version. *"I wouldn't personally say anything like that—even when I don't think anyone is filming me."* The quote was bad enough in itself—Kolt managed in a single sentence to be a supporter of a National Day and distance himself from his boss in both substance and form. He did it elegantly and it was a mark of Palle Enevoldsen having moved to the outer edge of his prime ministerial era. The *Express* could, of course, smell all that. Attacking a powerful man on his way down was a favourite, and usually harmless, journalistic discipline, including for the *Express*.

Benedikte and Frank Koch. Torp let his gaze slide from the small letter box up to the terraced house. The neighbour on the one side was a former EU Commissioner, and on the other, he could see that the chairman of the board of the country's major television station lived. How it was possible to get the small, old workers' housing to cost 12 million, even 14 million kroner, was beyond Torp's understanding. He noted the wealthy carelessness on the street—an old Citroën 2CV, a little clutter in the small, not very well-tended front gardens, several windows in need of replacement, and some food boxes of organic vegetables on the stone steps. In the midst of capitalism's most perverted example of supply and demand, it was important to signal a laid-back attitude and moderation. Torp didn't understand it at all.

The doorbell appeared to be broken. He knocked, at first in a friendly and discreet manner, then more powerfully than intended. Maybe the bedroom was upstairs.

"They're not home," said a teenage girl, on her way out of the chairman's front yard.

"I thought Benedikte Koch was ill."

"I don't know anything about that. They're not home."

She opened the gate and was about to move on.

"Where are they, then?"

"I don't know. They left a few days ago, I think. Maybe they're in the summer cottage."

Torp wanted to continue the conversation, but she was already heading in the opposite direction. Should he ask the other neighbour, the former EU Commissioner? A window was open, so she or her husband was probably at home. No, this was too crazy. He might as well take the Metro and get home while he still had one.

Karen was in the kitchen when Torp stepped into the hallway.

"I've found a flat," came bubbling out of her before he had taken off his jacket.

"Really?" said Ulrik, hanging his jacket on the overcrowded hook in the narrow, overcrowded hallway.

"Ingelis from school, her husband is a lawyer and property manager. He has a flat we can take over—outskirts of Østerbro. Right away. Isn't that amazing?" said Karen, almost hopping around with excitement. "The only problem is the deposit and the rent in advance."

"How much is it?"

"One hundred eighteen thousand five hundred kroner. Wednesday at the latest. But then we also get the keys right away."

Ulrik stared at his wife. "How on earth are we going to raise over a hundred thousand kroner? We don't even have enough for a new battery for the car."

"I've arranged a meeting at the bank at nine o'clock tomorrow morning."

"Why haven't we talked about this?"

"Because it's just happened," she said, turning to attend to the pots on the stove. They were going to have meat rissoles, he could see. And because if she didn't do something, then nothing happened, Torp thought she was close to saying.

He was tall and thin, tending to the skinny, with a bouncing Adam's apple, and Torp guessed he wasn't much over twenty-five. How could you be a bank adviser at that age? He and Karen must be at the bottom of the customer hierarchy. On the other hand, he had a hard time seeing any real adults as he looked around the small bank branch this Tuesday morning. In addition to their man, there were two other employees to be seen. A young woman of about the same age and then a slightly older guy with overly long hair gelled back so both his forehead and his ears were exposed.

"So, I understand you've found a flat you would like," said the boy, who introduced himself simply as Bastian.

Torp hadn't dared to have a meeting with the bank for several years and had never heard of this Bastian before. They were sitting in the branch's small meeting room surrounded by glass walls so everyone could see them. Both Karen and Ulrik declined coffee.

It was Karen who did the talking. That they were homeless from the first of the month. That they, via one of her colleagues, had the opportunity to take over a flat. That they had until the next day, and that 118,500 kroner had to be paid for the total deposit and rent in advance.

"And the interest rate is super low," she added.

"Well," said the boy, hesitating, "not for this type of loan." He looked up at Torp. "I don't see that you have any income."

Karen continued, now in a slightly feverish tone and tempo.

"Ulrik has just started at a freelancer office in the city with several regular customers, isn't that right, Ulrik?"

He nodded.

"Yes, because one hundred eighteen thousand five hundred kroner is a lot of money," said Bastian.

"That's not true," Torp heard himself say.

"What?" said the boy, his protruding Adam's apple hopping.

"That's not true—one hundred eighteen thousand five hundred kroner isn't a lot of money. It's what some of your customers pay to have the worktop in their kitchen changed."

Bastian took a nervous sip from a bottle of the mineral water he had also offered his guests. He pretended to flip a little through the papers.

"I see you've had a number of overdrafts on your account over a long period, and when there is nothing that looks like a payslip from you, then I'm afraid that we'll have to have some form of security for the loan." He glanced out to the boss with the gelled hair on the other side of the glass wall. Torp concluded that they had talked about this beforehand.

"We don't have any," interjected Karen.

"These are austere times," he replied.

"Austere?" objected Karen.

"The bank had a profit of seven billion in the last financial year," Torp recalled.

"Yes, yes, indeed—but these are still austere times."

There was a long pause around the table. Karen didn't know what to say, and Ulrik had decided not to be the one to break the silence. Bastian lost.

"I'm terribly sorry, but we can't. The rules after the financial crisis have become very strict. It actually isn't something we can decide for ourselves."

"Of course it's something you can decide," said Torp sharply. "Just say that you don't want to, so we can get this over with."

"How in the world do you think you can pay it back?" parried the boy, regaining his composure.

"That's probably beside the point if we can't borrow anything," exclaimed Torp, getting up. Karen remained seated, even when Bastian pushed his chair back and unfolded his gangly body.

A few hundred metres down the road, Karen and Ulrik had one of their rare quarrels.

"I'm not going to be talked down to by a boy," Ulrik stated, spreading his arms wide, so that he almost struck a passerby who witnessed the marital showdown.

"It just happened to be that boy who was supposed to get us something to live in so we wouldn't be homeless," she said with tears in her eyes.

"Argh, that decision had damn well been made before we sat down with the damn water bottles."

"So what are you going to do now?"

"We'll come up with something, Karen," said Torp, attempting to be placatory.

"We'll come up with something," she mimicked. "Nothing is happening! This is unbearable!"

She was right about the last bit.

CHAPTER 11

Everyone was sitting in their seats this Tuesday morning when Torp came in after the visit to the bank and, with a couple of nods, delivered a slightly delayed good morning. Axel was working on the book he had been writing these last few years. Emma was immersed in her computer, and Bertel was working on yet another of his invoice-friendly press releases for a small business that believed him when he said it was a good idea. Crabby was in the middle of an argument with his old friend from the School of Journalism.

"You can't fucking do that!" he shouted, his voice shrill and his eyes watery. "That was my story."

Torp looked over at Bertel.

"The *Express* has pinched his story. They have it on the front page today."

Torp tried to recall the newspaper's placard from Nørreport—something about a clash over millions. Was that Crabby's story?

"'Was' is the right word," continued Bertel. "Crabby told them yesterday that he hadn't finished researching it and it would take a few more days. Now they've got hold of the documents themselves and written the story."

"I'm going to the union and my lawyer," said Crabby with no conviction in his voice and hung up. His eyes were fierce and red. "They say they had the story already."

"Did they?"

"He offered a tip-off fee of one thousand kroner."

"Jesus Christ," exclaimed Torp, sincerely indignant.

"You refuse that, of course," interjected Bertel.

"Call the union. They have lawyers for that sort of thing," continued Torp.

"Then it'll take six months, and I still won't get anything," said Crabby, his voice cracking.

"You say no to the tip-off fee."

Crabby turned his red-rimmed eyes on Bertel. "That's easy for you to say. You have one thousand kroner."

He turned round on the chair to show that he didn't need any more good advice this time around.

Why didn't he go to Netto? Both to shop and work, thought Torp. But he knew the answer very well—the villa in Vanløse, mortgaged up to the hilt, three children, and a wife working part-time. After a sudden impulse, he dialled a number at Police Headquarters that he hadn't used for more than six months.

"Anton speaking."

"Hi, it's Torp."

They went quickly through all the courtesies, and like the uptight guys they both were, they effortlessly jumped over everything else.

"What are you up to?" Anton asked.

"What did Otto Brathenberg actually die of?"

"Brathenberg? Haven't you had enough of him?"

"What did he die of?"

Anton swallowed an urge to say "no-don't-start-that-again-do-you-really-think-we-should-go-down-that-road?"

"He probably died of a heart attack—or rather lack of a heartbeat. Why?"

"A hunch, Anton. Just following a hunch. I'll buy you a cup of coffee if you just take some notes from your system about Brathenberg's death. Café Europa?"

"Who are you working for now?"

"The undertakers. In an hour?"

Anton paused. Then he relented; a walk in the balmy spring weather was probably not a bad idea after all.

"Why are you so interested in Brathenberg's death?" asked Anton, sipping his fifty-eight-kroner cappuccino, which left a little foam on his upper lip.

"Have you investigated it at all?"

"An old man lies dead in his bed after, incidentally, having suffered a minor stroke a few months earlier," said Anton, shaking his head. "How do you think we have the manpower for border control and Koran burnings—by throwing eight men at such a case?"

"Was there anyone with him when he died?"

"His wife, Lise, was away all weekend. Why are you so interested in him?"

"Wasn't there anyone looking after him?"

Anton checked his transcript. It wasn't a case he had had anything to do with. It wasn't even a case, actually.

"A private service company, WeCare, came by every day. What are you looking for?"

"Have you talked to them . . . WeCare?"

"I really don't know, Torp," said Anton, putting his cup down and wiping the foam off his upper lip. "You know, it was just an old man who died in bed. It'll also happen to us someday if we're lucky. Why don't you answer my questions?"

"It may be nothing at all," apologised Torp.

"That's probably the most accurate thing you've said all day."

Anton got up. He was, in fact, just out to breathe some fresh air.

"Your round?"

Torp nodded, gave the waitress 120 kroner for the two cups of coffee, and told her to keep the change, immediately regretting it. On the way back, Lindskov called. He was going home to Bente; she had got worse. A sclerosis like this was unpredictable.

"The boss wants an editorial about Enevoldsen for tomorrow," said the *Daily News*'s society editor and leader writer. He was sitting in his car.

"The melody?"

"We're tightening the screw. It can't go on like this any longer. His own ministers are undermining him, blah, blah, blah—something like that. We're bringing an opinion poll tomorrow—support for him among the Liberals' own voters is plummeting. They love Kirsten Rolighed."

"Should it be a now-he-should-resign leader?"

"No, no," said Lindskov, laughing from his car. "It's too early for that, Torp."

"Too early?"

"It's like *Jaws*; do you remember that?" Torp did. "It's a contract between the audience and the film company. We don't show the shark until the end—it would spoil the whole dramaturgy."

"Dramaturgy?"

"Torp, for crying out loud, you haven't been out that long!"

No, Torp hadn't. He knew the game very well. The newspaper's leaders and the mood of the people should more or less walk in step—a gap of a couple of steps, no more. But the direction was given and the goal in sight. Enevoldsen was finished. That had been decided, whoever had done the deciding—Lindskov the survivor was obviously one of them.

"We're tightening the screw, but there must be room for a few more twists. It's fairly high priority, so it may well be around three thousand characters. You just write away, then I'll shorten it if necessary. Can you have it done by six p.m.?"

Torp looked at his watch. It was the middle of the afternoon. It was Tuesday and badminton night.

"You'll have it in an hour," he promised.

He had got back to the office during the conversation. He tightened the screw and wrote 3,200 characters while wondering what it really was that Palle Enevoldsen had done wrong, since it was obviously going to end this way. Now the *Express* was no longer alone. When the *Daily News* got on the bandwagon, others would follow. The shark was on its way up to the surface. Torp came to think about today's four medium obituaries. He hadn't even looked at them. They would have to wait. He googled WeCare, the private service company owned by a private equity fund with the ambition of filling the gaps on the top shelf of the welfare state, and called the main number.

"Ulrik Torp, journalist. I'm looking for information about a customer visit in Hellerup last Sunday."

"We don't have customers. We have clients," came the reply.

"Sorry, client visit. Who should I talk to?"

"What's it about?"

"That I am looking for information about a . . . client visit last Sunday."

"You can't just call about it as a journalist. Are you a client or a relative?"

"I'm a journalist."

"Oh, yes. We can't give information. Should I refer you to our press and information officer?"

"No thanks. Thanks for your help." He hung up.

"Come with me."

Emma was standing next to him with her hands on her hips.

"Come on," she insisted.

"Why?"

"Come on, now," she commanded and walked back to the corridor. "Look at this."

Emma pointed with her pen at a sheet of paper on her desk with three timelines.

"Erling Jensen was a member of the Parliamentary Control Committee from its establishment in 1988 and then for ten years after that."

She looked up at Torp, who nodded. He was well aware of that.

"Benedikte Koch graduated from university in 1989. She immediately got a job in Parliament, and then, take a look here."

Emma pointed to her sheet of paper and Benedikte Koch's timeline.

"She was secretary of the Control Committee for two years until 1992," Emma said.

"I had no idea that that committee had a secretary."

"What does the committee do, exactly?" asked Emma, looking up at him.

"The Control Committee monitors the two intelligence services: the police's and the military's."

Axel could hear what they were talking about and came in from the bay window. He could recall the debate when the committee was set up.

"The Minister of Justice and the Minister of Defence inform the members of the committee about some of the nation's biggest secrets," he added. "It's supposed to ensure parliamentary control over the intelligence services and prevent a deep state, a state within the state, and that sort of thing."

"And Brathenberg is Minister of Justice until 1992."

Emma leaned back smugly in her office chair and spread both arms out wide as if in a gesture of victory.

"Brathenberg, Jensen, and Koch meet in the Parliamentary Control Committee from 1990 to 1992," she said.

"What's all this about?" asked Axel, looking inquisitively at both of them.

"How do you find out what was talked about in such a committee thirty years ago?" Emma asked.

Axel shook his head. "You can't. The committee is shrouded in secrecy. No one knows where they meet or how often. The members' notes during the meeting are collected and placed in a safe box. There are severe penalties if you say the least thing to the outside world. A Defence Minister was once fired for saying what *hadn't* been talked about in the committee."

"So how can it be called a control?" asked Emma with genuine surprise.

"You may well ask," said Axel, nodding. "In principle, a member can go to the Prime Minister, but this has probably never happened."

"That's not control. It's hostage-taking," Emma remarked.

"But why are you talking about the Control Committee?" asked Axel, looking at both of them.

Torp shook his head. "Just a hunch," he replied. "A few too many coincidences."

"Who sits on such a committee?" asked Emma.

"A Member of Parliament from each of the five largest parties," Axel answered immediately. "It went fine until the Radical Left became the fifth largest in the previous election. The system hadn't foreseen that," he said with a laugh. "It's rarely the Super League."

They googled their way to the committee members over the years.

"Just look at 1990 to 1992." Torp pointed to Erling Jensen's name and the four other members of the Control Committee.

"Are the others still alive?" Emma asked.

"Bjarne died long ago. So did Henning Vistisen. Look at them—there are almost no women in all those years," Axel pointed out. They checked the other two names, which told them very little. Both had died more than ten years ago.

"Erling Jensen was the last one," said Torp.

"And Brathenberg," added Axel.

"That means that Benedikte Koch is now the only one left who knows what was talked about in the Parliamentary Control Committee between 1990 and 1992," muttered Torp, almost to himself.

"By the way, who's in charge of the till here in the store?" asked Emma. She sensed that the conversation between the two male dogs was about to glide out into nothingness. "I have to pay for half a month. Twelve hundred fifty kroner, is that right?"

"I'll just send you the account number," began Axel, but was interrupted by Emma, who was fishing curled banknotes out of the pockets of her holey jeans.

"Nine fifty, ten fifty, eleven hundred, eleven fifty . . . twelve hundred fifty. There you go," she said, stuffing the rest back in her pockets.

"Don't you use a card?" Axel was staring at her in amazement.

"As little as possible. I know what it can be used for," she replied, deadpan.

"I haven't paid my rent."

Crabby appeared from behind Torp. He hadn't uttered a word since the showdown with the *Express*; his eyes were still red.

"It's just come due. Can it wait a bit?" Crabby asked. He was squirming uncomfortably.

"Of course it can wait," said Torp.

"Then you'll owe for two months." Axel hesitated. They weren't used to this.

Crabby's eyes went shiny again. "I had been betting on that story for the *Express*. There were several good monthly salaries in it." He flung out his arms in resignation.

"Would you like two of my obituaries?" said Torp, without really thinking about it. Of the two, he was probably in the tightest fix; he would have no place to live in a couple of weeks. At least Crabby had that—for a little longer. "You can have all four of them. I don't need them!" he exclaimed. "It's four thousand kroner for less than a day's work."

Torp was getting intoxicated by his own mood.

"Bertel! You must surely have a press release or some ad-paid whore-article that Crabby can get."

Bertel was sitting at his desk and looked up from his computer. He pretended not to know what it was all about, but Torp had a firm grip on him.

"Out with something, Bertel."

"I can't accept that," objected Crabby half-heartedly.

"It'll go to the rent here, so it's actually more us who are doing the accepting. I'll just email the contact information to you; maybe you can get hold of some of the relatives right now. Then you're up and running."

Torp didn't know why he was so excited about the idea, but with the prospect of doing real journalism again, the obituaries were suddenly in his way.

"This is pure socialism," protested Bertel, while finding a task—an interview with the owner of a lamp factory in Viborg in connection with an advertising supplement which the trade association was bringing as an insert in the *Viborg Diocese Gazette* in a few weeks' time. "You can get three thousand kroner . . . no, probably more like twenty-five hundred kroner for it. Deadline on Friday; four thousand characters including spaces."

He made it sound as if it were the crown jewels that were being handed over, and it was received in the same spirit by Crabby.

"I really can't accept this."

"Of course you can," intervened Axel. "We need your rent."

Like Emma, he had no work to pass on, although the two of them were probably the most solvent in the group—Emma because she neither owned nor owed anything, and Axel because he had his old age under control.

"What a fourth state power we have assembled here," he mumbled, as much to himself as anyone, as he turned around with Emma's greasy banknotes in his hand and sat down in the bay window again.

They all knew that the relief they were offering was like asking Crabby to pee in his pants. All it did was postpone the sale of his house and the upheaval in his and his family's life. But Crabby acknowledged their efforts; it gave him a warm feeling inside.

Torp decided to give Erling Jensen's papers in the old Coop plastic bag a chance. Maybe they weren't just notes from a vain old politician after all. Maybe there was something about the Parliamentary Control Committee from 1990 to 1992, something that made Brathenberg, Jensen, and Koch call each other thirty years later and, apparently, decide to contact Torp. And something that could suggest an explanation as to whether the deaths of two old men within a few days were coincidental or not.

Torp had put the bag on the shelf by his desk. He knew it had been there the day before, just under the crumpled copy of the *Daily News*.

Now it was gone.

CHAPTER 12

B loody hell, that's way over the top!"

Axel Boas was shouting from inside the bay window. To begin with, no one took any notice of him—Axel often commented on things he read, but rarely as loudly as now. He got up and walked into the fine living room. Crabby was preoccupied with a relative of one of Torp's obituaries. Bertel had gone to a meeting, and Emma wasn't the type to get up until noon, as she had explained without elaborating on what she did to get the nights to go by.

"What's over the top?" replied Torp politely as the only one there who could address the outburst.

"Have you read the *Daily News*'s leader on Palle Enevoldsen?"

"It's just words, Axel."

"Just words? What do you mean by that? That's what we make our bloody living from."

"Yes, yes," interjected Torp, "but those are just words in a leader."

"Have you read it? They're disparaging him for being against a National Day on June the fifteenth. They're saying he's un-Danish."

"Well, not quite that directly," objected Torp.

"Have you read it?"

Torp tried to look down discreetly and muttered an answer no one would be able to decipher.

Axel was red in the face from a fury he was able to build up all by himself when he was outraged. It had been his driving force and motor throughout his journalistic life. It was the fire that had earned him the Cavling Prize as a young man. Torp envied him for a brief moment. Imagine never being indifferent. Ever.

"It's far more subtle than that."

Axel was holding the newspaper in outstretched arms—his reading glasses were lying on his desk. He interrupted his headlong spurt into reading aloud and turned his head again towards Torp.

"The leader writer has deliberately mixed things up. Believe me, he knows exactly what he's doing, that leader writer." Axel's finger was trembling menacingly.

"Are we sure it's a 'he'?"

A little smile pressed itself onto Axel's face, but it wasn't a proper smile.

"Believe me, Torp. It's a he."

He turned his attention back to the newspaper, which was again being held out in outstretched arms due to the reading glasses in the bay window.

"Is Enevoldsen in step with his core voters' original culture, when he turns his back on Dannebrog in this way? Can you hear that, Torp?"

Torp blushed a little and shrugged.

"Core voter and *original culture.* Do you think when he says *core voter,* he means Ali, who has been voting for the Liberals for twenty years? And do you think *original culture* is before or after the Olsen Gang films?"

"Argh," responded Torp.

"Those inserted sentences and tiny words that just accidentally happen to creep in. Like a cut with a razor blade, so thin and fine that no one notices it until it's too late."

"You really can't force such an interpretation on it."

"Oh yes, I can," dismissed Axel. "Okay, this may just be a superficial treatment, smooth and fine. But it's national romantic racism. That's exactly what it is."

"It's just a leader. People don't care about that sort of thing," said Torp, trying to defuse the situation.

Axel took out his phone, went on Twitter, and pulled the screen all the way up to his face.

"The leader of the Nationalists, Annegrethe Hulsig, wrote an hour ago in a tweet with a link to the leader: *The statement from the Prime Minister lacks spirit and history, but he won't be deciding this alone. The Nationalist Party demands that the matter be discussed in the parliamentary chamber, so that we can name and unmask everyone who disgraces Dannebrog in this way.* It's followed by a red heart emoji and a Dannebrog emoji."

Torp blushed even more, but said nothing. He had been looking for the Coop bag with Erling Jensen's papers ever since he discovered that it had disappeared the day before, and he was having difficulty concentrating on Axel's outburst. The bag was nowhere to be found; no one had noticed it, and Axel had solemnly sworn that he hadn't thrown it in the rubbish bin in the backyard, not even by accident. It was usually he who kept order in the tenancy. Torp was annoyed at not having leafed through the papers more thoroughly when he received them from Erling Jensen's son. At first glance, they had just looked like a vain politician's notes about his own—overrated—achievements. Could he perhaps have taken notes after meetings of the Parliamentary Control Committee? Torp was convinced that Emma had put her finger on something—there was nothing else connecting Brathenberg, Jensen, and Koch.

"A disgrace," sneered Axel. "There are six hundred sixty likes, one hundred eighteen comments, and eleven retweets in less than an hour. Just a leader? Just words?"

He turned and went back to his reading glasses. Torp cleared his throat without wanting to say anything. Maybe the leader had gone slightly overboard. He shuffled around a little uneasily on his chair. Lindskov had been very enthusiastic. *Not a comma,* he had written back the night before—not a comma had been deleted or added. Was it really worth six bottles of red wine? The box had just arrived. No one in the office had yet begun to ask about the deliveries. Ah well, harmless and immaterial leaders would probably still have to come out if Lindskov's wife's multiple sclerosis continued to cause him problems.

Torp extended his leg. He had—once more—stretched a tendon when they had been playing badminton the previous evening. "If you're in any doubt, then it's not a pulled muscle," the confident advice had been from the accountant as Torp had lain writhing on the floor at a moment when he and Karen had been hopelessly behind in the second set of their mixed doubles. He had been in doubt, so it was obviously not a pulled muscle. The strain had still been enough, though, for him to limp into the dressing room, to Torben's great irritation.

"Tine tells me you're going to be homeless from the first of the month."

They had been standing naked in the shower, Torben drying his swelling belly hurriedly.

"Yes," Torp had mumbled.

"We have the summer cottage, but we use it ourselves," Torben had continued.

"We'll find something. Don't worry about it."

"It isn't so easy if you aren't able to throw a tidy sum of money at it."

Karen, for Christ's sake!

"It's like the Wild West, the rental housing market. The Wild West. If you knew what I've experienced as an accountant."

"But I don't know."

Torben had bent down with his back to his badminton opponent to dry his thin legs. Torp had looked directly down at the accountant's flaccid buttocks before his reflexes had made him turn both face and body away. Then they had stood with their backs to each other. Torp had quickly finished drying himself and put on his underpants. That had helped.

"Money under the table. Fifty thousand kroner to have a floor sanded. Waiting lists that disappear in favour of a little brother, cousin, or mistress. I'm telling you, rental housing and cooperative housing is a market for the chosen few, if it isn't in Taastrup. Ha!"

"We'll find something."

"In fourteen days and without money? Forget it, Ulrik. Such things just don't happen."

On the way home in the Metro, the talk about housing had continued, only now with Karen.

"Why shouldn't I tell Tine about our housing problems? It's an honest case, and maybe she or Torben could help," Karen had said defensively.

"It's not you who has to listen to that fool with a bare backside," Ulrik had grumbled.

His leg was painful, he was tired, and he regretted that he had given four obituaries to Crabby. Medium ones, to boot. Karen mustn't find out about that.

"Tine thinks we can borrow the tiny shed in her sister's allotment garden in Brønshøj."

"An allotment house! In Brønshøj!"

"Why not? It could be very cosy. They aren't going to be using it over the summer, she thought. So it would be nice for them if there was someone to take care of it."

"An allotment house," Torp had repeated. "Tell me, Karen, don't you have any pride or lower limits?"

"So come up with a suggestion."

They didn't speak for the rest of the journey home. Torp convinced himself that they hadn't become enemies. Nor had it been a quarrel. Not really. There just hadn't been anything more to say.

"Hello!"

Emma stuck her pale face right into Torp's. It made him jump.

"Where were you just then?"

She smiled her neutral smile that only rarely showed itself.

Torp shook his head. Axel had finished his lecture on the *Daily News*'s Enevoldsen leader, and Emma had arrived in the meantime. She sat down on the edge of Torp's desk.

"I've been thinking about that Brathenberg guy."

"Yes?"

"You talked to the private service company that was looking after him?"

"WeCare."

"And what could they tell you?"

"Not much," said Torp with a shake of his head. "I tried to get in touch with the nurse who had been with Brathenberg the weekend he died, but the company refused to help."

"Because you were a journalist?"

"Yes."

"What if you'd been a relative?"

"Then it would probably have been another matter." Torp shrugged.

"Look up the company," said Emma, pointing at his computer. "There must be some numbers other than the main number. A regional number."

There was. She took out her mobile.

"Hi, you're talking to Katrine Brathenberg. My grandfather died last weekend, and I really want to get in touch with the home help who attended to him on his last day. The family would like to thank her for the excellent care she gave him."

She smiled at Torp and raised both eyebrows in triumph. He half-heartedly tried to protest.

"Hellerup, yes. Otto Brathenberg."

She wrote down a number and said thank you.

"Here you are." She handed him the note with a mobile number and name—Gosia, her name was—then turned around and went back to the passage. Torp followed her, trying to be reproachful.

"You didn't damn well learn that in the short time you went to the School of Journalism. Lying like that is against all the ethical rules."

"So don't call her."

Torp wanted to go back to his desk, turned back halfway, and handed the note to Emma.

"Can't you do it?"

"He was such a sweet man," said Gosia on the phone.

She was visiting a client and was a little busy but could easily chat for a bit.

"What was your name? Katrine?"

Emma confirmed and put the phone on speaker so Torp could follow along. You could hear she was from Poland, but the Danish sounded effortless, and she was easy to understand.

"I," she said and hesitated before continuing throatily, "I am sor-ry for your loss."

Emma thanked her and assured her that the family had been very happy for WeCare and especially for Gosia, whom she understood was her grandfather's regular home help. Gosia confirmed that. She had been coming to him since the stroke in the winter.

"He was in great shape when I was with him last Saturday. He always teased me a little about my accent," she continued, "and he was looking forward to the football match the next day. I wonder if he got to see it."

"Weren't you with him on Sunday? I thought you were supposed to come every day when Grandma was away?"

Emma was living right into the role; Torp was outraged and impressed at the same time.

"When we were about to start on Sunday morning, I was told that Otto was to be skipped. It happens sometimes that a client asks for that if they aren't going to be at home or a son or daughter has come by and they don't want to be disturbed."

"So there was nothing strange in that?"

"No, not really."

"Not really?"

Gosia hesitated. Someone was calling in the background. She had to get back to work.

"The woman who told me was a new colleague. I was actually wondering a little about how she knew."

"Could I get to talk to her?"

"I don't know. I only saw her that one day, last Sunday, but there is a lot of shifting around, so it's probably not that strange."

"Probably?"

"A little strange. Not a lot," said Gosia.

"Can you describe her? I'd really like to get in touch with her."

"She's not at WeCare anymore. I know that because I even asked about her when I heard that Otto was dead."

"What did she look like?" Torp tried to communicate his question with mouthing and a whisper.

"Can you describe her?"

". . . I only saw her briefly that Sunday morning. It was ten days ago." Gosia thought about it. "I think she came from one of the Baltic countries. She spoke English, but it sounded like she had a Russian accent. So it was probably Estonia." She thought further. "Mid-thirties, short, dark hair, slim. I can't remember more than that."

Emma thanked her and prepared for landing. Gosia did the same.

"I mean, I'm really happy I got to know Otto, and I'm really glad you've called. It means a lot to me, but I have to get on with my work. I still have to vacuum half of the house."

Before they ended the phone call, Emma assured Gosia that her grandfather had died an easy and gentle death and had been doing well for the last few months and often told the family how happy he was to have Gosia.

"You're full of lies, Emma," exclaimed Torp, with equal parts reproach and admiration.

"Just say when," she answered, straightening herself up. "Has the old man been autopsied?"

Torp shook his head. "I don't know. Why?"

"Then you can find out what he died of."

"Denmark is the country in the Nordic region that performs the least autopsies, so I doubt it. If the police want an autopsy, they have to pay for it themselves—and then there is less money for border guards. And Brathenberg's death wasn't remarkable in itself."

"Has he been cremated and buried?"

"Saturday. His funeral is on Saturday."

"So he's lying waiting in refrigeration somewhere. There's plenty of time."

She repeated her neutral smile.

Anton at Police Headquarters was of a different opinion.

"You must be off your head, Torp. You're asking for an autopsy of the country's former Justice and Foreign Minister, who at the age of seventy-nine dies in his bed a few months after a stroke, because you can't find the home help who cleaned and cooked for him last Sunday. You've totally lost the plot."

"You're forgetting that Erling Jensen, the Member of Parliament, died a few days later, and that the two of them had been in close contact in the preceding weeks."

"Didn't you say that Erling Jensen had come to the hospice with his whole body riddled with cancer?"

"Yes, but . . ."

"Torp, for Christ's sake," said Anton, now with a little concern in his voice, "surely you can hear for yourself—this is a bit out there, right?"

Torp was well aware of that. He admitted it.

"Roger. More?"

"No, no—no more. Roger—argh, forget it," apologised Torp and hung up.

"What an idiot," exclaimed Emma.

"Maybe Anton's right. Maybe it's too out there."

"Nonsense. We agree that there's a connection between Brathenberg's and Erling Jensen's deaths, don't we?"

Torp nodded. They agreed on that.

"Then we have two murder scenes. Let's go out to the other one, the hospice in Frederiksberg."

They were standing on the quiet residential street, looking at the building and the activity around it. A gardener was getting the green areas ready for when spring planned to align itself with the calendar. A hearse had just stolen away with a coffin. A man walked past with his dog. One of the hospice's residents was sitting in a wheelchair with a blanket over him and a cigarette in his mouth. His carer was sitting next to him. They were chatting away as if they had all the time in the world they could wish for. Torp thought about his own death. Would he be similarly relaxed if he knew there were only a few weeks left? Would he be able to come to terms with the fact that it was all over? The dying man took one last puff of his cigarette before stubbing it out in a tall ashtray standing next to the wheelchair. He was older than Torp, but not much. Why should one stop smoking when lying in a hospice? It was almost 6:00 p.m. Emma had argued that it was a good time to take on the hierarchies and command paths—people were going to eat, and the bosses had gone home.

"I think you should do it," said Torp, giving her a gentle shove.

"I think so, too," she replied without hesitation.

She crossed the road, went straight over to the death row inmate and what must have been one of his last cigarettes, and fell into conversation with him and the carer. They didn't speak all that loudly. Torp couldn't hear anything, but the man in the wheelchair laughed with a little difficulty and immediately had a severe coughing fit. She accompanied them into the building.

Torp looked around at the Frederiksberg villas that surrounded the hospice. Many of them were twice as big as they needed to be. Would he really be sitting in an allotment house in Brønshøj in a fortnight, just because his idiot son-in-law had made a mess of things? It was hard to get out of Sofie exactly what Jonathan had done or not done. Maybe she hardly knew anything herself. It would be a shame for her if it turned out to be something illegal, he thought. He didn't give a damn about Jonathan. Right now, it was Sofie who mattered. They had to get rid of the flat in Berlin in the next wave, the one Jonathan couldn't control, together with their villa in Klampenborg. Where were *they* going to live, for that matter? It seemed to Torp that once one had reached a sufficiently high level of prosperity, then the law of gravity that applied to everyone else was repealed. Then you never became really poor again. Then there was no allotment house waiting as a last resort.

Now Emma was coming out of the discreet door. She was smiling, more than he had ever seen her smile before.

"What are you smiling about?"

"They have a CCTV camera in the corridor."

"Yes?"

"It was also filming the morning Erling Jensen died."

"And?"

"It's just that we're not allowed to watch those recordings."

"No?"

"Not even if you're a relative. Erling Jensen is my grandfather, you know."

An even bigger smile spread across her face. It almost looked like a real smile.

"It couldn't be done under any circumstances, even though I really wanted to know if my sister from Jutland had been visiting—the family hasn't seen her for several years due to an annoying matter, which I didn't want to go into."

"Stop all that now, Emma—what happened?"

"Then we talked further inside the boss's office—the boss who had left for the day." She could see she shouldn't drag it out any more. "And hanging on the wall was a note with the code for the CCTV system."

"How do you know it's that code?"

She cracked up in a giggle. "Because it said above the code: *Code for the CCTV.* We're going back to the office to look at the recordings."

"What's the code?"

They were sitting at Emma's computer in the corridor.

"Hospice1234—you wouldn't believe it," she said, the last bit mostly to herself. Didn't people ever learn to take these things seriously?

They quickly found the day on the recordings. They were black and white, filmed by a camera in the hallway, which filmed the people entering from behind. On the other hand, you got to see them from the front when they left again. Even though the camera was high up, the images were sharp. There was no problem recognising people when they left the hospice. Erling Jensen was found dead at 10:00 in the morning, about half an hour after he had had some water and a little breakfast in his room. Their search was therefore initially concentrated on visitors who had arrived in the half hour between breakfast and when he was discovered dead. A gardener stuck his head in, was given a key, and left again. An undertaker came in with a coffin on wheels.

"There—next to the undertaker, to the right of the coffin!"

Torp pointed, while Emma slowed down the recording. They looked at the time code. It was 9:43 a.m. They could see the back of a youngish woman. She nodded to the undertaker, who nodded back. Then he went to the left in the hallway, while she disappeared on the right side of the picture.

"The crucial thing is when she leaves again," said Torp, mostly just to control his excitement. Emma ignored the obvious statement.

"There she is!"

Torp pointed again, his pulse pounding in his temple; he looked at the time code: 9:48 a.m. For a brief second, it looked as if she almost looked up at the camera, but it was so high up, as Emma had noted, and was so discreet in both size and colour that few people would notice it. Emma stopped the recording. They looked at the picture: under forty, slim, short, dark hair.

"I can see by looking at her that she speaks English with a strong Estonian-Russian accent," exclaimed Torp.

"We'll find out soon."

Emma took a picture with her mobile phone and sent it as a text message to Polish Gosia. *Is this person here the one who told you that my grandfather, Otto Brathenberg, shouldn't be visited last Sunday? Best, Katrine.*

It took less than a minute before a text message came back from WeCare home helper Gosia: *Yes, that's her.*

"Now you can call your Anton at Police Headquarters. Now they have to do an autopsy," said Emma triumphantly.

CHAPTER 13

Y ou look like crap."

They were sitting at the meeting table in the Prime Minister's Office preparing the noon press conference which had been convened a few hours earlier. Palle Enevoldsen nodded heavily. He was accustomed to, and usually appreciated, his special adviser's outspokenness. His cheeks were hanging flabbily, his double chin was merging with his throat, and his eyes were bloodshot. He hadn't slept a great deal in the last seven years and even less in the past couple of days.

Press conference with the Prime Minister in the Mirror Hall at 12:00 p.m.

That was all. No headline, no topic, no hint of what it was all about. The text messages flooded into the special adviser's mobile from hopeful journalists who thought it was time for a little confidential information. Could she tell them on the quiet what it was all going to be about? She served one master and one only—the Prime Minister—and didn't reply to a single message.

"By the way—don't forget Otto Brathenberg's funeral the day after tomorrow. Saturday at ten. It's in your diary."

Enevoldsen muttered an acknowledgement that he was well aware of that. His lungs hissed as he inhaled. Thirty fags a day for thirty years were catching up on him. He slapped his hand on the newspaper that was lying between them.

"Now Joshua Como can no longer play in the national team."

He shook his head so that his cheeks could barely keep up.

"I suggest we post this on social media as soon as you've finished the press conference."

She passed a sheet of paper—the Prime Minister preferred paper—over to his side of the table. Her mobile rang. It was the Minister of Health again. He had asked to speak to his boss several times over the past twenty-four hours. She turned off the sound. It really had to wait.

"The best left back we've had in a generation."

Enevoldsen again slapped his hand down on the front page of the *Daily News. Requirement for birth in Denmark to be on the national team.* FIFA had bowed to the political pressure and decided that only players born in a country could play on the national team, regardless of citizenship. The only exception was if one had been "adopted before the end of one's third year of life," as the federation's lawyers had put it.

"Joshua Como has Danishness coming out of his ears."

"I would just like you to approve the last sentence, too."

"Will they only be happy when all eleven are blond?"

She shook her head in despair and didn't want to ask who the boss thought "they" were. She knew him well enough to know that there was no time for the answer. The press conference was due to begin in less than ten minutes.

"The last sentence: *We love and support Denmark.* I think that should be included."

Palle took a sip of his coffee, which in the meantime had become so lukewarm that he spat it back into the cup and angrily squeezed another piece of nicotine chewing gum out of the pack and chewed extra hard to get the effect immediately. How he missed a smoke.

"*We love and support Denmark,*" she tried again.

"Yes, yes, for pity's sake."

Palle Enevoldsen brushed it aside with a quick, professional look at the text destined for the social media accounts. Even though he was both tired and under pressure, he was perfectly clear on what had to be done. "The political window will close in a day or two," as his special advisers and his totally loyal department head had all advised the night before. He could almost not bear to be Prime Minister any longer and had been looking for a dignified exit in this election period; it certainly wasn't going to be now. Why did so many political careers come to an ugly end? Furthermore, there were no international top positions he could reasonably expect to be in play for at the moment. Palle had almost decided to play his trump card, but wasn't going to say anything to his adviser— she would just argue against it. That was why she was an employee and would never become a top politician. A real man of power must sometimes be able to play precisely the card that no one has expected or would dare to play.

Enevoldsen dared.

He stood up, spat the nicotine gum out into his hand, and placed it on the edge of the saucer next to the others.

"Okay—let's do this fucking press conference."

Ulrik Torp had felt surrounded by pessimism and nay-sayers all morning when he set his computer to livestream Palle Enevoldsen's suddenly convened press conference.

Breakfast had developed into one of the by now no-longer-so-rare quarrels with Karen in their flat which they had on borrowed time, now less than two weeks.

"What have you done, precisely?" she had begun accusingly.

"You mean, like, hunter-gatherer?" he had snapped back.

"Oh, spare me your man talk."

"What has it got to do with man talk?"

He had snarled *man talk*. It was too late now. Torp hadn't been able to find a reverse gear, and he didn't know if Karen had one anymore.

"That I'm supporting both of us, and you can't stand that."

"And so you think I could at least find us somewhere to live?"

"But you haven't done anything, Ulrik. You do *nothing*."

"What the hell do you expect me to do!"

Karen had got up with a jerk, making the chair clatter backwards. She had looked at her husband with teary eyes and—Torp had thought—with a contempt he could fairly well understand. She had lowered her voice, almost in resignation.

"I've said yes please to the allotment house in Brønshøj. We can borrow it all summer, if need be. And we don't have to pay anything for it. That's what I've done."

He had wanted to say sorry. He had wanted to say he was ashamed of not being able to contribute. That there might be hope now. That the Adam's apple in the bank could get stuffed. That he admired her fervour and insistence. That the happy pills were just a transition. That he felt bad. That she should sit down. That they should talk to each other. That an allotment house in Brønshøj was fine, even though it was a lie, which they both knew. He had wanted to say all this, while instead he just sat there silently watching her grab her bag and leave the flat.

The next note of pessimism had come on the mobile from Anton, while Torp had been walking from the Metro to the office.

"Your idea for an autopsy of Brathenberg isn't that simple," he had begun.

Anton had sounded more than interested when Torp had called earlier and told him about the dark-haired home help who had disappeared from WeCare after having been with both Otto Brathenberg and Erling Jensen just before their deaths.

"What the hell are you doing at Police Headquarters? I thought the idea was that you look for a murderer when someone has been murdered."

"It's not that simple, Torp."

"Yes, it is—it's precisely that simple."

"We first have to talk to that Gosia from WeCare before we know if there's anything to go on at all."

"But she said that it was the same dark-haired woman who was with Erling Jensen at the hospice."

"I don't interfere in your work as a journalist," had been Anton's impatient response. "I admit that it looks a little strange, but there is a way to go before we can get the whole apparatus rolling and start cutting up Brathenberg, just before he's to be buried. And then, moreover, no one's talking about murder here."

"When do you get the apparatus, as you call it, rolling?"

"You look after your stuff, Torp, and I'll look after mine."

"If Gosia says the same thing to you as she said to me, that it is the same woman—will you open him up then?"

"Take it easy. Today is Thursday. We have all day today and tomorrow before the funeral," Anton had replied, trying to be conciliatory.

"And then you can get on with Erling Jensen afterwards. Even if you are lying dying in a hospice, you don't necessarily die a natural death."

Torp had hung up as he entered the stairwell of the office community. A pushchair hadn't been pushed completely under the stairs. It was far from the first time it had been in the way. Torp had released the brake and had been about to roll it all the way in when he had spotted some rubbish in the corner. He had pulled the pushchair out again and bent down completely to reach it with his left hand. The stairwell didn't deserve clutter—it was impressive, old, and well-maintained, with the original hundred-year-old glass mosaics in all the windows from the time a glazier had a workshop on the ground floor and owned the property. Torp had taken it all in one go, a plastic mineral water bottle, a 7-Eleven paper bag with some croissant leftovers, and an old plastic bag with a small hole in the left side at the bottom. Torp had stopped in mid-movement. It was the bag with the old Coop logo—the bag he had got from Erling Jensen's son with the notes, the bag he had put on the shelf in the office and couldn't find anymore. It was empty. He had looked around, but knew in advance that there wouldn't be anything else to be found under the stairs. Erling Jensen's papers were gone.

Torp had the bag in his hand when he entered the office but didn't have time to ask if anyone had noticed anything or seen the contents before Crabby came up to him in an agitated state.

"Have you seen the *Express*?"

Crabby held out the newspaper. His eyes were red, but then they always were, thought Torp, so you couldn't immediately make anything of it.

The story of Joshua Como and the national team players who in the future would have to be born in the country to play for the national team was a true tabloid story and filled most of the front page. At the top right, they had made room for another: *Top-Notch Cheats in Research Scandal,* read the headline.

"They're stealing my story every single day at the moment. And for a tip-off fee of one thousand kroner."

The last comment was no doubt mostly meant as self-reproach because he had swallowed his sense of shame and sent an invoice to the newspaper.

Apart from the headline, Torp didn't really understand the story, which he was hardly alone in. Something about research funding, Copenhagen University, and millions, as well as accounts and a gallery of characters that was so complicated that no one could fully understand it despite today's clarifying articles.

"Where did you actually get your story from?"

Torp looked at Crabby, who was clearly suffering, both over the injustice that had befallen him, but also because of the financial collapse that awaited him, his wife, and their three young children. Jumping down a social class could be hard. Skipping a class on the way down was the nightmare Torp himself had been through and still found himself in the middle of. Crabby looked away. Torp was immediately embarrassed at his unprofessional question.

"Sorry, I didn't mean it like that. I mean, it wasn't . . ." He was fumbling for words until they made eye contact. "You know what I mean, don't you? I wasn't asking you to . . ."

Crabby nodded. Of course, he couldn't tell anyone where he got the story from. And no, he hadn't seen any old papers that had been in an old Coop bag.

* * *

"That is why I am very pleased that my government is introducing a National Day, Valdemarsdag, on the fifteenth of June—the first one will be in two months' time."

Torp recognised Palle Enevoldsen's characteristic way of coming to a conclusion—with a twist in his last sentence. The Prime Minister looked out across the assembled political journalists, whom everyone knew he had divided into, on the one hand, a large pile of idiots and, on the other, individuals he respected.

"Will shops, workplaces, and everything else be closed that day?" That was one of the idiots.

"A National Day is a day off for most people. We will take up the exact details with the government's support parties." Enevoldsen paused and put the planned political pressure on parts of the opposition. "This is also an invitation to others who may wish to join in. I have a bit of a hard time imagining that some parties will actually be against Denmark."

He had an expectation that there would indeed be some parties that refused. This situation seemed tailor-made to create a split in the opposition, now that it finally needed to be split.

Torp was following the press conference together with Axel and Bertel, who were watching over his shoulder.

"How does this chime with the clip of the Prime Minister that we all saw on social media a few days ago, where you called supporters of a National Day idiots?"

Enevoldsen took a deep breath. The question was frighteningly predictable, and he had gone through the answer with his special adviser several times. He couldn't remember saying that at all, even though it actually corresponded very well to his position on the matter. The damage had been done in every way—"perception is reality" was the mantra from his special advisers. This was all about damage control.

"I don't remember using those words, and don't know exactly on what occasion that recording was made and by whom. In any case, it has been taken out of context, as the decision about a National Day shows."

"But you said that supporters of a National Day are idiots," continued the journalist, one of those he actually respected. A member of staff from the Prime Minister's Office tried to take the microphone away from him—only one question per journalist.

"I and this government will always love and support Denmark," maintained Enevoldsen. Those journalists who had known the Prime Minister through his long political life and had experienced his temper could see that he was about to explode. Sometimes they managed to push him all the way to the edge and a little over. On these occasions, his eyes would become evil, his breathing fitful, and then—for a brief moment—he would lose control. It made for good TV, and the journalist who had succeeded with the last thrust enjoyed a collegial pat on the back afterwards.

"How can you say something one day and the exact opposite the other?" tried the next journalist who had been given the microphone.

"I love and support Denmark and always will. So does the entire government," intoned the Prime Minister. That was the sentence they had decided should be the main message of the rescue attempt.

"You're not answering the question," said a new journalist.

Were they ganging up on him? He was usually able to control them.

"Why has it taken you several weeks to find out that you side with Denmark?"

They smelled blood. Enevoldsen, who in his seven years as Prime Minister had controlled most of the press corps with the divide-and-rule strategy that only absolute power allows, suddenly looked like a wounded wildebeest on the savannah surrounded by hyenas. The evil eyes flickered for a brief moment. His narrow, clenched lips seemed to dry up.

"My God, he's in a hole," said Axel from behind Torp's left shoulder.

"He just doesn't give a damn about Denmark," said Bertel from behind Torp's right shoulder.

Palle Enevoldsen pulled himself up to his full height. He embodied everything the National Board of Health warned men in their mid-fifties against: obesity, alcohol, cigarettes, stress, pressure, lack of exercise, and lack of sleep. Maybe that was why he was still a fearsome opponent—he had very little to lose. He had made his decision. This press conference hadn't gone as his advisers had hoped. He didn't have charge of the agenda; he was only reacting to it—until now.

"And finally, now that there are no more questions, I would just like to make a comment on recent writings about my person."

The few seconds of uproar among the journalists in the Mirror Hall ended. The Prime Minister had their total attention.

"There has been a degree of criticism of my leadership of both the government and the party lately. It's a criticism I neither can nor want to live with."

Torp stared silently at his computer screen. Even Bertel withheld any fresh comments.

Enevoldsen let the pause hang longer than others would have dared, but just as long as his power allowed him.

"Later today, I will therefore be convening my party's national executive for an extraordinary general meeting seven days from today with one item on the agenda: my continued leadership of the party and therefore also of the country. Thank you for your time."

Enevoldsen turned his body ninety degrees and left the Mirror Hall with remarkably brisk steps, with his especially surprised adviser on his heels.

"Bloody hell," Torp mumbled to himself, looking up at Axel and Bertel. "The old man just took charge of the agenda."

Social media was overflowing with joy at the prospect of political victory in the form of a National Day. In the minutes after Palle Enevoldsen's press conference, comments about Valdemar's Day outdid the large numbers of comments about only those born in the country being allowed on the men's national football team. *It's about bloody time, too. It was getting to the stage where you couldn't see the difference between the Danish national team and Cameroon's. Now we can be proud of our national team again. No more monkey sounds.* Suddenly, comments like these had been replaced by victory tweets about the National Day that was to save Denmark's honour for those "who love Denmark."

Torp followed the comments in astonishment—it was party time on social media.

"Half of them are trolls—you know that, don't you?"

Emma was standing with folded arms next to Torp, thus preventing Bertel from being part of the gathering. He tried to squeeze himself in again to get a view of the computer screen, the focal point of their attention.

"Maybe, but there's no doubt about the direction," objected Bertel. "This is a popular no to the Great Replacement," he continued with victory in his voice.

"The Great Replacement! What's this replacement you're talking about?" Axel turned his attention to his office companion. There was only sincere curiosity in his voice.

"Yes, well, you know. Muslims, of course," replied Bertel, a little uncertainly. He sensed the criticism between the lines and was manning himself up. "That we Danes become a minority in our own country. Then you'll just see Sharia law and all that."

Emma took over.

"The Great Replacement is the idea that, in the space of a few decades, the Danish population will have been replaced by a Muslim population due to uncontrolled immigration and high birth rates."

She didn't take her eyes off the computer screen, where the comments were continuing to roll in. Nine out of ten were jubilant about a National Day on 15 June.

"It isn't only Denmark that's facing a change in the population, they say. It's the whole of Europe," she continued.

"Who are *they*?" Axel looked puzzled. "I guess it can't just be you, Bertel." He smiled and they all laughed, except for Emma.

"Kirsten Rolighed used exactly that expression at the demonstration. The Great Replacement. She said that," said Torp eagerly. He hadn't given it much thought on that occasion.

"It's become a marker. The gate all true national conservatives must step through to be accepted in those circles. The dog whistle the believers respond to," continued Emma.

"Dog whistle? Which circles? Where do you get all that from?" Axel looked at her.

She smiled at him—almost lovingly. "Wake up! This is what the world looks like in those circles. Europe is lost, now it's time to save Denmark. That's how they think."

"And now *they've* got their National Day. I wonder if they get their hunger satisfied by being fed or just get hungrier," said Axel, staring into thin air.

"And an all-white national football team. Don't forget that," finished Emma before turning around and walking back to her place in the corridor.

"But who are *they*?" asked Axel again, a little to himself and this time without expecting an answer.

Torp's mobile phone dissolved the gathering. Axel crossed the passage to the bay window. Bertel went off to his desk with a slightly restrained but clearly well-satisfied smile.

"Hi—it's Vivi."

Torp leafed through his memory. He didn't know many people and certainly not many who would call him. The voice presented itself as if it were obvious that he would know who it was.

"Vivi?"

"From the west coast."

The voice was trying to hide its disappointment at not being recognised right away. The west coast? Torp forced himself not to look at his computer screen and instead concentrate on the conversation that hadn't yet become a conversation.

"Vivi!" The voice now sounded a little offended. "Vivi from Østerbro with the halfwit ex-husband!"

Suddenly, it dawned on him. The two-week spa break with psychotherapist Dion. The sessions with a full serving of bullshit, and yet two weeks that had helped. And the walks on the beach, most often with Vivi, when they could be allowed to just be the two of them. That Vivi. The social educator with an ex-husband and stress. He became unusually happy and went into a hectic apology.

"I was just somewhere else completely, sorry. Hi, Vivi, how nice."

"Hi, Ulrik."

"How are you?"

"I'm fine, thanks," she replied, pausing just long enough to indicate that she wasn't. "I've been thinking about you a lot. Could we meet up?"

Dion had encouraged the participants to meet each other according to desire and need. "You're like fellow soldiers who have been in the trenches together. Use each other," was the advice he had given before they went their separate ways. Ulrik hadn't thought any more about it, but the only one he could bear seeing again actually was Vivi. The only one he really felt he had got to know. Vivi's request sounded completely innocent.

"That could be nice," he heard himself say. *Nice* was an innocent enough word, but he actually really wanted to. He couldn't on Saturday due to a funeral and some work, but what about Sunday? They agreed on Sunday at 2:00 p.m. at a café by the Lakes, not far from where she lived. They assured each other of how much they were looking forward to it. Sunday.

CHAPTER 14

For the first time in a long time, Ulrik Torp felt like a real journalist—a permanent job, an editor, an assignment, and some readers waiting for his words. He let the Polo's flimsy engine labour in fourth gear and positioned himself in the inside lane to get onto the Holbæk motorway. It was self-deception, of course. He had a single, real journalistic job for a lousy fee, but he was looking forward to the interview, looking forward to writing the article, and looking forward to being able to live in the illusion for just a moment that his existence both hung together and made sense.

In the morning, he and Karen had tacitly agreed not to mention the quarrel from the day before. Karen reminded him in a neutral way that they were going to the closing dinner of the badminton season on Saturday night—the couples' dinner, which neither of the men had had any say in. She immediately saw the reluctance on his face.

"It'll be nice," said Torp, in an attempt to be positive, while pretending to be busy with the news on his smartphone, which was partly true.

The political commentators agreed that Palle Enevoldsen's move at yesterday's press conference had been smart. The national executive wouldn't have any other choice but to back a beleaguered, but wily, party leader, and then the little revolt would be crushed before it grew out of control. Kirsten Rolighed and her supporters didn't have a chance, the analysts agreed. They also agreed that the Prime Minister's decision to give in to a National Day on Valdemar's Day was populist but wise, especially after the fatal clip on social media where he had called its supporters idiots.

As one commentator remarked, "The funny thing about populism is that it is so popular." Ha, ha.

Torp noticed a small article about a powerful flu-like virus that wasn't the real flu and apparently came from China. The Minister of Health had no comment.

"I'm getting a key from Tine for her sister's allotment house. Just in case it proves necessary," remarked Karen, before saying goodbye with a light touch on his shoulder.

She always got to work early. In the space of one day and without discussion, the allotment house in Brønshøj had gone from Plan over-my-dead-body to Plan B—in fact, it was Plan A; he knew that was how it was going to turn out. How far was he really from the man in front of the Coop who sold the newspaper for the homeless? Five years and a divorce? Karen took care of her bad conscience by always buying a magazine and bringing it home, without it ever being read. Torp had always ignored him and his homeless colleagues as best he could—until today.

"I'll give you fifty kroner for your magazine if you help me for five minutes."

The homeless man, whose name was Birger, was happy to help. They just had to push a car to get it going. Torp had observed the man on the quiet—they must be roughly the same age. Aside from his black teeth and a few that were completely missing, he didn't look like a homeless person. A little down-at-heel maybe, unshaven, and clearly unwashed hair, but that was how many people looked. Aside from the teeth, he looked like an ordinary, unkempt citizen with an ID number, an overcoat, and a bad conscience. Had Birger also been married, with a good job and healthy children?

"You keep pushing when I shout—it only needs a few metres, then it's up and running."

Torp stood on the driver's side and pushed with one hand on the door frame and the other on the steering wheel to get out on the road in front of the flat. Then they ran with the car as best they could, and he jumped in—clutch down, second gear, clutch up.

"*Now!*"

Birger was fairly powerful, and after the promised metres, the Polo's engine started. Damn it, he should have got hold of a cheap battery; this was too stupid for words. Birger waved, and Torp tried to wave back with his left arm. A car behind him honked and couldn't get past, and he tooted to Birger, who waved back and smiled with his whole set of impoverished teeth.

Torp tried in vain to overtake another vehicle on the other side of Roskilde. He was a little late and had to give up because of a slight incline on the motorway. Until a few hours ago, it would have looked like an ordinary Friday, if he could even use that appellation for his short period in the shared office and his new life. Neither Emma, Axel, nor Bertel had been in. Emma one never knew about, Axel came and went a bit at random, and Bertel was—once more—off to his summer house. But Crabby had been sitting there, as usual, trying to get a freelance life up and running before his mortgage provider said stop. Torp couldn't bear to listen to more about the *Express*'s theft of his story. There was probably at least one more version of that theft, and Crabby had been too sluggish in getting the story out. If he had just written the story right away, the *Express* wouldn't have become impatient and got in ahead of him.

A little unexpectedly, there had been three medium obituaries for Torp. *The shop has suddenly got busy*, wrote Erik from Funen. *I think this is going to be our breakthrough.* Before he could make coffee for himself and his self-pitying office colleague, the editor of a newly started political online magazine, *Around Borgen*, had called. They knew each other from the old days at Christiansborg.

"Can you get going on something right away, Torp?"

He skipped all the courtesies, even though they hadn't talked to each other for a dozen years or so.

"We need a perspective on the National Day that Enevoldsen has announced. The whole movement behind it," continued the editor.

He was up in a completely different tempo to Torp, who after a brief hesitation had let himself be swept along.

"Did you see the demonstration at the Liberty Memorial? Okay—you were there yourself. So you saw Per Frost, the old anti-Communist of the '80s, risen from the dead. He's in it, right up there, as their chief ideologue or something like that."

Torp had only managed to contribute to the conversation with few yeses, noes, and uh-huhs in the avalanche of words and commands that his old Christiansborg colleague rolled out.

"I've talked to him; he'd like to be interviewed, but it has to be at his home today at one p.m. We get him first. It has to be online tonight. You'll have to take photos yourself. Are you up for it?"

Torp was up for it.

"You'll get fifteen hundred kroner for everything and mileage at the low rate."

It would have been a poor rate even when they were interns thirty years ago. Nowadays that was just the way it was.

"You can get three grand more if you record the interview on video and edit out two excerpts of four to five minutes, which we can post online in a few days."

Torp had heard himself say it was okay. Bertel had a tripod he could borrow, so he could use his mobile as a camera, and Crabby had gratefully received the three dead. The obituaries were to be done right away, but that was no problem at all.

Torp turned down a narrow gravel road with deep tracks and a strip of weeds in the middle. The roads had become smaller and smaller as he had progressed. If an oncoming vehicle came now, one of them would have to reverse.

He switched off the car radio and *Radio News*. Rather as anticipated, several other international sports federations were beginning to follow FIFA's lead and require sports people to be born in the country to be on a national team. *Born in the country.* Torp had never noticed that expression being used before. Now it was the swimming federation and the volleyball players.

The gravel road wound through the West Zealand landscape for the best part of a kilometre to its only building, a small, cosy, thatched and whitewashed house surrounded by individual trees and a flagpole with the Dannebrog. The Polo left a trail of dust—it was hard to arrive unnoticed. A man was standing at the front door, waiting with his hands behind his back. Torp recognised the elderly author. Instinctively, he looked for an opportunity to park the car so that it would be easy to push-start again. Per Frost had to be close to eighty years old. If he was alone, how would they get the car started? Fuck it. Torp stopped with a small jerk between some trees by an outhouse.

"I remember you well."

Per Frost was friendly but reserved. They were sitting in the small kitchen that merged into one with the living room. The furniture was heavy for the size of the house, but it was neat and tidy. Torp instinctively felt comfortable in the surroundings—it was his host who prevented him from completely relaxing.

"It's been a few years since I was at the *Daily News,*" said Torp, after setting up the tripod and mobile phone, making sure that the picture was sharp, handing Frost one of his new business cards, explaining his status, and accepting the offer of coffee.

"Even if you were one of the politically correct, you were fair," said Frost, smiling. "For the most part, anyway."

He didn't try to hide the bitter tone. He had been uncompromising in his critique of Communists and fellow travellers in the 1980s—*cultural Communists,* as he had called them—to an extent and with a tone that had isolated him both professionally and socially. Torp was sure that, like so many other journalists, he had written critical articles about the fierce, humourless anti-Communist and author, but he couldn't remember one.

"I was present at the demonstration in front of the Liberty Memorial. How central are you to Friends of Denmark?"

"Were you participating, or just watching? My guess is that you were just watching," replied Frost, trying to tease his guest.

Torp smiled politely and began filming. There was no need to answer.

"I'm just one of many patriots," continued Frost with false modesty.

"Patriots?"

"Yes, patriots. Since when has there been anything wrong with being a patriot?" Frost didn't wait for an answer—it wasn't meant to be a question. "Actually, you're right—in fact, there *has* been something wrong with being a patriot in the decades in which religious globalisation has taken a grip on everything." He smiled amiably. "That seems to be over now."

"How do you see it to be over?"

"Borders are re-emerging; citizens are daring to be proud of their country again; the people are electing a new type of politician." Frost spread his arms. "Look around."

Torp nodded, not only to show that he was looking around and had understood the reply, but also that he thought the analysis was correct.

"It's our epoch," said Frost, searching for how to formulate it, "our time to run the show, as the young people would probably put it." He smiled genuinely and confidently.

"You talk a lot about the Great Replacement. Could you say a few words about that?"

Frost leaned forward. "Do you remember the oil crises in the 1970s?"

Torp could clearly remember them: the winter with the car-less Sundays, shops without lights in the windows, his mother sewing a five-metre-long curtain to divide the living room in two so that they could turn off two radiators, the unheated sports hall where he played indoor football all winter in just a few degrees of heat.

"The Western world saw its existence crashing into rubble. But then it blew over. Have you ever wondered why it was so easy?" Frost continued without waiting for a reaction. "European leaders made an agreement with the Arabs on oil from the Middle East. The price was a political distance from Israel and the United States and acceptance of Muslim immigration."

"Where did you get that from?"

Frost got up, pulled a book out of the bookshelf, and laid it in front of Torp.

"*Eurabia*, written by the Egyptian author Bat Ye'or. It's from 2005 and explains everything."

"Where does the Great Replacement come into the picture?"

The elderly man was surprisingly agile in going back to the bookshelf, grasping another book, and putting it in his guest's lap.

"*Le Grand Remplacement* from 2011. Written by Camus—not *that* Camus," said Frost with a laugh; it was a joke he had used before. "Renaud Camus. He describes here how Muslims, partly as a result of the secret agreement on oil for immigration, will be in the majority in Europe in a generation or two."

Torp looked up.

"As Yasser Arafat said about the Palestinian struggle against Israel: *Our strongest weapon is the womb of Palestinian women*. Half the Egyptian population is under fifteen years of age. Do you think they will stay in their country, or do you think the regime will help them to cross the Mediterranean?"

"Do the Friends really believe that?"

"It's pure mathematics, Torp—death rates, birth rates, immigration. The only hocus-pocus in it is the ability of the political elite not to see it." Frost sat down and poured more coffee for both of them.

"And if what you're saying is true?"

"Then we'll go under. As a people and as a civilisation." Frost said it matter-of-factly, as if he had just run out of baked beans.

"But why all this effort for a National Day?"

"Because, Torp, that's where it all begins and ends—with the nation. A national awakening is the only vaccine against all this."

"And a vaccine is essential?"

"A vaccine is absolutely crucial."

"What can you use a national awakening, as you call it, for?"

"The appointment of a competent political leader."

"Appointment?"

"Yes, election, that is." Frost spread his arms disarmingly.

"What about our Prime Minister?"

"Palle Enevoldsen has had all the chances he deserves. Can't we agree on that?"

"So what should a new political leadership do?"

"Permanent borders, stop immigration, dissolve the EU." He hadn't hesitated for a second; it seemed like a litany learned by heart.

"It sounds like the good old days. Are you a reactionary?"

Torp tried to show with his facial expression that he was teasing. Frost burst into a roar of laughter.

"Reactionary! Yes, you can bet your sweet life I am. That's what I've been trying to explain to you ever since you arrived. It's a new era, a showdown with modernity and the oh-so-correct."

"And what about your—our—old enemy: Russia and Communism?"

"The Russian people were never my enemy. The system was the enemy and a threat to our homeland. But that's no longer the case." Frost was becoming eager. "Russia today is exactly what we aren't yet—a proud, Christian country. The Russians are the true national conservatives."

"Weren't you once a liberal?" Torp asked with genuine interest, without a hint of criticism in his voice. Frost received the question in the same spirit. In a way, the interview was over.

"A conservative is a left-winger who got beaten up in Central Park the night before."

Frost's face took on a triumphant expression at his last words, as if he was expecting a round of applause he could bow to.

"Who said that?" Torp laughed.

"Irving Kristol, the father of neoconservatism and founder of the magazine *The National Interest*. Incidentally, he started as a Trotskyist."

"He must have taken some heavy blows."

They both laughed.

"Who beat you up?"

"No one has beaten me up" replied Frost, suddenly becoming serious again. "But someone has been beating up our homeland."

"That's probably a good way to finish up," said Torp, leaning forward to stop the recording.

"I hope you can use it," said Frost, almost making it sound as if a theatrical performance was over. "More coffee?"

There was a knock on the door. A young man with cropped hair and a white shirt stepped in without waiting for an answer, walked straight over, and laid the day's edition of the *Express* on a small sideboard.

"Pages five, six, seven, and eight," he said. "That woman, the associate professor at the University of Copenhagen, has now been named."

Frost cleared his throat and made eye contact with the delivery man.

"May I present Ulrik Torp, journalist. We were right in the middle of an interview—which is also being recorded."

He nodded in the direction of the tripod with Torp's mobile phone. The voice was reproachful, and the words came as clipped commands. It made the short-haired man jump as he turned his head and saw a stranger in the armchair.

"Excuse me," was his flurried response, "I didn't know there were guests."

"Now you know. We'll manage," said Frost sharply. It was made plain that the short-haired man should leave, which he did immediately.

"One of the young people in Friends of Denmark, who helps a little with practicalities," said Frost apologetically. He folded the day's edition of the *Express* and placed it on the shelf under the sideboard.

It turned out that the short-haired man had an equally short-haired and white-shirted mate. Together, it was a simple task for them to push the Polo out of its ill-conceived parking space. A little shove and the engine started immediately. Torp could see them standing there in the rearview mirror until the dust from the gravel road and the distance made them disappear. The old man was nowhere to be seen.

Torp regretted his decision to park the car close to the office, even before he began looking for a parking space. Even though the Friday afternoon rush hour went out of town and he was coming in, it would have been faster to park at the flat and take the Metro to Nørreport, but now it was too late. He finally found a parking space and decided that three hours would be enough. The parking meter asked him to say okay to a deduction of 114 kroner from his card. It looked like a mistake, but it wasn't. There was no hint of a slope, but he postponed the concern. Now it was time to write. The footage would have to wait.

One of the ideologues behind Friends of Denmark, the author and anti-Communist Per Frost, who was a high-profile figure in the 1980s, is fighting against globalisation and modernism. "The current Prime Minister has played his role, regardless of whether he is allowed to continue or not," he explains from his refuge in the provinces, "the concrete Denmark," as he calls it.

"The concrete Denmark is where the real goods are produced, where public administrators' PowerPoints and endless meetings are replaced by people who are slaving away for themselves and their loved ones," emphasises Per Frost.

The article almost wrote itself; the old man had been very generous with quotes. "The concrete Denmark," thought Torp to himself. Spending 114 kroner for three hours of parking was concrete enough for him. He sent the article, attached without comment an invoice for the 1,500 kroner plus mileage at the low rate, and announced that the clips for social media would come in a few days as agreed.

Torp's phone rang a few minutes after he had sent it off. Either it was to thank him for the article or to get the clips ready more quickly, he thought, reaching for his mobile. It was Lindskov from the *Daily News*.

"I know it's Friday and late, but I just don't have the time. Can you write the leader for tomorrow? We're tightening the screw on Enevoldsen and suggesting that Kirsten Rolighed could be a sensible replacement. Everything has its time and blah, blah, blah." He was sitting in the car on the way home for the weekend.

"Should he resign soon?"

"No, no. Not yet. Remember *Jaws*. That doesn't come until the end," bellowed Lindskov into the car's not terribly effective hands-free setup.

Torp glanced down at the crates of red wine. How much sense did it really make? He would do it, within the hour, of course.

Palle Enevoldsen can probably twist the arm of his base of support in the national executive on Thursday, but many will be left with a nagging fear that his time is over and that he may not be able to deliver more results or election victories. Kirsten Rolighed seems like . . .

The phone cut him off. He prepared himself to say that it would take him a few days to make those clips with Per Frost. In fact, he had no idea how to do it technically.

It was Anton from Police Headquarters.

"We've talked to that Gosia from WeCare."

"Yes?"

"She thinks that the dark-haired woman who said she shouldn't visit Brathenberg on Sunday is probably the same as the one in the grainy picture you sent her from the hospice."

"That's what I told you."

"Probably, Torp. She says it's *probably* the same person."

"So what are you waiting for?"

"The waiting is also partly the problem," said Anton hesitantly.

"What's the problem?"

"Well . . ." Anton paused. "It turns out that Brathenberg was cremated the other day."

"What?"

"The family wanted a private funeral."

"The burial is tomorrow."

"The burial is when the body is laid in the grave. The funeral is when it is driven to the crematorium."

"Okay, the funeral."

"Yes, but that was held the other day."

"So what is it tomorrow?"

"I don't quite know. Probably just a burying of the urn, or whatever it's called. With an audience."

"So what about the autopsy?"

"Yes, well, we can't do that now. Brathenberg no longer exists."

Anton made it sound like a minor detail.

"But why haven't you done it?"

"Everyone was probably thinking the funeral was tomorrow. That the old man was lying in the freezer. But he wasn't."

"Then we'll never know how he was murdered."

"If he was murdered. No one really believes that over here. The man was old and had a heart attack this winter. His life was by no means certain anymore."

"What about the dark-haired woman?" Torp was looking for a way out. "Have you found her?"

"No," replied Anton irritably. "We haven't bloody looked for her, either."

"What the hell are you doing?" Torp could feel the anger pressing up through his stomach and chest. It had to get out.

"I've had enough of this, Torp. I'm just calling to say that your story is thin, that the lady wasn't sure, and that Brathenberg has been cremated anyway. Case closed, if there ever even was a case." Anton hung up. No more this time.

On paper, it hadn't been such a bad day. Torp had done a current interview that had already been posted online and shared lots of times, and he had written an editorial for the *Daily News* about a Prime Minister on borrowed time. Even so, he was almost ready to cry as he stood by the Polo with the yellow parking ticket in his hand. He had been there fifteen minutes longer than allowed by the 114 kroner. Torp put the fine back in the windscreen wiper again and walked home.

CHAPTER 15

With a pair of old-fashioned, slightly worn dark trousers, and a—in his opinion—nice black sweater over a white shirt, Ulrik Torp thought he had got the most out of his meagre wardrobe. Besides, it wasn't a burial, not even a funeral. Torp had never thought deeply about the difference. The sky was bright blue, the sun felt like that of a summer's day, and those spring buds that hadn't already burst into bloom looked as if they would over the weekend. He walked in the direction of the church bells from the regional station and could feel the sweat breaking out under his shirt.

Torp placed himself at the back of the church, right down by the organ. He had no desire for, or possibility of, a place on the bench. He noticed the large number of wreaths. Should he have brought flowers with him? And incidentally, where was the damn urn? The church was full, but hardly as full as Otto Brathenberg would have expected. He had died in that intermediate phase so critical to funerals, where power was gone and friends were in nursing homes. Those present had to be voluntary or healthy.

The widow sat with their children and grandchildren right at the front on the left. The bench to the right was reserved for the few who found it necessary to come, including the Labour Party's leadership, led by the chairperson and opposition leader Pernille Hjort. She demonstratively made room for Prime Minister Palle Enevoldsen when he was one of the last to arrive, while the church bells were still ringing, just before 10:00 a.m. They briefly whispered a few remarks to each other; everyone in the church knew that there was great mutual respect between the two.

The local priest had been replaced by one of the Brathenberg family's lifelong friends, a retired bishop. He didn't make much of an impact now, thought Torp, as he waited for the words of remembrance that were clearly on their way. In American fashion, a microphone stand had been set up in front of the baptismal font—several people were to pay tribute to the deceased.

"My father loved my mother, his children, and his grandchildren. But first of all, he loved his country," began the eldest son.

Could someone really love his country more than his family? Torp noted that several on the rear benches reacted as if they had had the same thought.

"He never asked what was best for himself or for the party. He always asked first what was best for Denmark," continued the son.

Did he have no shame, or didn't he know his father in the slightest? Certainly, all that remained of Brathenberg were ashes in an urn, which must have been somewhere in the church, but the memories of his lust for power and many years of disappointment at not having become Prime Minister hung heavy in the church space. Torp imagined Pernille Hjort and Palle Enevoldsen sitting in the front row struggling with an inopportune giggle. This was a bit rich, perhaps even more so than the obituaries that Torp had come into close contact with over the past month. After all, the obituaries of ordinary people merely required the omission of certain details.

Finally, the son was finished. He received a hug from a woman who must have been his wife and who was fumbling with a handkerchief and dark glasses. His mother, Lise Brathenberg, seemed more composed, as if she found her daughter-in-law's behaviour theatrical and her son's praise embarrassing.

"Otto Brathenberg made the Labour Party broad and popular. He was a rock of knowledge and a lifeline I could always count on," began Pernille Hjort.

Could was the key word. Torp knew she never did. To say that they detested each other was an exaggeration, but Brathenberg didn't like Pernille Hjort as leader of "his" party. She was too young, she was a woman, and she had attained the leadership too easily, thought the old man.

"He was a man of principles. Thank you for your achievements, Otto," she ended and sat down.

Torp came up with his own translation: She hadn't been able to use his advice for anything; both his questions and his answers were from a different time.

Then Palle Enevoldsen took over the microphone, and a very special calm spread through the church.

"As a former Minister of Justice and Secretary of State for Foreign Affairs, Otto Brathenberg knew the importance of being able to keep his mouth shut at the right moments. He had access to his country's deepest secrets for decades, and knew that confidentiality could be a matter of life and death."

Prime Minister Palle Enevoldsen was an eminent speaker; he loved the attention and was gifted with an ability to misrepresent even the most important events plausibly.

"Even so, I'm glad he broke his promise of silence when I had just become Prime Minister and invited him for a cup of coffee in the Prime Minister's Office he had trotted in and out of for decades—sometimes out more often than he cared to talk about."

The Prime Minister looked up. A subdued lightness spread in the church. So little was needed, thought Torp. The elephant in the room could be shown the door so simply and elegantly. Everyone knew that Brathenberg had desperately wanted to be Prime Minister—so why not just hint at it? Palle Enevoldsen held one of his famous pauses, smiled faintly, and began an anecdote about the main person of the day, who many years ago had picturesquely explained to a young and ambitious Minister of Housing why a government can certainly have a Ministry of

Housing, but absolutely shouldn't have a housing policy—it just makes the voters insecure.

"I need hardly say that Otto was able to comfort that young minister who actually just had to sit and sharpen pencils until he got a real ministry. Brathenberg not only understood those closest to him, he understood his voters, he understood Danes." Fresh pause, fresh eye contact with the audience. "I promised never to tell the story of the advice to the despairing Minister of Housing to others. I hope Otto will forgive me this indiscretion," said Palle with a smile. He took a brief rhetorical pause before delivering his punchline. "I must of course emphasise that this is definitely not how it is today."

You're not supposed to laugh at funerals or memorial ceremonies— and certainly not in church, so everyone did their utmost to hold back. It was as if the ordinary laws of nature didn't exist for Palle Enevoldsen, thought Torp. At a time when almost all the media, more than half the country, and at least as big a proportion of his party and government were working to get him out; at a time when he had fought fire with fire and demanded a renewed mandate from his national executive; at a time when, with the ease of a figure skater, he had turned 180 degrees in relation to a National Day—at that very moment, he was standing on a Saturday morning and discoursing a gathering of mourners into a good mood, as if there was no other moment in life than this one. How Torp would miss Enevoldsen if it all ended on Thursday.

Beer and canapés would be served in a nearby restaurant, announced the son, with pathos in his voice, before the organist with an excessive prelude began playing the hymn "Always Joyful as You Leave" as a sign that the service was over. Either the urn had already been laid to rest or the burial would take place at a later time only for close family. Torp stood outside the church feeling a little self-conscious, that there were some places where he didn't really belong. Perhaps he shouldn't have come at all, he thought, and decided that the wake and canapés were hardly intended for him. The Prime Minister nodded at him reservedly from a distance, as did the leader of the Labour Party. There was a general feeling of a change in atmosphere on the church gravel; a queue of condolence was forming by Lise Brathenberg, who was standing upright in an elegant, dark designer jacket, surrounded by her family.

What would they all say if they knew it wasn't just a heart attack? If they knew that not only Brathenberg but another political colleague of his had been murdered by a young Russian-sounding woman, if that was indeed how the case hung together? Would the sun then still shine on this select flock of privilege-blind people who had always taken the sweetness of life for granted? Torp felt his bitterness rising up like nausea. How many of them would end up in an allotment house? How many would even demean themselves to have one? What if he shouted all over the churchyard: *Your Otto Brathenberg was murdered!* Would they then finally begin to doubt that life was all about having a fantastic kitchen, an Audi with leather upholstery, and good wines? Could they even count the people they had stepped on—perhaps inadvertently—in their quest to get to the top or stay up there? Were they at all interested in having their carefree lives disturbed? Torp sensed the gathering was preparing for a cosy lunch with beer and open sandwiches at the nearby restaurant. And of course, there was a terrace on the sunny side, so Otto Brathenberg could be remembered in the right spirit.

The damn sunny side.

He felt a hand on his shoulder.

"Hello, Ulrik Torp."

It was the Prime Minister's special adviser. She had been an intern at the *Daily News* back when Torp was in favour both with the management and at Christiansborg. He remembered her as skilled and purposeful and wasn't surprised when she jumped over to the other side.

"Christine. Hi."

"Sad about Brathenberg. You knew him well, if I remember correctly."

Torp nodded and had to remind himself that when he was her age, Brathenberg's time as Minister of Justice and Minister of Foreign Affairs was a different era—it could just as well have been before World War II.

"A fine speech your boss gave. Did you help him?"

"There can be a lot of hassle with Palle, but with that kind of speech, he doesn't need a special adviser or secretary," she said with a smile, almost proud of her boss.

"That one about the Minister of Housing—he has told that story before—many times," said Torp.

Christine wanted to laugh, but then remembered where she was.

"Are you staying for the wake?"

Torp shook his head.

"Me neither. Palle has to go, but I have time off now. Almost," she said, holding out her mobile. The 100,000 kroner she was paid a month included bodily contact with Apple around the clock.

"What about the national executive on Thursday?"

"I guess I should almost be asking you about that. As a special adviser, I live in a bubble," she said in a voice thick with irony.

She saw Torp's puzzled facial expression and explained how sick and tired she was of the public criticism of the walls within Christiansborg, the regime dominated by the professional classes, and the distance between the people and the so-called elite.

"If you read the editorial in your old newspaper, we have one of the lousiest Prime Ministers in history right now."

"Ah, that's a bit much."

"Do you think so?!" She held his gaze firmly and took half a step forward. "Those leaders are below the belt. You're welcome to tell your old colleagues that. To be perfectly honest, it's amateurish."

"What about Thursday?"

"The people around Kirsten Rolighed will get a mega going-over. Mega," she repeated as if to emphasise her point, but said it in such a way that it weakened the message.

"Is she the one behind it?"

"Her and those Friends of Denmark. I read your interview with Per Frost. I think Kirsten is more being controlled than she is in control. I don't bloody know which is worse."

"It isn't so fucking smart either to call Friends of Denmark idiots a few days before you bite the bullet and introduce a National Day." Torp said it without a hint of criticism in his voice. It was just a banal statement of fact.

"Palle doesn't think he has ever said that."

"He's probably not the first politician to think that," said Torp with a laugh that Christine mirrored warily and without such great delight. A few reproachful glances reminded them that they weren't standing in the lobby at Christiansborg. They both lowered their voices.

"Yes, sure, I know what you mean. But to be perfectly honest, he simply doesn't remember saying that."

"Doesn't he think they're idiots?"

"Of course he does. But he doesn't run around saying what he thinks." Torp nodded.

"Actually, That clip's a little weird. It was someone on Twitter who calls himself monkeybusiness who posted it. Does that mean anything to you?"

Torp shook his head.

"Not to us, either. I don't really understand it. I think it's from a meeting at Marienborg three weeks ago with some employers and the trade union movement. He had an almost new tie on that day, and he has that on in the clip too."

"Yes?"

"I was there myself. He talked a bit about a National Day, but I just remember it as a couple of neutral remarks. No more."

"It certainly wasn't smart in any case. Everyone runs around recording what a Prime Minister says."

"Yeah, yeah," said Christine, hesitantly. "I think you should be a little more interested in Per Frost and his relationship with Kirsten Rolighed."

"Because?" Torp sharpened both his senses and his tone. So, it had arrived—the eternal barter and the eternal spin, never a regular conversation with the guard down. He suddenly remembered how natural it had been. Christine sensed his reaction immediately.

"Even though I'm a special adviser and have to take care of my boss, what I'm saying may also be true."

"You're afraid of Kirsten Rolighed," said Torp.

"We don't really know what's going on. That's not the same as being afraid."

"And the mega going-over on Thursday?"

Christine smiled. "Feel free to call if there is anything."

She handed him her business card, turned around, and walked over to her Prime Minister, who was in the middle of a comforting embrace with Lise Brathenberg. He was good at that, too.

Torp caught sight of Ebbesen, a long-term Member of Parliament who had been nicknamed Sir Ebbe, because he had been overly happy when, after the obligatory ten years of membership in Parliament, he was offered the Knight's Cross by the Queen and had defied the Labour Party's principle of not accepting orders from the royal court. Ebbesen was standing a little by himself, sheltering from the sun under a large oak tree. Torp remembered that his name was on the list of former members of the Parliamentary Control Committee when he reviewed the names with Axel. Torp went over to him.

"Torp," he said, greeting him with a smile. "It's been a while. Are you on your way back into Christiansborg?"

Torp shook his head. "Sad about Brathenberg."

"He was a power hungry shit. That's the short version."

Ebbesen barely tried to muffle his voice. Torp suddenly remembered how Ebbesen had been more or less bullied by the party leadership for many years. Perhaps it was even Brathenberg who had come up with the nickname Sir Ebbe.

"You sat on the Parliamentary Control Committee for many years."

Ebbesen nodded, puffing his chest out and exposing his Knight's Cross, which was dangling on his chest on the black jacket, which would have been too small even many years ago. Torp had no doubt that it was hanging in the right place in line with protocol.

"I was on it for fifteen years from 1994. Right up until I left Parliament."

"Were you there at the same time as Erling Jensen?"

"Erling? He's just died, too, hasn't he? I thought I saw his obituary." Torp nodded. Ebbesen continued. "We were on it together for four or five years, I think." Then he stopped.

"What were those meetings actually about?"

"Why do you ask?"

Ebbesen tilted his head suspiciously to one side and looked Torp in the eye. Many people laughed at Sir Ebbe, but Torp remembered that he shouldn't be underestimated. Ebbesen was a wily politician, although it had never amounted to much despite him being inordinately fond of the royal family, decorations, and the Home Guard.

Torp shrugged as if to signal that there was no particular reason.

"What was Erling Jensen like?"

Ebbesen deflated his chest. It was clear that his political antenna was working impeccably even after more than a decade out of politics.

"Erling was okay as long as he stayed away from the secretaries. He was a good colleague."

"Did he take notes at the meetings of the Control Committee?"

"Have you gone mad, Torp!" Ebbesen laughed. "We were allowed to do bugger-all at those meetings. Bugger-all." Ebbesen thought about it for a long time. "Erling didn't actually say much in the committee, but he took great interest in it."

"Do you think he might have made notes after the meetings?"

Ebbesen paused, wiping the sweat off his forehead with one of his jacket sleeves and folding his hands over his voluminous belly. The heat was hard on him.

"Funny you should say that. I remember that there were actually several of us who suspected him of doing so. Without completely remembering why."

"There was a lot about Moscow and the fall of the Wall in the Control Committee back then, wasn't there?"

Ebbesen regained his suspicious demeanour. "Tell me, why do you ask?"

"I can't say."

"Hmm."

He looked briefly past Torp. The guests were getting ready for the wake. Ebbesen clearly didn't want to miss that. Then he turned his gaze back to Torp.

"Can you keep a secret, Torp?"

"Of course." Torp lowered his voice and moved his head closer to Ebbesen.

"So can I." He laughed, slapped Torp on the shoulder, and joined the gathering, which had already begun moving towards the canapés and the cold beers.

Ulrik went into the office to pick up two bottles of Lindskov's wine as a gift for the evening's host. Karen emphasised over the breakfast table that they should take the regional train to the badminton couples' dinner no later than 5:30 p.m. He had refused to take the car with the reasonable explanation that the battery was dead, and a half lie that he would like to be able to enjoy the wine without thinking about his driving licence. Actually, he had no desire to get drunk with that accountant idiot, but if the wine was particularly good, which it would most probably turn out to be, it was a pleasant option. The Polo stayed in the parking space with its yellow fine in the windscreen wiper. Ulrik decided he wouldn't do anything about it until Sunday. Maybe he could find a used battery online really quickly.

No one was sitting in the office on a Saturday afternoon. It was nice and homely here, with those quirks family life brought with it. Axel Boas's desk was filled with books, papers, and folders—he didn't use much computer power on archives despite the heavy PC that was standing under the desk. A few old coffee cups, a picture of some grandchildren, and three neglected green plants in the bay windowsill completed the picture of the laid-back man that Axel was. Emma's desk was completely clear, as in completely. She didn't go anywhere without her laptop and didn't have anything else. Bertel's desk was divided into systems. His papers were carefully placed in three plastic trays. The trays were in a small stand, and Torp was sure that the three different colours each had their own archival significance. Bertel had the large bookcase in the living room, and here the choice was between placing the books alphabetically, by size or by subject. The alphabet had won. Torp was certain that Bertel had a compost grinder at home and couldn't understand why other people hadn't also acquired one. Crabby's desk looked like him—total chaos with no obvious attempt to sort it out.

Torp turned on his computer while glancing again over at Crabby's desk and yesterday's issue of the *Express*, which lay just far enough on the desk to prevent it falling on the floor. It was the edition that one of the white-shirted men had brought in to Per Frost, precisely to ensure that he would read the story that Crabby was actually the instigator of. What was it the young man had said? *That woman, the associate professor*.

The editor of the online magazine *Around Borgen* had sent an email. He was very happy with the Per Frost interview. *It was spot on—you've still got it*, he wrote. What the hell did he mean by *still*? Was it meant as appreciation, praise, or modern leadership? *Still?* Two things: they needed a "damn good" photo of Per Frost for a print edition—if Torp could have one taken over the next few days?—1,000 kroner. And lastly: could Torp do a similar interview with Kirsten Rolighed, Monday at 2:00 p.m. in her office at Christiansborg? Not about the power struggle and Enevoldsen, but about the National Day, Friends of Denmark, and "suchlike," as he wrote. Remember to record two clips of four to five minutes for social media. Again, Torp was taken aback by the small word that might seem random, but rarely was: "suchlike." *1,500 kroner, we have a photo. Plus 3,000 for an edited recording*. Torp replied "yes" immediately. Although the fee was insultingly bad, *Around Borgen* could possibly be a good opening back to real journalism and politics. Perhaps he could even make a living from it at some point. He emailed Per Frost immediately— was he coming to Copenhagen one of these days? He wanted to take a good picture of him for a print edition of the article in *Around Borgen*.

Torp sat down on Crabby's chair, reached for the newspaper, and flipped to pages five, six, seven, and eight. And there she was—on page seven—the associate professor, in a small two-column black-and-white portrait photo. It was Benedikte Koch, the third wheel on the Brathenberg-Jensen carriage, who, according to the Jensen son's somewhat vague account, had been in contact with them in the week leading up to their deaths; Koch from the Kartoffelrækker, who had called him up without saying a word and not answered the phone since. Koch who, according to the neighbour's teenage daughter, hadn't been home for several days and who, according to her department, was ill. Torp skimmed the page to find the relevant words in the article.

The scandal at the institute is spreading . . . bank account in which the money was deposited . . . no control over private research grants . . . Benedikte Koch . . . source outside the university . . . no one suspected the nice and reputable associate professor . . . luxury housing . . . at least 2.3 million kroner, but probably even more . . . Koch is, as revealed in recent days in the Express, *far from the only one . . . the Minister has no comment . . . a case for the police.*

Torp hesitated for a moment, grabbed his mobile phone, and omitted the initial pleasantries.

"Anton. What do you know about the case of researcher fraud at the University of Copenhagen that the *Express* is running?"

"You've certainly got varied interests these days."

"What do you know?"

"Not much. Some researchers have been reported to the police. There have apparently been scams amounting to quite a few million. It resembles a case from the Rigshospitalet a few years ago." Anton suppressed a deep sigh. "But it isn't a case I'm involved in."

"Can you check it out a little?"

"Of course. I'm sitting here at Police Headquarters just waiting for the opportunity to help you with your research."

"Could you especially check what an associate professor at the university, Benedikte Koch, has done? She was mentioned in the article yesterday."

Emma had entered the office before Torp finished the conversation. He smiled at the sight of her. She smiled back.

"Why are you sitting at Crabby's desk? And in such nice clothes?"

Torp replied with a couple of half sentences about a funeral, the *Express*, and Anton from Police Headquarters, while he went over and sat down at his own desk.

"Doughnut?"

She threw one to him from a takeaway bag without waiting for a response. He only managed to catch it after it had first landed on his sweater and left some chocolate cream melting in the spring sun. She giggled. Torp didn't care and finished it off in two bites. He was hungry and regretted that he hadn't accepted a couple of Brathenberg's sandwiches.

"Next time you get hold of that Anton, ask him to find out who that dark-haired Russian is."

"We don't even know if she's Russian."

"Gosia from WeCare thought she had a Russian background. Poles know about such things."

"Anton has already talked to Gosia."

"But that's not enough, is it? He has to get hold of the Russian."

"How is Anton going to find her? We know nothing about her."

"If she killed Brathenberg and Erling Jensen, and if she has a Russian background, then she will no longer be in the country."

Emma stuffed doughnut number two in her mouth. Unlike Torp, that kind of food was her primary diet.

"Is that supposed to make it easier?"

"I bet you she left the country from Kastrup a few hours after the visit to the hospice, where Erling Jensen died."

"And?"

"If she has flown directly to Eastern Europe, then she will have gone through passport control, and a picture will have been taken of her, her passport, or both. Then it's just a matter of comparing it with the picture we have of her. They must have plenty of staff who can go through it," she said in a neutral voice.

Torp understood what she meant. The question was whether Anton would, too. Or more accurately, would want to. His old contact at Police Headquarters didn't seem particularly easy to impress these days.

His mobile emitted the familiar sound of two bamboo sticks hitting each other. A new email. It was Per Frost; he was coming to Copenhagen on Thursday, so could they take a photo of him in the morning? Torp wrote back immediately. What about 10:00 a.m.—he hesitated a moment—at the Liberty Memorial? Less than half a minute later, Per Frost replied. *Excellent idea. See you, Frost.*

"These must be yours," said Emma, handing him two yellow parking tickets she had curled up in her back pocket. "They were sitting under the windscreen wiper on your car."

"My car?"

"Old Polo, just down there," she said, pointing in the direction away from Strøget. "Some of your business cards are inside the windscreen— *everything in journalism.*"

"Two of them?"

"That's all there were."

"But I've only parked once. Yesterday."

"Two twenty-four-hour periods. Two parking fines." Emma immediately sensed that it was no laughing matter.

CHAPTER 16

Torp felt a slight headache and a taste of ammonia in his mouth as the mobile's ringtone pulled him out of the depths of sleep. It had to be the combination of too much red wine, too little water, and the happy pills. Torp didn't think he had had such problems earlier in his life. Could you get bad breath from happy pills? It had gone on until late with Torben the accountant and his wife. He hadn't got drunk, as in drunk, but enough that the atmosphere had been surprisingly good. Karen had become clearly intoxicated just like Torben and Tine, without it being embarrassing in any way.

He would have given a lot for a glass of water before answering the phone with a hoarse "Torp speaking."

"Anton here. Did I wake you up?"

Torp looked at the alarm clock that was beside his bed. *You are one of the last people to have a real alarm clock instead of using your mobile,* Karen had teased him at one point and proclaimed him *boomer of the year.* He didn't care; in his opinion, an alarm clock with battery and luminescent numbers belonged beside a real bed.

"Yes."

"It's almost ten o'clock. Even though it's Sunday, it's about bloody time. Shouldn't you get up and pee?"

Torp should, in fact. He got up with a jerk, waking Karen, who was lying with most of her head under the duvet, and went out a little too fast to the small bathroom. The acceleration made him dizzy. He supported himself against the wall with his right hand while holding the mobile to his ear with his left shoulder and got ready to pee. The taste of the ammonia in his mouth became more distinct as he spoke.

"I'm peeing now," he said.

But that wasn't entirely true. He should be peeing and was trying hard. Then there came a trickle—dark yellow, as a sign of the mismatch between alcohol and water the night before. It was probably also one of the reasons for the ammonia taste.

"I've just checked up on that Benedikte Koch you asked about."

"Yes?"

The trickle stopped, even though it had only just begun. He could feel that he needed to pee a lot; it just didn't come.

"What did you say?"

The dizziness subsided, and as such, his other hand became available. Now it went better. The trickle came back in spurts.

"Benedikte Koch, associate professor at the University of Copenhagen. Tell me, what are you doing?"

"What about Benedikte Koch?"

"You asked me to check up on what was in the *Express* the other day."

"Yes, have you found anything out?"

"Well, it's a real mess with those research funds. The *Express* has got hold of a good story; there are many millions involved."

"So it's true?"

"More than that. Just between the two of us—tell me, are you still pissing?—it's pure fraud. Some very grand and self-assured people are going to end up in jail when all this is over."

"And Benedikte Koch?"

Anton hesitated.

"On the face of it, that's a bit weirder."

"Yes?"

Now the stream was coming in small spurts again, but it was okay. He could feel that he was almost empty and tried to squeeze the last drops out. It went fine.

"The *Express* has a document with her name on it, which really isn't a good sign."

"I saw that. She's asking for research funds to be transferred to something that looks like her private account."

"But it doesn't look like the money has been transferred."

"So she hasn't actually done anything?"

"Argh," said Anton, sounding like he was biting into a bread roll. "We at least want to talk to her, but we can't find her right now. No one is at her private address and her phone is dead."

"I've heard she's on sick leave."

"Yes, we've also been told that. That doesn't make it any less weird, though."

"What do you mean?"

"There's a lack of clarity about where the *Express*'s document comes from. It would be nice to talk to her or find out where the newspaper got it from."

"Where do you think it's from?"

Torp shook off the last drops and felt a single drop flick up on his cheek. Done!

"We have no idea—that's what I'm saying." The bread roll was gone; he sounded irritated. "You'll have to talk to your journalist friends about that." Anton was about to hang up.

"Now that I have you—thank you for that, Anton—now that I have you . . ."

Torp wiped his cheek with his arm.

". . . the woman from the hospice and Brathenberg, the murderer . . ."

Anton ignored Torp's swift conviction of the woman.

". . . if I'm right in what I'm saying, that she actually killed those two old men, and that she's Russian, or something like that."

"Yes?" Anton was getting impatient. It was Sunday morning; he wanted to have his time off.

"Then she almost certainly left the country a few hours after being in the hospice."

"Yes?"

"From the airport. With passport. Then there will be a picture of her and her passport, name and all. Isn't that right?"

Torp repeated Emma's arguments as he went out into the kitchen. He would need a glass of water to rinse his throat and mouth as soon as this conversation was over.

"Only if she has travelled to a non-Schengen country."

"Precisely."

"Do you want me to review thousands of travellers on that basis?"

"You must have done it loads of times. I have the picture of her from the surveillance camera at the hospice; I'll send it to you right away. In these computer Big Brother times, it must be fairly easy to do. Aren't you at all curious?"

Anton avoided the question. "I'll have to think about it," he replied briefly. "More?"

"Roger. No more."

Ahh, he really needed that glass of water. Torp immediately texted the picture of the dark-haired woman from the hospice to Anton.

"Do you have any plans today?"

It made Torp jump. Karen was standing in the doorway of the narrow bathroom wearing her old bathrobe. Her hair was tangled after her heavy sleep of the night and morning.

"I'm going into the office at some point. That was Anton from Police Headquarters. It's a long story."

She turned around without a word at the clear rejection. Torp instantly regretted it, even though he didn't feel up to telling the whole story and certainly not that he had started giving the obituaries to someone else—his only real income apart from Lindskov's red wine from *Daily News* stories, if that could be called income, and the small projects from *Around Borgen*. He knew she would respond with an "okay" if he told her about it, but where she put the stress in her "okay" was crucial to its meaning. She would give him the critical "okay," and he couldn't blame her. He was throwing out a little secure income in favour of what was at best an unremunerative story, at worst no story at all.

"I have to correct assignments today, so it'll be fine if you're at the office," came the message from the living room. She made it sound as if she couldn't get rid of him quick enough.

They could have chatted about her assignments: *Are they good? Who are they? How is your class doing, actually?* They could have exchanged impressions and views on the atmosphere last night at the couples' dinner with Tine and Torben, which to Torp's surprise had been both pleasant and boozy: *Such a lovely place they have; such delicious food; we just about caught the lumpfish roe season; my goodness, what a nice starter; did you also drink too much wine?* Or she could just ask about his work once more, and this time he would be willing to answer. *I think there is something completely wrong with Brathenberg's death; the Prime Minister is at risk of being toppled on Thursday; Torben was actually a great help when we went into his office right after dinner.* That is how they could have talked over their morning coffee. He could have gone and fetched rolls and pastries. They could have laughed at the expense of Torben's bulging stomach and childishly happy appetite. They could have talked about the key to the allotment house in Brønshøj, which Tine had received from her sister and passed on to Karen with an assurance that they shouldn't think about it at all; they could use it as much as they wanted the entire summer. They could have made love with ammonia breath and tangled hair, gone for a long walk in the spring sunshine afterwards, and grabbed a cappuccino at a café in town. They could have done a thousand other and better things than what they ended up doing—spending Sunday separately and without exchanging a word.

He took the Metro to Østerport and walked past the Kartoffelrækker and Benedikte Koch's home. As there was no one at home, he took the decision to ring the doorbell of the neighbour with the sullen teenager.

"I'm looking for Benedikte Koch. Do you have any idea where she might be?"

It must be the teenager's father.

"I don't know anything about that," he replied very quickly, without opening the door completely and with signs of closing it again.

"They say at the university that she's off sick."

"Then she must be."

The father was trying in vain to close both the conversation and the door in a polite manner.

"But then she should be at home, wouldn't you think? I mean, if she's ill."

"As I said, I don't know anything."

"I talked to your daughter the other day. She hadn't seen Benedikte and her husband for several days. Do they have a summer cottage?"

The father hesitated and froze in mid-movement as he was closing the door.

"She said they might be at the cottage," continued Torp.

"They don't have a summer cottage. I don't know anything."

Until a few seconds ago, Torp had been intending to end the conversation, say thanks for nothing, turn around, and walk away. Now he stood his ground.

"Maybe I could ask your daughter again."

The father's gaze wavered.

"She's not home. I have no idea who you are and I don't know anything. Goodbye!"

Torp stood in front of the closed door and, at first, ditched the idea of ringing again. It had to be the article in the *Express* and the police's futile enquiries that had made the neighbour so protective. You couldn't really blame him for that. Goodness knows how many journalists had stood where he was standing right now. Then Torp plucked up his courage and rang again. After waiting in vain, he knocked on the door, not heavily, but nicely and insistently, or so he believed. After a long time, he heard footsteps on the other side.

"I said goodbye," came a voice through the door.

"I'm not from the *Express*. I haven't come because of the story about fraud at Copenhagen University."

"And what should that have to do with my neighbour?"

"No, precisely," replied Torp immediately. "I would very much like to talk to Benedikte about something completely different, and I think she would also like to talk to me."

The door was opened again. At first, a little ajar, then completely.

"Who are you?"

"Ulrik Torp. I'm a journalist." Torp rummaged in his windbreaker for one of his new business cards. "Here you are. If you see her or hear from her, could you please give her this card and say that I just want to talk to her? I'm sure she'll know what it's about."

"So what is it about?" The father had accepted the business card and was looking suspiciously at the journalist—*everything in journalism?* His eyes narrowed a little; he was still standing with one hand on the door, ready to slam it quickly if need be.

"It's a bit complicated," replied Torp evasively.

"I'm sure it is," he said, closing the door again, this time more calmly.

Torp sat resignedly at his own desk. He wasn't meeting Vivi in Østerbro for another hour, but he sensed that Karen wanted to be alone with her assignments, and he had also excused himself with work at the office. He logged into the databases that Torben had introduced him to the night before and checked some of the PDF files that the accountant had downloaded and emailed to him while they had been sitting in his office after dinner, and before Tine had come in and a little reproachfully told them that coffee and cognac was available in the living room.

The evening had somehow fallen into place as soon as they arrived, even before they had got their jackets off in the hallway, which was almost as big as the bedroom of their two-bedroom flat on borrowed time. The enchantment had taken place the moment Torp had handed the host two of Lindskov's bottles of red wine.

"Wow," the accountant had said, as he looked at the labels with outstretched arms.

"Have you seen this, Tine? A Barolo from Monforte d'Alba."

He had delightedly shown his wife the two bottles, interrupted the presentation, and this time brought the labels all the way up to his eyes.

"It's from the Mosconi slope. 2014! The year we were down there."

Then he had looked up at the donor.

"I must say, Ulrik, you really didn't need to do this."

Torp had felt the accountant's firm and full stomach press against his as he embraced him, still holding the two bottles of Barolo. All of Torben's defences had collapsed, and thus so had Torp's. No bitterness over the magnificent villa, the car in the driveway, the art on the walls, and the life at the top that they clearly took for granted. No bitterness over the key to the sister's allotment house and the exposure of their situation that it symbolised. No half hidden remarks or the quiet sulking that Torp increasingly often lapsed into. It was as if the two—obviously expensive—bottles of Barolo and the recipient's childish delight had created a fellowship between the four people in the hours that awaited them.

During the dinner, Torben—"we'll drink the Barolo with the cheese"—had asked about Torp's interview with Per Frost, which he had read with great interest. *What's he like? He seems a bit over the top. Wasn't he more ordinary in the 1980s?* Their unforced chat had got Karen and Tine to relax. Without having talked to each other about it, they had both been worried about the evening.

After dinner, the accountant had introduced Torp to a world full of accessible information: databases with accounts, names of board members, company histories, and new companies that owned the first ones but were controlled by some completely different ones. A maze of open information, which was Torben's daily life. It turned out that Per Frost, in addition to being an elderly author with small print runs and a modest home in West Zealand, was both wealthy and discreet. The ramble through businesses, registration numbers, private limited companies, and limited partnerships with one faceless name after another showed not only that Per Frost had assets worth millions of kroner, but also that several of the companies ended up with Russian-sounding names on their boards, after which they could no longer be traced in the databases that Torben had access to.

"There isn't necessarily anything illegal in this at all. Believe me, I've seen strange set-ups that were only just about legal, or at least not illegal," he had said with a faint smile. Torp couldn't really see the difference, but the accountant clearly could.

"But this one is a little strange."

"Why?"

"Because there doesn't seem to be a practical reason for the structure of the companies. The only reason I can see is that they want to hide the Russian connection."

"But what do these companies do?"

"Import and consultancy, it says. That could be anything."

"They have the same accountant on virtually all the accounts. Do you know him?"

"By name only. And not for anything good, without being able to remember why."

He had smiled disarmingly and looked at his guest with slightly floaty eyes—the Barolo, which they had brought into the office with them, was making an impact.

"Just as there are scumbags among journalists, there are also bandits in my profession."

Torp had thought about the change of atmosphere when they, happily and tipsily, had said goodbye to Tine and Torben with hugs and jovial comments of *we'll-beat-you-next-season* and *your-serve-is-miserable*, and he and Karen were on their way alone to the train station. Suddenly, there had been nothing to talk about, as if the hangovers had already turned up and revealed the mute atmosphere between them.

Torp looked at his watch—he had to go now to get to the coffee date with Vivi on time. He was looking forward to seeing her.

She was instantly recognisable as she sat outside the café, soaking up the April sun with closed eyes. She was wearing the gentle expression he remembered her for when they used to walk on the beach by the North Sea and mostly talked about her. It was impossible to guess that here sat an unhappy, stress-stricken, and almost newly divorced woman with depressive tendencies.

"You look like a million dollars," he exclaimed spontaneously as he sat down next to her. She opened her eyes calmly, smiled warmly, and put a hand on his cheek. Exactly the same greeting that she had used several times on the west coast.

"Ulrik. How glad I am to see you. What would you like?"

He saw she was sitting with an Aperol Spritz.

"I'll grab a beer."

They sat at the table for almost two hours until the sun refused to shine on them any longer. They recalled the weeks on the west coast, talked about their depressions, about her ex-husband, who was still an idiot, about a job centre that insisted that Vivi should move on, and for the first time, Ulrik spoke about himself in more than headlines; about his journalistic comedown, about suddenly counting the years to a pension he had no ambitions for, but which were becoming increasingly restrictive despite everything he tried, about his new office, about Karen and the silence between them. Vivi even got to hear about his problems with producing powerful jets of pee. She listened. They laughed. They swapped the Aperol Spritz and beer out with coffee and back to beer again. A small pat on the shoulder, a slow hand on the thigh, her touch on his cheek. Ulrik hadn't been so relaxed for as long as he could remember.

And then the sun disappeared. They got up, knowing it couldn't continue. That the last hours had been a parenthesis that they could probably recreate, but which was nothing more than that. Vivi looked at Ulrik and put her hand on his cheek again. Then she hugged him, he let it happen, and she pulled her head back, looked at him again, gave him a quick kiss on the mouth, and smiled her farewell.

CHAPTER 17

Ulrik Torp saw himself from above when he shouted, but he still couldn't stop himself. It was as if his world was falling apart when he first spotted the parking warden farther down the street, followed by the yellow parking fine she was about to put under the Polo's windscreen wiper.

"Hey! *Hey*!"

The parking warden turned her head; it was a woman in her early thirties. Torp instinctively despised her. Who did she think she was?

"You can't fucking mean that."

Obviously used to that kind of reaction, she said nothing and tried to get her yellow jacket with the municipality's logo to be her authority. When Torp reached her and the car, he grabbed hold of the lightly laminated fine and took a series of quick steps towards her.

"Here; I've already been fined for this parking."

"It's not a fine. It's a fee."

"It's over five hundred kroner."

Torp stood in front of her and handed her the paper, as if it were a gift she couldn't refuse.

"You've been there since Friday," she replied calmly.

The distance between them was just exactly wide enough not to be intimidating.

"This is the third fine for the same parking. You just can't do that."

"Fee. That's the rules. You haven't paid for your parking."

"Fucking power freaks. It's Monday; it's a little past nine. Don't you have anything else to do?"

And no, Torp knew, the moment the words left his mouth. Of course, she didn't have anything else to do. His mind changed strategy without him planning anything.

"I'll move it right away. Can't you just take this one back?"

He handed the fine to her.

"Sorry, can't be done. Once it's been issued, it's in the system," she said with a slight shake of her head.

"Nothing works in this town. Nothing except the parking wardens."

"I'm just doing my job."

She turned and began scanning the licence plate of a large SUV. The parking fee had obviously been paid. She tried to move on, away from Torp.

"Why are you leaving? You forgot this," shouted Torp, his voice cracking up into equal parts spite and powerlessness.

"Visit our website. It tells you how you can complain."

It looked as if she was ignoring the next parked vehicles just to get farther away from him. It was probably something she had learned in a course, thought Torp. He could feel his eyes going watery, not so much over the size of the fine—that was bad enough—but more over his legal incapacitation. He could have been her father, yet was being treated like a child. Everywhere he looked, it was as if he couldn't reach anything at all. A hand was laid on his shoulder. It was Emma's.

"Don't pay those things. I don't."

She had apparently been watching the whole scene. Torp was suddenly embarrassed by his behaviour.

"But you don't have a car."

"Metro and trains—I never pay."

"What do you mean?"

"What do you mean, what do I mean?" she fired back with a laugh.

"You can't just not pay."

"You will see that you can. Someday they'll forget it, or else it'll disappear from their system, become out of date or something." She shrugged. "Or else it won't."

"And what if they don't forget it and it doesn't become out of date?"

"Those fines are a money machine I can't be bothered to be a part of. Come on, let's go up to the office," she said, giving Torp a tug.

When they came into the office, Bertel was sitting prostituting himself with another article for a chamber of commerce, coughing heavily, and apologising with yellow snot running out of his nose. Crabby was battling with the last obituary he had received from Torp. Axel was sitting at his desk pretending to write his book, but in reality, he was just surfing around between the newspaper websites. He looked up as soon as Torp and Emma came in, happy to be distracted from his displacement activity.

"Have you seen the front page of the *Daily News* today?"

Torp shook his head. He hadn't seen anything.

"Annegrethe Hulsig from the Nationalists is proposing that politicians in Denmark should only be able to stand for election if they were born in the country."

"Nobody will take that seriously," said Emma, waving her pen, *Ulrik Torp—everything in journalism*, as if to emphasise her point.

"Ha! That's what you think!" exclaimed Axel. "Pernille Hjort from the Labour Party and Kirsten Rolighed from the Liberals think it sounds interesting. That's Newspeak for them being about to join in."

"What does the Prime Minister say?" said Torp, pouring himself coffee from Axel's jug.

"Nothing. Not a word from the government."

Axel read out loud from the article: *Being a politician in Denmark is also a question of being a politician for Denmark. We propose that birth in the country should in the first instance apply to candidates for Parliament, but we would also like to see it extended to municipal councils, says Annegrethe Hulsig.*

"There's no way that can be done," objected Torp. "If you can vote in a parliamentary election, then you can also stand for election. It says so in the Constitution."

"Hulsig is also asked about that in the article," continued Axel. "Here's what she says about such a minor detail: *It isn't without reason that the US Constitution requires the President to be born in the country.* Born in the country! Can you feel how those words are permeating everything?"

"What about the Constitution—what does she say about that?"

"She takes it very calmly: *The Constitution is supposed to protect Denmark and Danes. I refuse to believe that it will be a problem, but if it is, then we will just have to change it.*

"Just. It won't get anywhere."

Torp turned and went back to his own desk. He still had the parking ticket in his body and couldn't concentrate on a proposal that was clearly just meant as a provocation.

"It doesn't sound all that crazy," said Bertel, coughing. "It's just like being born in the country to be able to play for the national team. What's so wrong with having to be born in Denmark to look after Denmark in Parliament? I don't understand that at all."

He shook his head and directed his attention back to his chamber of commerce article; it was neither to provoke nor initiate a discussion.

"Can't you see what's going on?" continued Axel, this time almost to himself. "It's spreading deeper and deeper."

No one was listening.

Torp made another round of all the offices in his search for Erling Jensen's papers from the old Coop bag, which he had folded and placed on his shelf after finding it at the bottom of the stairwell. It made no sense, and after talking to Sir Ebbe, he became increasingly convinced that the papers in the bag had been some of Erling Jensen's notes from the meetings of the Control Committee. Axel, Bertel, and Crabby could no longer be bothered to pretend to help him look for them. No, there was nothing between the piles of paper on the shelf either—Bertel had a hard time hiding both his irritation and his astonishment. Only Emma understood.

Torp sighed despondently and instead turned to his screen and googled Kirsten Rolighed. He knew most things about her and what the interview should focus on—especially when the editor of *Around Borgen* had made an agreement with her that it wasn't to be about the power struggle and Palle Enevoldsen. It was perfectly sensible of her and therefore natural that there was that limitation in the agreement. Yet the many so-called contracts between journalists and politicians irritated him. He knew there was especially something wrong with TV interviews. It was there that the risk for politicians was greatest, and thus it was also there that the many—often intense—negotiations between press advisers and journalists took place. How long is the interview going to be? Will there be inserts during it? What is in the introduction? What is the first question? Will you be getting into other topics? We don't want to be asked about this and this and this, otherwise we won't even turn up. We? It was a mental and sometimes almost physical power struggle, in which any differences between male dogs and female dogs were blurred. The winner was the one who didn't withdraw. And the editor had quickly withdrawn in the face of Kirsten Rolighed's press officer. An established media organisation would hardly have been so easy to dance with, but *Around Borgen* was new, had to make a name for itself, and both Per Frost and Kirsten Rolighed were taking advantage of that. Was Torp also being taken advantage of? *Ask Torp; he's hungry, he's out on a limb and not in a position to make demands. He needs to get back in and will do it for 1,500 kroner per article without making special demands. Give a hungry man the opportunity to eat out of somebody's hand, and he doesn't have any choice.* Was that how it was?

He found one of the many portrait interviews, conducted five years earlier, back when Rolighed had been elected to Parliament for the first time.

Kirsten Rolighed at home in her villa in Humlebæk. There is a direct view of the Sound, Hven Island, and Sweden when the sky is blue and the sun is shining. And it almost always does when you are with the newly elected Member of Parliament for the Liberals, the single businesswoman Kirsten Rolighed.

It was a women's magazine, but Torp still took his time reading it. He knew from experience that politicians relaxed a little more when it was journalists outside the Christiansborg clique who were doing the inter-viewing. And it was precisely in these kinds of situations that politicians could expose themselves a little, without either the interviewee, the journalist, or the readers noticing it.

Kirsten Rolighed established her company when she was very young and hasn't looked back since. Were there any clichés that the women's magazines refused to use? Hardly, Torp thought to himself and skimmed through the article with the well-known story of the woman who, without qualifications and in her mid-twenties, jumped on the computer wave and the internet before they really got big, and was today a multi-millionaire and an icon for many entrepreneurs. A business article about entrepreneurs from long before she became a politician told the story of a good idea helped along the way by a nice inheritance and an eighty-hour working week that turned into a thriving business. An eighty-hour working week! Torp was astonished every time those numbers of hours appeared in portrait articles about successful businesspeople. Was there no one counting, then? He continued to click on articles in the Google search results. Why she chose to enter politics—*I want to give something back to my country.* Why she had never had children—*there have been men in my life, but never in such a way that I wanted to share a child with them.* Why she liked going to church—*Christianity is a very strong part of my identity and our country's identity.*

Torp clicked on today's edition of the *Express. Rolighed slays Enevoldsen,* tempted the headline. In a way, it wasn't an exaggeration. Then came the predictable polls, which were particular in that their very existence was a disaster for a party leader and especially a Prime Minister. Seventy per cent of voters would prefer Kirsten Rolighed as Prime Minister over Palle Enevoldsen. The man was bleeding, and Torp knew there would be more polls ahead of his all-or-nothing national executive committee meeting on Thursday. The Fourth Estate rarely missed that kind of opportunity.

Torp turned back to his computer. He was finished with Kirsten Rolighed; it would have to wait until 2:00 p.m. when he was scheduled to meet her. Now it was Monday's promise to himself and, in fact, also to his obituary pusher on Funen—no more obituaries for Crabby. Four new ones had arrived, three medium and one small one and a message that it was okay to let someone else do the obituaries if he really had a lot on, but that there was an agreement between him and Torp, not an agreement that Torp could send the obituaries to a mass of other people. It wasn't a criticism, it said, but then it was anyway, concluded Torp. He again felt he was being talked down to, even though he both understood and accepted the objection. *All right, it will just be me in the future, just had something urgent on*, he wrote back and started with *Hanne Lindblad, eighty-one years old, former school teacher, Mågevej, Glamsbjerg*. If he was lucky, he would have time to do all of them before the interview with Kirsten Rolighed. The editor from *Around Borgen* had written and reminded him of the agreement: approximately 6,000 characters including spaces, deadline at 6:00 p.m. Remember camera for clips to come later.

CHAPTER 18

S ometimes the world changes in an instant, from functioning reasonably well, being cohesive, familiar, and predictable, to toppling with such a violent force that nothing remains as before.

Ulrik Torp felt life disappearing from under him when, on the big flight of steps outside Christiansborg, he switched off flight mode and re-established his mobile phone's connection with the rest of the world after the interview with the Liberals' political spokesperson, Kirsten Rolighed.

Torp thought it had gone well. He was still having a hard time getting used to the special entrance with security checks, like an airport, for guests and journalists who didn't work at Borgen on a daily basis. As a young journalist, he had just swanned in without thinking about it. The guards in the glass cage back then had been intended more as a service to guests who weren't familiar with the building than as protection for anyone or anything. Now Christiansborg had been terror-proofed with large stones, bollards, a cordoned-off inner courtyard, and lots of visible security guards, as well as some who were invisible. The Prime Minister, a select few ministers, and particularly controversial Members of Parliament were protected by bodyguards around the clock. That was how it had become, and most people thought, quite frankly, that it was very un-Danish.

Kirsten Rolighed laughed when he began the interview with that observation. She was one of the selected Members of Parliament with bodyguards since a speech on nationalism and Islam some years earlier. Torp noted *laughed* on his notepad and thought about her doing precisely that: laughing. There weren't many who did that any more.

"It isn't Danes who are a threat to my life. So I suppose it is a little un-Danish," she said with a smile and an apology for a dry cough.

They were sitting in her Christiansborg office, which had been reserved for the Liberals' political spokesperson for decades. It was the size of a small flat, with stucco, a split-level, and a huge window overlooking the riding arena. Torp had sat there several times in his earlier life with other politicians sitting across from him, including Palle Enevoldsen, when the current Prime Minister had been young and aspiring—like the journalist who had been interviewing him. Torp rigged up his mobile phone on Bertel's tripod, focused the camera, and pressed "Start," while he watched her pouring coffee for both of them and pushing a small plate of biscuits over to him.

"British gingersnaps bought at the airport on the way home from the delegation trip to China."

They sat down on the office sofa arrangement farthest away from a huge desk that—apart from her thin computer and the high-gloss, chrome-plated, PH table lamp—was completely bare. Kirsten Rolighed radiated control and neatness. Torp was convinced she had never in her life had visibly sweaty armpits.

"I well remember the speech that started it all. The summer festival at Mossø, where you argued that there must be a convergence between people, state, nation, language, and church for Denmark to be peaceful."

"Ah, now I know where you're heading." There was no hostility in her voice. She reached for today's copy of the *Daily News* on the service table next to the armchair. "Annegrethe Hulsig's proposal that parliamentary politicians should be born in Denmark."

"You don't distance yourself from it in the article."

"No, of course I don't."

She paused briefly, thinking about how to express herself. That was the difference between her and Annegrethe Hulsig from the Nationalist

Party. Hulsig knew she would never become a minister and certainly not Prime Minister. Rolighed knew that both weren't just possibilities, but also within reach. The tightrope was therefore thinner.

"I'm well aware that the Constitution makes it impossible and that in practice it isn't possible to change the Constitution. But that doesn't mean we can't discuss it openly and perhaps also agree that being born in Denmark gives one a special feeling for the country."

"Many Turks, Pakistanis, and Somalis in Denmark were born here."

"And they are welcome to become Danish," she interrupted.

"And also become a politician?"

"Yes, indeed, that too." Kirsten Rolighed pushed the biscuits towards Torp again. "Did you know that after Struensee—the king's German private physician—was executed in 1772, the state introduced the right of citizenship?"

Torp shook his head. Of course he didn't know, but he knew that the question wasn't meant to be a question to be answered. She would certainly do that herself.

"They didn't want to risk a new German or other foreigner coming in and turning the Denmark they knew upside down. The right of citizenship was to ensure that state positions were filled only by people who had been born in Denmark."

"But we also had no Constitution then," interjected Torp.

Again Kirsten Rolighed laughed, that contagious, disarming laugh, which Danes knew and were comfortable with, according to the opinion polls.

"It was very progressive at the time—completely unique in a European context, but part of a national programme. Struensee and the Enlightenment had shaken the national guy-ropes rather too much. They didn't want such a situation repeating itself."

"Do you think such a law would be a good idea today?

"Of course not." Her expression changed and became more serious. "But it is thought-provoking that a few years after Struensee was executed and hacked to pieces, right where our national football stadium stands today, the best and wisest Americans drafted a Constitution which states, apparently as something perfectly natural, that the country's president should be born in the USA."

"Americans are patriots, not nationalists," objected Torp. He was suddenly sounding more like a debater than a journalist.

"Are you sure?" Kirsten Rolighed looked at him with a little triumph in her eyes.

Torp hesitated. "Well, that's how it once was, at least."

"Is there any difference?"

"Patriotism is about the fatherland. Nationalism is about the people." Torp's reply came faster and more aggressively than he would have liked.

"I wasn't aware that there was any difference," remarked Rolighed, again with the smile that could be both disarming and charming at the same time. She was interrupted by a coughing fit.

"Sorry. It's the long hours of air conditioning in the plane."

She took a glass of water from the carafe that stood on the table. Torp didn't want any.

"In reality," she continued, "the central question is whether the threat to a country comes from outside or from within."

"And what's the answer?"

"If the country is a well-functioning nation state, as Denmark still is, then the threat always comes from outside. That's self-explanatory."

There was a pause between them.

"How passionately do you want to become Prime Minister?"

Rolighed's breathing stopped for a split second, then she looked searchingly at the journalist in front of her and tightened her face a little bit, indicating that this was in breach of the agreement. She cast a quick side glance at the camera tripod.

"I'm pretty sure my press adviser and your editor made an agreement on what we were going to talk about."

"Seventy per cent of voters prefer you to Enevoldsen. That must have some effect on you, surely?"

"The national executive meeting on Thursday is a party matter. I take it for granted that it will confirm that Palle is, of course, our leader and thus also the Prime Minister of the country."

"Do you know any top politician who doesn't want to become Prime Minister?"

Rolighed's gaze fell on Torp's business card, which he had given her when they met.

"*Ulrik Torp—everything in journalism*. You can say that again."

She apologised for another fit of coughing and looked over at him.

"I've only been in Parliament for five years and don't actually know your name. But my press secretary does."

Now she had a broad smile. Torp knew who her press secretary was and could hear from the Liberals' political spokesperson that she had been given the whole story. He felt convinced that the version she had been given was without extenuating circumstances. Maybe there weren't really any extenuating circumstances.

"Was there anything else, or were we finished?" she said, with a glance at her wristwatch. An hour had been set aside for the interview. Forty minutes had passed.

"One more little thing," said Torp. "Just a detail, really. Because in addition to it being a topical political article, I would also like some of your own background for that part that has to do with business policies and the whole startup business."

"Yes?" She didn't make any effort to hide her impatience.

"Startup capital is often the jumping-off point from having a good idea to its execution. How did it start for you? Who believed in you? How did you get the money to start your own business?"

The question was meant innocently and completely without ulterior motive, but Torp could see that he had hit a nerve—the slight tightening at the corner of the mouth; the breathing that stopped again, this time for more than a second; the look that wasn't as fixed as it was trying to be. It was as if the last surviving remnant of trust had disappeared inside the large office.

"It was sort of a little at a time. That kind of initiative didn't require large sums of money. Anyway, it was many years ago," she said defensively. "It's completely different nowadays," she continued, regaining her self-control. "That's why we're proposing special credit options for good ideas." She misunderstood Torp's slightly disoriented facial expression. "Yes, you know, what I was talking about earlier."

He nodded, also as a sign that he had no more questions.

Out in the front office, Torp nodded to the press secretary who had made the agreement with *Around Borgen* with a guarantee that they wouldn't talk about power struggles and prime ministerial dreams.

"Thanks for your time, Torp. Did it go well?"

"It went fine, thanks," replied Torp. He recognised the short-haired young man in the white shirt sitting at the farthest desk, working at his computer. It was one of the young people from the visit to Per Frost.

Out in the corridors, Torp instinctively sensed the atmosphere of a power struggle in the Liberals' corner of Christiansborg: closed doors, no jovial talk in the corridor, a few glances that registered that he had come out of Kirsten Rolighed's office. It was all about power in the country's second-largest party and the battle to be the next Prime Minister.

"Well now, Torp—have you been interviewing Rolighed?"

Torp stopped and shook hands with one of the elders from the parliamentary group.

"Iversen. Long time no see."

"I hear it's for the new magazine *Around Borgen*. Who took the initiative for an interview? Not you, I assume."

"Iversen, you old poison-monger, you're well informed," said Torp, with no attempt to hide his amusement. "I don't know who took the initiative. Is it important?"

Iversen looked around. "Everything's important in war, you know."

"Is there a war?"

Iversen just rolled his eyes. There had to be limits to how stupid even a burnt-out journalist could be.

"I'm assuming you're on Palle's team," Torp said.

"You bet your life."

"Will he win on Thursday?"

Torp was really only asking the question in order to have it confirmed that the party leadership, despite distorted polls, was of course in control.

"If you had asked me last week, I would have been totally certain. But she is shifting things. *They* are shifting things."

"And who are *they?*"

"The small-minded, everyday nationalists." Iversen made this last comment with a sneer in his voice and walked on, after saying goodbye to Torp.

Powerful sections of prime ministerial parties had previously flirted with the idea of overthrowing their leader and appointing a new Prime Minister well in advance of the next election. On one occasion, it had been very close. Could it really happen? Torp went through the bulletproof glass sluice at the exit and stood in the April sunshine on the broad flight of steps in the inner courtyard. It took a few seconds for his smartphone to reconnect with the telecommunications company and the internet. In less than an hour, five text messages, seven emails, and over a hundred notifications had come in on Twitter and Facebook.

He opened the text messages and saw that two of them were from Karen. The first just said: *What the hell are you up to?* The next one, which had arrived a few minutes ago, apparently in frustration at him not having reacted to the first one, was more detailed.

I can't take any more. There is a suitcase in the stairwell with a key to the allotment house in the front pocket. I need time to think. So do you.

What in the world had happened?

CHAPTER 19

S he wasn't answering her phone or his text messages.

Ulrik Torp was standing on Christiansborg's broad flight of steps frantically trying to get hold of his wife.

Karen, call me. It's not what you think. It's important we talk. All my love, Ulrik.

He didn't think he had ever written *all my love.*

It was always just *love/u.*

I don't understand anything. The video is completely false. Call me.

Had Vivi kissed him? Yes, quickly on the mouth. More than that? She probably wanted him to be tempted, but that was it. A light touch, a long hug, two lips in a dry, quick meeting and that was that. He couldn't get it to tally.

Ulrik went on Facebook again to see the recording, the comments, who liked it, and who had shared it. Nearly 200 shares, even more likes and comments, and 15,000 views in just one hour.

"STEAMY SPRING" was written over the clip, which lasted almost two minutes. It had been edited with close-ups and snapshots, and it all stood out sharply. Vivi strokes his cheek. They toast, lean towards each other, and laugh. She puts her hand on his thigh, letting it stay without him protesting. All of it affectionate, but not devastating. On the other hand, you couldn't say that about the last minute. A long embrace and a kiss that apparently just kept going, deep, heartfelt, and long. It hadn't been like that, but Ulrik had to admit that from a distance it looked like that. The last five seconds were a still image of Ulrik turning his head away from the woman's mouth and apparently looking directly into the camera.

Some comments noted that it wasn't his wife. Others protested over the use of the word "steamy" and lauded the kiss, the good weather, and springtime. Some were moved that such old people still had blood coursing through their veins. *Why shouldn't old people kiss each other in the spring?* wrote some young people, thinking that it would be understood as support. It spawned a longer thread for and against old people, spring, and libido. Old people? Ulrik switched to Twitter, where the recording had also been posted. Here, just with the hashtags *dkpol* and *torpcomesout*, so many of his journalist colleagues couldn't help but stumble across it. The sender on both Facebook and Twitter was called monkeybusiness and was impossible to identify. The person in question had apparently only existed on social media for a few weeks.

Ulrik tried to call Karen again. It went straight to voicemail, which presumably meant she had turned off her phone. Karen, for Christ's sake! How can you believe that?

He got a sudden urge and called Sofie.

"Hi, Dad, is something wrong?" Had she already seen the recording? She misunderstood his silence. "I mean . . . it's not often that you're the one who calls."

"Have you heard from Mum?"

"No, I haven't. I'm divorcing Jonathan."

"When was the last time you talked to her?"

"Dad, did you hear what I just said?"

"Yes. Have you talked to Mum?"

"Is Mum okay? Has something happened?"

"No, no, I just can't get hold of Mum. You don't know where she is?"

"Jonathan and I are getting divorced, Dad."

"And so you should. Sofie, do you mind just calling me if you hear from Mum?"

Ulrik hung up. Did he have a phone number for Karen's old school friend Ingelis? He didn't. Tine? Her neither. It dawned on him that they had very few mutual friends. They did have, back when he had been in demand, or maybe it was just his friends who had fallen by the wayside the last few years. Sofie was getting divorced. That was good. Then he would also escape the recurring humiliations in Klampenborg. Conversely, it could be that an economic and social downturn would become Jonathan. Maybe there was, in fact, something good in him, as Karen occasionally tried to say. Karen! He called again. Straight into the answering machine. At least it was good that they hadn't had children, then it would have been a mess. Maybe Jonathan's comedown was just the opportunity for the divorce. It would probably have happened at some point anyway. Was it Sofie? It had to be. He couldn't bear the thought that it was that idiot who had broken it off. She would get over it; she had always been good at moving on.

Ulrik moved from the main stairs and the inner courtyard at Christiansborg down to the library garden at the National Archives. It was a small, easily overlooked, and therefore peaceful spot in the middle of Copenhagen. When he had been working at Borgen, he had enjoyed sneaking off down here for a break and sitting on a bench with a coffee and a newspaper. Now, for him, most things had a hazy quality to them. He noticed that there were a few other people in the garden—a young couple sat kissing on a bench; a handful of Chinese tourists were crossing the garden with a guide, taking the shortcut from the Black Diamond. They were probably on their way to Strøget. Ulrik saw them and yet didn't see them. He would never be able to describe what they looked like, how they were dressed, or the atmosphere between them. Ulrik sat down heavily on the bench farthest away from the kissing couple and put his head down between his legs to get oxygen to his brain. He felt dizzy and tried to breathe deeply.

All the way in, all the way out. Calmly. Once more. All the way in, all the way out. Calmly. It helped a little.

Twice in their nearly thirty-year marriage, Karen had been so tired of him that he had forced himself to think what it would be like to be divorced. Both times, he had been horrified. Ulrik had no illusions—children and friends would choose Karen. They wouldn't reject him, but they would choose Karen. Would he become lonely and weird? Even weirder? Both times, the thought had filled him with so much self-pity that he became disgusted with himself. Was he really so selfish, fragile, and miserable? So dependent on Karen, so little able to give of himself? Was dependence on another human being the same as love?

Head down. All the way in, all the way out. Calm. Once more. Better.

Several of their acquaintances had been divorced over the years, and that had strengthened Ulrik in the knowledge that there are only a few happy divorces. At least for men. The illusion that the grass could be greener on the other side was precisely that, an illusion—it was a wilderness of weeds on the other side. Some of his peers had found much younger wives, which also brought new children and nappy changing, new mothers-in-law and parent-teacher meetings.

It wasn't a life that made them young again. It was a daily reminder of one's own decay and mortality.

Ulrik glanced over at the bench with the kissing couple. Where were they? There—with their arms around each other, continuing on their way. At the bottom by the National Archives, he recognised an elderly Member of Parliament who was talking to a woman who was probably his young secretary. They were standing too close for it to be work. They made eye contact; the man recognised Torp and withdrew half a metre in one quick movement.

His mobile rang. Karen!

It was a number he didn't recognise. Ulrik let it ring out. He checked Facebook again—soon up to 300 shares and more than 20,000 views. What would he have if she wanted a divorce? He didn't even have anywhere to live. His parents were dead and he rarely saw his much older sister in North Jutland. He had nothing. Once again, this self-pity which he could neither endure nor keep away. Maybe the municipality would be obliged to find something for him. He dismissed it. Of course, she didn't want a divorce. What was it again she wrote? He checked the text message: *I need time to think. So do you.* They both had to think.

You didn't do that, surely, if you were going to divorce. Torp felt a little better.

A little.

Maybe he could call Vivi and get her to call Karen and tell her it was all a misunderstanding? He shot the idea down right away. But they hadn't kissed, not in that way. Ulrik couldn't understand that it had got this far, even though he had to admit that he had enjoyed being with her. He googled his way to the phone number of Ingelis; he could remember her strange last name—Brage.

"It's Ulrik, hi. . . Do you happen to know where Karen is? I can't find her right now and she isn't answering her phone."

She said she didn't know, but he could hear she was lying. And yes, she would be certain to say he had called. That was, if she saw Karen. He sent her a new text message. *This is a huge, huge misunderstanding. Love you. Call me.*

The phone rang less than a minute later. It was the editor of *Around Borgen* who wanted to hear how the interview with Kirsten Rolighed had gone. It had gone well.

"Are you in the process of writing the article?"

He was indeed.

"No later than six p.m. I want to have it on the website before I go home today."

Ulrik tried to call Sofie again. He hadn't reacted very seriously to her news of their divorce. Maybe he could save it. And maybe she had heard from her mother by now. She didn't answer, and in a way he was relieved. Maybe she had now seen the recording on Facebook or Twitter. She would see it at some point. And at some point, he would also have to explain to her—and Jesper. Jesper would find it easier to believe him, to understand and accept. Sofie was difficult. She was like her mother. Had Karen been as patient with him as Sofie had with Jonathan? His stomach contracted—perhaps their friends were surprised that Karen had endured him for so many years. He went on Facebook again. It was absolutely crazy; now almost 400 shares and 30,000 views. How could it go so fast? Thousands of likes and hundreds of comments. He didn't feel up to reading them, but he could see that several people—he had no idea who they were—wrote that "it certainly wasn't the wife he was snogging." Some even tagged Karen to make sure she saw it. Why couldn't they just be indifferent?

Brathenberg, Erling Jensen, and Benedikte Koch were suddenly far away. Ulrik's thoughts were all over the place; he couldn't hold on to one thought at a time. This monkeybusiness also bothered him. What the hell was that monkey up to? What had he done to him? What had the Prime Minister done to him?

He received a text message. His heart jumped, but it wasn't Karen. It was the editor from *Around Borgen* who had gone home and was giving him another email address where he was to deliver the interview with Kirsten Rolighed. But still no later than six p.m. The readers had been promised that the interview would be there this evening. Torp answered okay, got up, nodded to the embarrassed, older Member of Parliament, who was still talking to his secretary at a proper distance, and left the library garden.

CHAPTER 20

The Liberals' political spokesperson is carrying a mild spring cold and a dry cough as she offers Around Borgen British biscuits in her office at Christiansborg. Ahead awaits an hour of political analysis of both the crisis among the Liberals and the problems for the country's entrepreneurs. The first is dismissed with unreserved support for the party leader and Prime Minister. The latter reveals that the entrepreneurial environment she herself has been shaped by is her lifeblood.

May we present: Kirsten Rolighed, perhaps the Liberals' next leader and the country's next Prime Minister.

Was that too much? It was, but Ulrik Torp had a good feeling that the editor certainly wouldn't think it was too much. Besides that, it just had to be that way. He forced himself to write the article—6,000 characters before 6:00 p.m.—because that was the agreement; it was the deadline that his entire professionalism and many years of journalistic experience decreed that you didn't miss. Everything else. Not that. Like an actor who had lost a spouse yet a few hours later was standing onstage in front of the audience. Torp couldn't quite remember any concrete examples, but knew that he had read about it in several biographies.

The article had to be delivered, even though his thoughts were scattered in all sorts of other directions. Or rather, one special direction—Karen.

Axel had asked sympathetically if there was anything he could do. There wasn't. Crabby said nothing, Emma had gone, and Bertel had a fever and had gone home. Torp wrote on.

Kirsten Rolighed rejects any talk that Palle Enevoldsen is finished as leader and Prime Minister, and refuses to take part in any discussion about "what-if."

Should that be a "but" instead of an "and"? "But" would suggest a connection between Enevoldsen and her ambitions. "And" was the innocent choice. Torp chose "and." That was what he had written first. It was more in line with the agreement on the framework for the interview. And all things considered, it was also more in line with his experience. Not that Torp believed her for a moment, but sometimes you had to accept what was said. Moreover, he was past that place in the text—it would cost time to go back.

Now it had to be finished and sent.

He continued writing about Rolighed. Now he had 5,100 characters. A few hundred more. Torp added some more sentences about small and medium-sized companies, which wouldn't have been included if he had had time to make a proper article, but now it just had to be padded. He didn't have the energy to find the exact quotes from the recording of the interview, so he wrote the section as indirect quotes and with loose formulations that may not have made much sense but weren't wrong either. Rolighed had hesitated when he had asked about her own business career and startup capital, which had surprised him because he thought he had read in several articles that she had used inherited money for the startup. Torp dismissed it—it didn't matter now. He skimmed the article, put his by-line on, didn't even bother to suggest a headline, and sent it off.

Done.

Torp remained seated, staring out into thin air. He registered that Axel came in and told him that he had just talked to Bertel's wife. Bertel had been admitted to the intensive care unit at the Rigshospitalet; the doctors didn't really know what was the matter with him—it was something to do with both liver and lungs.

"She says he's not the only one," added Axel.

The phone rang. Maybe it was Karen at last.

"Nice article, Torp. It's a perfect fit for *Around Borgen*."

"Thanks."

Torp promised to be available for more interviews and articles.

"I'm pleased to hear that. You still write well—it's important that we get off to a good start. Remember the recordings for social media."

Still? We? Torp assured him that he was ready and thought that, all things considered, the project was promising, and apologised for being a little busy. Axel had turned around and gone back to the bay window. Neither Crabby nor Torp had reacted strongly to Bertel's condition.

He went into Facebook and saw the recording again. STEAMY SPRING—didn't people give any thought to privacy? Even though it had taken place in public, you weren't allowed to do such a thing, Torp remembered from the law lessons at the School of Journalism. You weren't allowed to zoom in on individuals without permission. His thoughts were like a bluebottle fly in an empty jam jar. If only he could get in touch with Karen and explain everything. But explain what? The meeting with Vivi had been too intimate. He hadn't planned anything, but he had let her put her hand on his thigh, let her stroke him on the cheek, given her a long hug, and let her kiss him on the mouth. But only for a moment. Not a real kiss. Or was it?

"What a spring you're having online."

Emma entered the office smiling with her laptop under her arm. Torp looked up, surprised she could be smiling as she was. He noticed that Axel was trying to get her to shut up.

"What?"

She looked back towards Torp.

"What?" she repeated, when she was simply greeted with two tomb-like faces. "The sun's shining, people are happy," she continued, lightly reproachful of the old men she shared an office with. It dawned on Torp that she had never met Karen. She thought, of course, that it was his wife he was with on the recording.

"It's not Karen on the video."

Emma swallowed a remark about "videos" and "boomers."

"Oh, shit," she exclaimed as she sat down.

"It was recorded yesterday. It's someone I know, but not in that way."

Torp thought he should explain himself or apologise, but could see that Emma immediately accepted the situation or maybe was just indifferent.

"Who posted it?"

"His name is monkeybusiness. That's the only thing you can see," replied Axel.

"He?"

"Do you really think it could be a woman?" continued Axel with a hint of disbelief.

Torp could see that Emma was forcing herself to hold back, an exercise she wasn't used to. She was probably wondering why men his age didn't think women could come up with something like that. How was it possible at one and the same time to convince themselves that they believed in equality, and then couldn't imagine women being evil, going to war, being bawdy, committing abuses of power, or killing people for money? How could they convince themselves that they were modern and believed in equality when they quite simply didn't? She was probably holding back a lengthy lecture that monkeybusiness could of course be a woman, that it could have been herself if the purpose had required it. Torp imagined that she was holding all this down in a single deep breath while going online and checking out monkeybusiness.

"Created a few weeks ago with a few followers on Twitter and even fewer friends on Facebook. It's clearly a troll," she stated. "*He* also had the recording with the Prime Minister, in which he called supporters of a National Day idiots."

Emma put the stress on *he* in a way that made it clear that she didn't immediately accept Axel's sexist conclusion.

"Can you see who monkeybusiness is?"

"It's not a bot, whatever it is."

"What's a bot?"

Emma had difficulty suppressing a sigh. Didn't they know anything?

"A bot is a Web robot. It is, in fact, a computer program that controls a profile. It just throws things out on the web, sometimes sharing content ten, fifteen, twenty times an hour. Its sole purpose is to spread other people's content so that people get the impression that it's very popular."

"Who does such things?"

"The Russians are experts at it. It's fairly easy to figure out, but it works."

"How does it work?" asked Axel.

Emma looked at him. She guessed that Axel probably had a Facebook account to be able to see pictures of his grandchildren, but she was almost certain he wasn't on Twitter and certainly not on Instagram.

"It generates traffic and creates the illusion of many followers. When the Americans elect the president, when the British vote to withdraw from the EU, or when the Greeks have a referendum on changing the name of Macedonia. Every time a referendum means something geopolitically. You name it. There are plenty of examples, and not only with Russia as the sender."

"But this isn't a . . . bot, you say."

Emma shook her head.

"No, this is an anonymous identity. It seems to have been created just to post things online. At least that's all it's been used for so far."

"And he's a Russian?" Axel was persistent.

"We don't know, neither if it is male nor if it's Russian. It could just as easily be a suburban woman."

Emma was trying to be patient. She turned her attention to Torp, who was just sitting staring at his computer screen.

"Speaking of Russians, have you heard if Anton from Police Headquarters has found that female Russian killer at passport control at the airport?"

She tried to say it as sensitively as possible; maybe it could even get him to think of something else. Torp shook his head. No, he hadn't heard from Anton. All in all, Anton didn't seem as enthusiastic about their theories as they were.

"And what about Benedikte Koch? Has she been located?"

Torp once again shook his head.

"It's all a total mess," he said.

Torp made a sudden decision and stood up.

"Maybe Karen's at home. Of course she is. Is there anyone who can be bothered to help me push the Polo and get it going?"

Both Emma and Axel volunteered. Crabby didn't really say anything.

It was almost 8:00 p.m.; the sun was about to set, but it was still light, so Ulrik couldn't see from the street if there were lights on in the flat and if Karen was home. He parked right in front of the gate, left the engine running, and tried to call again, in vain. Then he let himself into the stairwell and saw the suitcase standing in front of the door into the flat as she had written. He rang the bell several times, knocked on the door, knelt down, and looked through the letter box. If she was home, she was doing a really good job of hiding it. Ulrik was about to unlock the door but held back. Somehow or other, Karen's text message and the suitcase were denying him access to the flat. Maybe she had changed the lock? No, you probably couldn't get that done in such a short space of time, and she would never do that, either. She trusted him. The fact that the suitcase stood where it stood meant that he shouldn't go inside. But then again, she didn't trust him. That was precisely why the suitcase stood where it stood. Ulrik hesitated with the key, pulled it out of the lock, and put it back in his pocket. He had to show that he respected her decision. He grabbed the suitcase and shoved it onto the back seat of the Polo, which was waiting patiently with the engine running, and typed the address of the allotment house into his smartphone after making sure the key was in the front pocket of the suitcase. Away.

During the day, spring in April could fool you into thinking that it was summer, but when the sun was about to set, as it was when Ulrik arrived at the allotment association in Brønshøj, the cold suddenly penetrated, abruptly and without warning. Ulrik was only wearing a thin shirt when he walked the last bit from the parking area up to the allotment house with his suitcase. He shivered in the evening cold. Damn spring. An elderly, overweight couple was walking towards him on the wide gravel path. They could see each other from a long way off despite the evening twilight. He was clearly a stranger and restrained his feeling that he owed them an explanation.

"Evenin'," he mumbled at the obligatory one and a half metres' distance.

They nodded back. He had no doubt that they would get wind of the fact that he had moved into number 42 and the next day would tell the others about "him with the suitcase," whom everyone thereafter would be keeping an eye on. Some people called it neighbourhood watch. Ulrik could feel that it was on the verge of suffocating him.

It was a small but, from the outside, well-maintained allotment house with roofing felt, white painted wooden walls, and a small outdoor kitchen and outdoor shower by the terrace. A privet hedge beginning to display new leaves surrounded the plot, which unlike several of the other allotments wasn't planted with herbs, vegetables, and flowers. This plot was pretty much only grass. Ulrik took hold of the rusty metal gate that creaked and groaned when he moved it. It wasn't just oil and paint that it lacked. It was hanging on one hinge, so you had to give it an extra twist, and that made it squeal heartbreakingly for a brief moment.

The key fit. An acrid smell of overwintered summer cottage came to meet him. The smell wasn't unpleasant; it was just unnatural. It would take more than fifteen minutes of airing to get rid of it. The living room and kitchen were so small and so close together that it would be impossible to say where one began and the other ended. Torp checked the bedroom, which consisted of a three-quarter-size bed that literally filled the whole space. The door could only be opened because it opened out of the room. He lit the small wood-burning stove that seemed to be the house's only source of heat and looked for the toilet. Surely there must be a bathroom? He found a privy in a small extension with an entrance from the outside and strained for a long time to pee. The bathroom had to be the outdoor shower that hung crookedly next to the outside kitchen.

Ulrik hadn't eaten anything since the biscuits in Kirsten Rolighed's office. He had forgotten to buy food, but he found a can of tuna in oil and a can of cod roe left in the cupboard next to a handful of teabags. It was dark outside, the heat was beginning to spread through the few square metres, and he tried with partial success to regulate the air damper so it didn't get too hot.

Torp let the tea brew an extra long time, searched in vain for the half teaspoon of sugar he usually rounded it off with, and sank into the allotment house's only armchair with the cod roe and tuna by his side.

CHAPTER 21

Ulrik Torp stayed behind the truck. Everyone else was overtaking, but he had with time become so conscious of the lack of horsepower in the Polo that it wasn't worth trying. Emma was sitting in the passenger seat, scrolling through her smartphone. The trip was a long shot but a welcome opportunity not to think about Karen and the recording that was still circling on social media.

A text message from her had woken him up in the morning in the allotment house, which was icy cold after the wood-burning stove had gone out during the night. How on earth could there be frost at night when it was almost summer during the day? Karen had simply texted that Sofie and Jesper had now heard about the recording and since then also seen their father intensely kissing a total stranger. The least he could do was explain himself to them. Torp didn't feel up to calling them. As it was, he wasn't good at that kind of conversation, and this one was in a class by itself. He texted them both at the same time.

Dear Sofie and Jesper, I know you have seen a recording of me with a woman. It's not at all what it looks like. Mum and I will work it out. Will call later. Love, Dad

Initially, he wrote it without the correct punctuation. It was as if the rules didn't apply in the texting universe. Moreover, correct punctuation might suggest that he didn't take it seriously enough when there was time to think about that kind of thing. It was probably a generational difference. He regretted it just before he was ready to send it, and went back to the text and put in the commas and full stops as they should be. *Will call later*—should he leave it at that? It gave the impression that he would call during the morning, or at least sometime today. Could he cope with that at a time when he generally couldn't cope with anything? He deleted it, and at the same time felt like a coward. Couldn't he even talk to his grown-up children about this? He couldn't. He had to talk to Karen first, but she hadn't responded to the text message he had immediately sent back to her. He changed his mind again and added *will call later*.

Emma looked up from her smartphone.

"We go straight ahead at the roundabout."

The Hillerød motorway had long since ended, and they were still driving behind the truck, which seemed excessively slow. It was also going straight ahead at the roundabout.

"Are you sure about this?"

He looked at her resolute face.

"Rågeleje is straight ahead."

Torp looked despairingly at her. That wasn't what he meant.

"You say that her teenage neighbour said that Benedikte Koch might be in the summer cottage, right?"

"Yes."

"That is, *the* summer cottage. Not *a* summer cottage, but a specific one."

"Yes."

"And you're sure about that?"

Torp was getting irritated. It had been a brief conversation with a mute teenager several days ago. Of course he wasn't sure.

"I think so. That's how I remember it."

"So that's the assumption we're working from," concluded Emma, sounding unconcerned and matter-of-fact. "To the left here—follow the truck."

* * *

Emma had come out to the allotment house a few hours after she had called to hear what he was doing and where he was. There had been a sense that she sounded worried. Torp heard the squeal of the rusty iron gate and was standing in the doorway when she came.

"Cool allotment," she had exclaimed appreciatively, proffering a bag of buttered rolls.

He had eaten gratefully while making tea for both of them. Emma was already working on her computer, which she had connected to her phone's mobile data, before Torp had managed to serve the tea.

"The neighbour said that Benedikte Koch and her husband didn't have a summer cottage," Emma said.

Torp nodded.

"And that fits with the land registry. The neighbour, on the other hand, has a cottage in Rågeleje. Maybe it was their own cottage that the daughter was thinking of when she was guessing where they could be."

A quick decision, a little push, and they were on their way.

Torp followed the sign and the truck turned off towards Gilleleje, so he could speed up a bit. He had lived most of his life in the area in and around the capital, but never been on the north coast of Zealand. It was as if it was reserved for others—as if it had nothing to do with him. The place names Hornbæk and Tisvilde conjured in his mind celebrities, shorts with ironed creases, a cabriolet, and Aperol Spritz—everything he felt repulsed by and at the same time attracted to, an unattainable lifestyle he both despised and envied. A reminder of his own ineptitude. Here he came, Ulrik Torp, fifty-seven years old, a partially unemployed journalist in an old Polo with a flat battery, without a permanent home, with a marriage on the rocks and a girl with a ring in her nose as a passenger. What right did he have to come here in the first place? Now they were on what must be the coast road towards Rågeleje—how many of these cottages had eaten canned tuna in oil and cod roe for dinner? He couldn't help but notice the fleet of Volvos, Mercedes, Range Rovers and Audis carelessly parked in front of many of the summer cottages.

"To the left and two hundred metres ahead." Emma was focused on her phone, which was showing the way.

"What do you think about this?"

"About Benedikte Koch?" she said, looking up.

"About all this," he said, pointing at the surroundings.

"I don't have any idea what you're talking about."

Emma was disoriented for a moment, then she regained her concentration.

"There, on the right; it's number ten."

Oh my God, how Torp envied her.

He drove carefully past the cottage—an older one, well maintained in classic black and white. There was no car parked, the curtains were drawn, no one on the terrace. He crept on, put it down a gear to get up the hill, and turned around. If they were going to stop, it might as well be with the nose pointing downwards, now that there was finally a hill. Torp stopped at the top, slightly out in the verge.

"What next?"

"Now we walk past and enjoy the lovely weather," commanded Emma, getting out of the car.

It was a large cottage, and at first sight, there was no sign that anyone was living there. But the second time they passed, Torp noticed a thermos standing on a small table on the terrace. Would one forget to take it in when one left a cottage? They agreed that one would not.

"Shouldn't we just knock on the door?"

Emma liked to keep things simple.

"What should we say?"

"That we think it's odd that she's on sick leave from the university when she's obviously not sick. That we want to hear how she can explain the articles in the *Express* about researcher fraud. What Brathenberg, Erling Jensen, and she were so busy with before the two died? Why she called you and hung up without saying anything? What happened in the Parliamentary Control Committee from 1990 to 1992, when she was its secretary? Why she's in hiding?"

Emma looked reproachfully at Torp.

"Do you honestly think we lack a good enough reason to knock and disturb her?"

"If she's there. We have no idea, Emma."

Torp still took the lead in the direction of the front door of the cottage, stood on the stairs—he could feel his heart thumping—hesitated initially, and then knocked, first in a friendly way, then a little less friendly. He could hear the sea, which lay a few hundred metres away on the other side of the slope, and immediately recognised the sound—it was the buzz that had been in the background when Benedikte Koch first called without saying who she was.

A well-groomed, tanned couple was standing on the road watching them.

"Hans and Benedikte have probably gone to Gilleleje to do some shopping. Can we give them a message?"

It was the woman who spoke. Torp noticed how amazed he was at how tanned they were at such an early time of the year. So Emma had hit the spot with the land registry; they exchanged a quick triumphant look. The couple were clearly not asking in order to help, but to check.

"We're from the Jehovah's Witnesses. Could we tempt you with a talk about Jesus and an invitation to a Sunday afternoon in our Kingdom Hall in Helsinge?"

Emma took four quick steps towards the couple on the road proffering a piece of paper. It gave the pair of them a jolt. The woman stretched out both hands to avert the piece of paper and in the movement dropped her tennis racket.

"It's not really us, that sort of thing," said the man in a voice that showed he was used to being obeyed. "And it's not something for Hans and Benedikte either, so you can safely move on."

He was polite but wasn't contemplating a discussion or an exchange of experiences about either salvation or damnation.

"Judgement Day is closer than ever," proclaimed Emma earnestly.

"I'm sure it always has been," mumbled the man, picking up his wife's dropped racket from the gravel road. "Now I think you should move on, and preferably to a completely different place. There are no potential

Witnesses here," he said, showing with both tone of voice and body that the conversation was over.

Emma thanked him, and muttered, "Come on, Father." Torp followed, away from the cottage down to the beach.

"You're such a mad liar, Emma."

They were several hundred metres away from the cottage and the couple who were watching their progress.

"Sorry, Father," she giggled.

Torp tried not to laugh, and he almost succeeded.

"What was that piece of paper you were offering them?"

"My notes about Brathenberg, Erling Jensen, and Benedikte Koch, where you can see that they met in the Control Committee."

"And if they had accepted the flyer from Jehovah's Witnesses about the meeting in Helsinge?"

"Are you crazy? That sort of thing works like garlic on Dracula."

"You couldn't know that."

"Believe me," said Emma, suddenly very serious, "that's actually something I know all about."

They walked silently for a while along the water's edge and eventually each of them bought an ice cream cone at the kiosk and sat down on a bench overlooking the sea. Sweden lay clearly to the right on the horizon in the form of Kullen. The beach was almost deserted, even though the waves were gentle and the sun was warming. Only a few of the beach huts had been transported down to the beach from their winter shelter up at the cottages. They had it all to themselves.

"Do you think it will ever get better?" Emma asked.

"Better?"

Torp looked at Emma.

"All of it—Friends of Denmark, National Day, border controls . . . It's not only in Denmark that kind of thing is happening at the moment, you know."

Torp nodded. "Politics isn't rational. If it was, we could just let the experts run the country. Politics is about catching, formulating, and sometimes also moderating the currents in the population. If the simple answer to a very complicated question is border control, then that's how it is."

"So it won't get any better. Is that what you're saying?"

He shrugged. Until a few years ago, he hadn't had any doubts—everything was getting better. Now, he wasn't so sure. He looked at his ice cream and knew he couldn't swallow another bite. Karen was weighing down his whole body. Imagine if their marriage was over.

"Why are you doing this?" asked Emma.

"Doing what?"

"All this stuff—the interviews with Frost and Rolighed, the articles, and the obituaries."

"I don't understand what you mean, Emma," said Torp, giving her a puzzled look.

"If you don't think it will get any better. You can't even make a living from it."

She screwed up her eyes in the sunshine and maintained her firm gaze. Torp took a bite of his ice cream anyway and waited a while before responding.

"Maybe I can make a living from it," he said, moving a little uneasily on the hard bench. "Some years ago, when I was young and promising, I received an inquiry about a position as communications manager in an international company that makes water pumps. Big salary, nice car, travel, the lot."

"What happened?"

"It never really turned into anything. Damned if I know if it was them or me. But I've thought ever since about how lucky I was. Imagine spending a lifetime on water pumps."

"Isn't that incredibly arrogant?"

Emma said it without a hint of criticism.

"Yes, it is," replied Torp straight away. "A water pump can save more lives than a front-page article in the *Daily News*. But I'm a journalist, you see. I ask on behalf of the common good, independence, hunting down the truth, and all that." He turned towards her. "Why did you want to be a journalist?"

"I'm not a journalist—I dropped out, remember."

"Emma, seriously. Why?"

"It's a way out. I would like to experience Africa."

"Not just to get away and experience, surely? Also to use journalism to point out problems, hold those in power accountable, change things."

"Now you're being a bit naive, don't you think?" she replied with a smile.

"You're thirty years ahead of your time, Emma. It's not until you reach my age that you're supposed to lose your ideals," he said, smiling back.

"Do you think it's all going really well, then?"

Torp shook his head. "There are some things that are sliding at the moment, but it isn't because of too much journalism. It's because of too little," he argued. "Fake news, conspiracy theories, echo chambers, populism, fear."

"And then you come riding on a white horse with a pen as a lance. Come on!"

"That's what I can do," he said, spreading his arms so that the melting ice cream went flying out of the cone and landed in the sand. "So other people will have to make water pumps."

"Yes, but you can't make a living from it," repeated Emma with extra emphasis this time.

"If you want to take the last remnant of dignity from me, then be my guest."

Torp enjoyed talking to her. There was no filter, but at the same time, there was no condemnation or criticism. It was down to earth, direct, and no beating around the bush.

"You'll be a great journalist, Emma," he said suddenly.

She shook her head. "I'll never accept just looking on. What was the name of that book, *The Naked Journalist*?"

"Now, then, he wasn't completely naked, the guy who wrote it," replied Torp. "But yes, the naked journalist who observes, reveals, and describes. Him—her—I believe in them."

"I think the naked journalist is showing its face a little at the moment. Don't you think so?" She was teasing.

"It's up to you, Emma. You're the one who's going to be taking over. I'm just trying to hold the fort as best I can until then."

Emma evidently regretted her sarcasm and the small hole in their bubble of intimacy on the bench. She ate the last of her ice cream cone and spat the crumbs out as she continued talking.

"Sorry, Torp. I didn't mean it like that."

They sat there, silent again, staring out at the water.

"What about your wife and that allotment house?"

Didn't she understand anything at all about privacy? Emma, who didn't reveal anything about her own life and background. He didn't even know what part of the country she came from, whether she had a partner, and if she did, whether it was a boy or a girl. He knew nothing about her. And then she was asking him—a man thirty years older— about the most private and painful thing she could think of.

"That's a little private, don't you think?"

"If you're looking for a definition, we're probably already well past that with that recording," was Emma's dry response. This time too, without judgement, just a quiet statement of fact.

"I still don't understand it. Don't misunderstand me. I might well have wanted to kiss her. She probably wanted to kiss me, too." He looked at Emma. "But I didn't experience it like that at all. And I can't get hold of Karen. That's the worst bit."

Once again, they let the silence sit between them and allowed the background noise from the gentle waves to take over. This time a little awkwardly. There were limits, after all, to how much they cared to reveal to each other. Although it was liberatingly harmless, they were both unfamiliar with such conversations.

"I wonder if Benedikte and husband have come back from Gilleleje."

Torp broke the silence in an attempt to ease an atmosphere that had suddenly become more serious and personal than intended. Emma gratefully seized the opportunity and got up immediately.

"Jehovah's Witnesses don't give up so easily when someone is to be saved from Judgement Day."

* * *

At first glance, it didn't look as if anyone had returned to the cottage. The curtains were still drawn and there was no car parked in the driveway. But a blue Golf was parked a hundred metres further up the hill which hadn't been there before. It could be someone else, but why park right there? It was Emma who noticed that the thermos had been removed from the terrace.

Torp knocked again, first gingerly, then more clearly and more insistently.

"Hello!" came a loud shout suddenly from Emma, who was standing on the stairs just behind Torp. She shuffled forward, insisting that there was room for them to stand next to each other in front of the door. "We know you're in there. We just want to talk."

Torp looked at her reproachfully. "Emma, damn it," he whispered.

"Benedikte Koch. It's Ulrik Torp out here. We want to talk to you," she continued undaunted, hammering her palm on the door several times with great effect.

The door opened, just as Emma was about to strike her palm against it again. The blow in mid-air sent her off balance and she staggered inwards slightly over the man standing in the doorway.

"What do you want? There is no Benedikte here," he said in a futile attempt to sound brusque. His wavering look revealed that he was scared.

"Hans Koch?"

Torp looked him in the eye. They were almost the same age and had the same sloppy look about them, although Torp was aware that the sloppiness of architects was more elegant than that of journalists. Hans Koch fitted the mould with his bare feet, worn designer jeans, and everyday blazer over a chalk white T-shirt, perfect for both the Kartoffelrækker and Rågeleje, had it not been for the hunted expression that spread from his eyes to his whole body.

"Who's asking?"

"Ulrik Torp. We just told you," replied Emma. She had regained her balance and insisted on standing on the step next to her colleague, even though strictly speaking there wasn't enough room.

"I don't know anything about it," he said, making as if to close the door again. "I must ask you to leave."

Torp tried amiably to put his hand on the door; he didn't put any effort into it but signalled thereby that they should continue the conversation that hadn't really started yet.

"We aren't from the *Express*. It's very, very important that I get to talk to your wife, and I actually think she herself would like to talk."

The move was misunderstood by Hans Koch, who gave an extra jerk on the door.

"You simply have to leave now, otherwise I'll call the police."

The door was slammed shut.

Torp knocked again. This time, he didn't wait for it to be opened, but used it as an introduction to give a message.

"We're going to sit down on the road, right by the driveway. Then Benedikte can come out to us when she's ready. Maybe you just need to talk a little first. I understand that."

He didn't wait for an answer but took Emma by the arm and pulled her down the stairs and out onto the gravel road next to the cottage.

"Now we sit here until she comes out. In the meantime, you can tell me about how you want to be a naked journalist when I'm not here anymore."

Even though the sun was still shining—albeit from a lower angle— the cold from the ground seeped up into them. After an hour and a half, Emma was ready to give up.

"She's not coming; maybe she's not even in there."

Finally, they heard the door open and a slender, short-haired woman in her early fifties came down towards them. She didn't have to introduce herself. Torp recognised her immediately from the photo on the university's website.

"I'm Benedikte Koch. Would you like to come inside?"

CHAPTER 22

Benedikte Koch was sitting with a small handful of papers in her lap, while her husband, with affected grumpiness, set about placing cups and coffee on the small table in the living room of the summer cottage. Even though the sun was beating down on the terrace and the heat was penetrating through the large curtain, there was no sign that they were going to sit outside. On the contrary.

"I guess there's nothing odd in wanting a little peace," she said when she noticed Torp looking at the curtains that had been drawn throughout the house. He just nodded.

"These papers," she explained, holding them up without any indication of wanting to hand them over to Torp and certainly not to the young lady accompanying him, "these papers clearly show that there has been massive fraud with researcher accounts at the university. You won't find my name in a single place. I have had nothing—absolutely nothing—to do with it."

She made her presentation calmly and without a sign of agitation, as if she was reading out loud from a baking recipe, thought Torp.

"That's not why we're here," interjected Emma.

Benedikte Koch ignored her and kept her eyes on Torp.

"It's important to me that that is clear," she continued, handing the papers over to Torp.

"Emma is right in a way. This isn't at all why we are here," said Torp, in an attempt to involve Emma, while still accepting the papers. He quickly flipped through them—transcripts, lots of numbers, bank statements for researcher accounts, emails to banks about changing accounts and transfers. He didn't doubt for a moment that Benedikte Koch was right—she had nothing to do with it.

"Why didn't you give these papers to the *Express* well before now?"

"You're asking me that! As a journalist for more than thirty years, you must know how it works."

Torp knew very well. The *Express* had no desire to exonerate innocent people; it didn't happen like that, but one usually ate from the hand that fed. The *Express*'s source had arranged it deftly and convincingly. And once the angle had been firmly put in place, it could be impossible to change it. Absence of evidence was technically not the same as absence of guilt. Yes, thought Torp, he knew very well how difficult it could be when the roles of heroes and villains had been assigned by the media. He knew it better than most of his journalist colleagues—through his own pain.

"I don't have direct access to any newspaper," continued Torp. "I'm not in a position to clear your name."

"What did I tell you?" said her husband, who was standing in the background.

"My husband thinks I shouldn't have invited you in."

"This isn't getting us anywhere," continued Hans, only to her.

"You called Ulrik and hung up immediately. Why did you do that?" said Emma, forcing herself into the conversation.

Benedikte hesitated. "Some people thought it would be a good idea to talk to you. I was in doubt."

She went quiet for a while.

"And to be honest, I still am."

"It was Otto Brathenberg and Erling Jensen who wanted you to talk to me, wasn't it?"

"Yes," she replied, without a hint of wanting to continue.

No one had touched the coffee.

"Do you think they died naturally?" Emma was insisting on the attention she wasn't getting.

"That's it. It would be better if you left now. Right now," said Hans, taking a step forward and clapping his hands, as if it was a command. His wife waved her hand defensively.

"It's no use, Hans."

"We think something happened when you sat on the Parliamentary Control Committee as its secretary in the early '90s."

Torp leaned forward in the uncomfortable chair. There was total silence in the small cottage. A woodpecker was hacking for food under the bark of a tree out in the garden. That—along with the hiss from the thermos that wasn't closed properly—was the only thing that broke the silence. Now the woodpecker paused. There was only the thermos left.

"And we can keep a secret," he continued.

Benedikte Koch allowed herself a slightly scornful smile.

"Then you are bad journalists," she exclaimed and took another long pause, which everyone in the living room knew only she could break.

"She has to leave."

Benedikte nodded towards Emma.

"You can't be serious!" spluttered Emma.

"She has to leave," repeated Benedikte, keeping her eyes fixed on Torp. "It isn't up for discussion."

"Emma—go and take a walk on the beach."

He tried to make it sound amicable, but it was completely impossible. Emma stared at him.

"You don't mean that."

"Now, Emma."

This time it didn't sound amicable. Nor should it. Emma got up without a word, went out into the hallway, and quietly closed the door behind her.

"Okay, I'm ready."

"I can't say very much."

"You have to tell me everything," continued Torp with a sudden and quite unexpected authority in his voice.

Benedikte shook her head. "You have no idea what you're asking for, Torp. This isn't a solemn journalist's toast speech about source protection. We're talking about state secrets and a harsh penal code."

"It's thirty years ago," replied Torp.

"It makes no difference. States only have secrets because some people can keep their mouths shut." She pointed behind her. "Even my husband doesn't know anything. Nothing."

Torp nodded. Everyone has someone they confide in. Someone to whom they entrust deep secrets. Someone who receives the story with a whispered "you mustn't tell anyone." But when everyone has someone, there are no secrets left.

"This stops here," said Hans. "You must leave now."

"No, Hans," said his wife, shaking her head. "No, Hans. I think perhaps it would be a good idea if you went for a walk too, so I can talk to Ulrik alone. It's about time. Go for a long walk in the lovely weather."

Hans Koch stopped in the middle of a movement, his arms falling limply down by his sides. He turned slowly and left without a word.

"He'll be all right again. But it will probably take a while." She smiled slightly apologetically. "Don't take it as an expression of me having decided to tell you everything. I'm still working on that," she continued.

They didn't say much to each other in the car on the way back to Copenhagen. Torp's brain was working on the things Benedikte Koch had told him, and Emma was upset. Torp had expected her to be angry, but she wasn't. It was much worse—she was simply upset.

"You let me down, Ulrik. You let me down," she contented herself with saying when he came up to the car.

It wasn't locked, so she had just sat in it after being thrown out of the cottage. Up to a point, Torp agreed that he had let her down, but what else could he have done, he half-heartedly tried to argue while praying that she wouldn't start crying. He would rather she was angry. Fortunately, she didn't have to help with the car—the hill was so steep that it was just a matter of releasing the handbrake and letting gravity do its work.

Without it being agreed between them, he turned off towards the allotment house in Brønshøj. She registered it and didn't protest. It was evening, the sun would set in a little over an hour, and the spring weather was already getting cold. There was no more canned tuna or cod roe in the house, so Torp stopped at a petrol station, left the engine running, and with Emma remaining in the car, he bought the essentials, namely coffee, bread for toast, cheese, jam, a litre of milk, and six chocolate-covered marshmallow treats.

"It's state secrets we're talking about. Benedikte can go to prison for telling anyone what happened in the Parliamentary Control Committee. Even though it's almost thirty years ago." He felt he owed her a more detailed explanation before they arrived.

"It's lovely how you're on first-name terms with each other."

"Give it a break, Emma. That sort of behaviour is unprofessional."

"I'm sorry," she said, so quietly that it pricked Ulrik's conscience.

Behind the hard exterior, the ring in the nose, the very short hair, and the quick remarks, Torp hadn't seen until now that she was fragile. And he had let her down. He suddenly felt sorry for her and made a quick decision.

"Okay, we first have to have something to eat. If you promise you can keep a secret, I'll tell you."

Benedikte Koch had set the conditions from the start.

"You may not take notes. You may not record with your mobile phone, and you must never publish what I'm going to tell you."

"Isn't that going a bit far?"

Torp withdrew his hand from his inside pocket, from which he was just about to fish out his mobile to record the conversation.

"Those are my conditions. Otherwise, you can follow that one you came in with and tell my husband he can come in again."

"It's my impression that Brathenberg or Erling Jensen wanted to tell me something."

"And that's the only reason we two are talking together right now."

"But since they could—or wanted to—then you can, too, surely?"

Benedikte sighed.

"They're politicians. I was a civil servant. The difference is vast. You should know that better than most, Torp."

He nodded reluctantly.

"I can go to prison for this. For a pretty long time, even. So, no notes or recordings. You haven't got it from me, and you can't publish it."

"Then I can't use it for anything."

"Those are my conditions." She was completely calm now, having made her decision and fenced off the playing field. From here on out, it was easy.

"Okay. Tell me," said Torp in agreement.

"Do you know what the 'Gold from Moscow' conceals?"

Torp nodded immediately. It was the term for the money the Communist Party of the Soviet Union had passed on to Moscow-loyal Communist parties in the West. Until the very last, the Danish Communist Party had been one of the most Soviet-loyal parties that existed, and in relation to the size of Denmark and the party, it had received a disproportionate amount of money over the years.

"Much was written about it in the years following the collapse of the Soviet Union and the partial opening of the archives," continued Benedikte. "The intelligence services, and later the public, too, quite quickly gained an insight into some of the money traffic that went between Moscow and Copenhagen."

This was almost home ground for Torp. He remembered it clearly, had written lots of articles about it, and also done a series of critical interviews with the last chairman of the Danish Communist Party, who later got his bearings on the changing times and ended up a successful minister.

"There was division in the party in the last years between the traditional Communists and a reform wing that supported Gorbachev. The last chairman was a supporter of reforms," recalled Torp.

"At least he became one when the reform wing got power," was Benedikte's dry response.

"How is the Gold from Moscow connected with the Parliamentary Control Committee?" asked Torp, beginning to get a bit impatient.

"The Soviet Union supported the Danish Communist Party in two ways. One way was by systematically overpaying for services to companies controlled by the DCP. As you know, the party had, among other things, its own newspaper and its own printing house, and it controlled a travel agency. It was easy enough."

"And the other way was direct cash," added Torp. "I remember how the last chairman of the party sweated a great deal over those details."

"Precisely. The money—in the final years it was thirty hundred fifty thousand American dollars a year, but in several portions—typically came by diplomatic post from Moscow to the Soviet embassy in Østerbro, and then someone picked up the cash, sometimes dollars, sometimes D-marks, sometimes Danish kroner."

"The chairman denied that he had done it himself, I remember. There was a huge hoo-ha—he was completely out on the ropes at one point."

"He was indeed. But maybe that was the truth," continued Benedikte Koch. "Maybe it wasn't him personally who picked up the money, even though it was his name on the list."

"The list?"

"The Smirnov list. In 1991, the Danish intelligence service obtained access to the so-called Smirnov list, named after the head of the Central Committee's international department, Anatoly Smirnov."

Once again Benedikte Koch spoke as if she had memorised a shopping list for the Coop—no dramatic emphasis, the same flat tone of voice, and completely neutral.

"Smirnov had simply transcribed the journal in their archives. Each time a sum of cash was handed over to a Moscow-loyal party in the West, it was journalised in the Central Committee with the date, amount, and to whom the money was directed. Always a name."

"And that also applied to Denmark?"

"Yes, of course. All this has been out before—it's not a state secret," said Benedikte with a smile. "The special thing about Denmark is that in the very meticulous journals, there are two dates that are especially interesting."

She got up, went over to a desk that stood as a room divider between the kitchen and the living room, and picked up a book.

"This is the book, *The Gold from Moscow*, which was published several years ago—we are still nowhere near a secret. At least not since the early 1990s."

She flipped to page 237 and handed the book to him. Here were the figures from the Smirnov archive, appropriations for 1988, 1989, and 1990 with dates, amounts, and names.

"Can you see that something is missing?" asked Benedikte.

Torp went through the list. That wasn't difficult. "On the fifteenth of February 1988, one hundred thousand dollars was paid out, and on the third of April 1990, one hundred fifty thousand dollars was paid out. But there is no name next to the amounts. By all the other amounts, there is the name of the party chairman."

Benedikte nodded. "Don't you think that's strange?"

"Two hundred fifty thousand dollars. Wow."

"Yes, wow—over one and a half million Danish kroner thirty years ago. That's equivalent to about three million kroner today."

"Transferred at a time when the party is entering a power struggle, and world Communism is dying," Torp exclaimed.

"Precisely. And now comes what you mustn't know," she said with a smile. "In the spring of 1992, there was a meeting of the Parliamentary Control Committee. Minister of Justice Otto Brathenberg informed us that he had been told on the quiet who received the money in February 1988 and in April 1990. He could even tell us that all the cash had been paid out in Danish kroner, not in dollars."

"Really?"

"It was a young woman who wasn't even—at least as far as was known—a member of the party."

"And?"

"Her name was Kirsten Rolighed."

"That Rolighed?"

"There probably aren't many of them. Yes, that Kirsten Rolighed, who may become the country's Prime Minister in a few days, if a majority in the party actually succeeds in overthrowing Palle Enevoldsen, which there are indications for at the moment."

Torp just had to let his mind catch up.

"Are you alleging that she is a kind of Manchurian Candidate, brain-washed and deployed by a foreign power?"

"Not at all. At least, there was nothing to suggest that at the time," said Benedikte in a hurry to establish that fact.

"But how could she get so much money? You couldn't just walk into the Soviet embassy off the street and pick up what is the equivalent of three million kroner in today's money, surely?"

"The Danish Communist Party's long-standing and powerful international secretary was a hardliner and in opposition to the new chairman. He had strong contacts in Moscow who had set themselves against Gorbachev, and in addition, he had a very young mistress."

"Kirsten Rolighed!"

"Precisely. Brathenberg told the Control Committee that there was so much disintegration and so many power struggles in both Moscow and Copenhagen that more and more people were running their own game. The international secretary wanted to weaken the new leader, and at the embassy and in Moscow, there were lots of people who opposed Gorbachev, control was poor, and hey presto—then he announces that a young woman is coming to pick up the money and that no names should be on the papers."

"So neither his nor her name is anywhere to be found at all? That's hard to believe," objected Torp.

"Maybe it's written on a piece of paper somewhere on the one hundred seventy-second shelf in the president's archive in Moscow. We won't get to see that in our lifetime."

"What about the money?"

"The most important thing was that it shouldn't go to the reform wing. And the international secretary was clearly so horny and so much in the pocket of his young mistress that she—or they—to begin with just kept the money. And that's how it stayed. According to the Police Intelligence Service, the international secretary died in Kirsten Rolighed's bed in the summer of 1990, apparently very aroused and on his back."

Benedikte let out a brief giggle and thereby revealed a whole new side of her personality to Torp.

"It wasn't only monotonous enumerations."

"So she just kept the money?"

"That was what they thought in the spring of 1992."

"They?"

"Yes," continued Benedikte, "that's the funny thing—or . . . well, I guess it's not that funny," she corrected herself. "The Police Intelligence Service wasn't on to that story in the slightest. In fact, they couldn't confirm it, either. It all allegedly came from a single source outside of it all."

"Why did nothing else happen?"

"What should have happened?"

"Black money, a foreign power, spies, prosecution," said Torp, listing them in a way that was meant to signal that he could have gone on.

Benedikte shrugged. "I finished as secretary of the Control Committee six months later, and I don't know if anything came of it, but what could even happen? The intelligence services couldn't confirm it. The international secretary was dead, and the chairman of the Communist Party wasn't exactly going to report that some people had snatched the money he should have had from Moscow."

"And Kirsten Rolighed?"

"There are no indications that she was, either then or later, a Communist. I'm guessing that they just said, oh, so what . . . But then . . ."

"But then, what?"

"Well, then she suddenly has the opportunity to become the country's Prime Minister. You're the one who used to make political analyses and could explain what people like Otto Brathenberg and Erling Jensen did, thought, wanted, and feared. But suddenly they started calling me."

"Could you remember it from back then?"

Benedikte shook her head.

"When I was given the details, I could easily recall it. It was Erling Jensen who remembered the story. I think he had broken the rules and written down a lot from his time in the Control Committee."

So he had been right. The notes must have been the ones that had been in the missing bag from the Coop, thought Torp.

"What about Brathenberg?"

Benedikte thought about it for a long time.

"Otto Brathenberg got it confirmed somewhere—he wouldn't say where."

"Holy shit," exclaimed Emma. She had said this several times during Ulrik's retelling of the information to the Parliamentary Control Committee at a meeting in the spring of 1992, the year she herself was born. They were sitting in the small living room of the allotment house; it was close to midnight, and the wood-burning stove was giving off so much heat that they had had to open a window.

"Brathenberg had of course been following the fuss around Friends of Denmark, the Great Replacement, nationalism, and that whole movement. What if the national conservatives in Moscow have their hand up Denmark's next Prime Minister?"

"And we can't use all of that for anything, because you've promised a university lecturer not to reveal anything that was said at a meeting at Christiansborg thirty years ago?"

"Yes."

"You told me," said Emma triumphantly, "so you've already broken your promise."

Ulrik had thought a lot about that during the evening.

"Well, yes and no. She said twice that I wasn't allowed to make it public. Telling you isn't making it public."

"That argument won't bloody hold in the City Court."

"Then I'll have to rely on the High Court."

Emma laughed. He was happy she was no longer upset and feeling let down, and surprised that she was apparently so fragile. He had given her the bed in the microscopic little bedroom. He insisted on taking the slender sofa in the living room. It was no problem, he lied. And there was toast, jam, milk, and two chocolate-covered marshmallow treats for breakfast, he argued when they agreed that it would be easiest for her to spend the night in the allotment house. There was something she had said in Rågeleje that had taken him aback. He couldn't remember what it was, but it was something that might go some way to explaining her.

"Be honest—what can we use all this for?"

Emma looked at Torp as she was about to close the door to the bedroom.

"We can only use it if we can get Kirsten Rolighed to tell it herself."

"Then that's what we must do," she announced and said good night.

Yes, thought Torp, then that was what they must do. He hadn't heard from Karen since she had asked him to contact Sofie and Jesper that morning. She still wasn't answering either calls or text messages.

He had to get hold of her tomorrow.

CHAPTER 23

Ulrik Torp almost routinely passed on the day's obituaries to Crabby, who gratefully accepted his lifebuoy. Five medium and two small. It was getting better and better for the former editor on Funen, who was rather morbidly pleased that the influenza season had apparently been extended well into the spring—all the dead today were old people. Maybe it was also that his concept was making breakthroughs with a number of undertakers. Maybe a little of both. The editor had begun communicating directly with Crabby—this was probably a sign that Torp would soon lose the initial birthright to the dead unless he pulled himself together.

It wasn't going to happen today.

Axel Boas came in from the bay window with both the *Daily News* and the *Express* in his hand. The political rumpus had given an unaccustomed comeback to printed newspapers in the office. Both were full of political obituaries of Prime Minister Palle Enevoldsen. Phone rounds to the Liberals' eighty-member national executive were indicating that the next day's meeting was a formality.

Two out of three national executive members supported Kirsten Rolighed—most of them even willing to be quoted.

"We need fresh energy. Palle has had his time. I think Kirsten seems like a girl with strong principles. If we are going to win the next election, something

has to happen. Have you read the voices from the deep?" Axel was waving both newspapers in the air.

"Maybe Enevoldsen actually has had his time," remarked Torp, without great conviction in his voice. It was more meant as an underlining of the prevailing argument for change.

"I don't think he loves Denmark. I've heard Kirsten Rolighed say she does. That's the analysis from a pharmacist in Djursland who is going to the national executive meeting tomorrow." Axel shook his head.

"There is nothing wrong with loving one's country," tried Torp again.

"There is something wrong with having to declare it constantly," continued his office colleague. "Like parents who in every other sentence tell their children that they love them. Or the man who constantly posts pictures of his partner on Facebook and tells the world how beautiful she is and how much he loves her."

"Is there anything wrong with that?"

"You can bet your life there is," Axel assured him, suddenly becoming more serious. "My wife is a psychologist. When she hears parents talking that way or sees that kind of thing on Facebook, her alarm bells start ringing."

"Why?" Torp was genuinely curious.

"Because it's a sign that something's wrong. It means you have to have it confirmed because you're insecure, jealous, and afraid of losing someone. So the relationship is dysfunctional."

"Says your psychologist wife."

"Says my psychologist wife, whom I love very much!" Axel laughed.

"Any news about Bertel?"

Axel shook his head. He had an agreement with Bertel's wife that she would call if anything happened. They agreed to send a joint bouquet to his ward at the Rigshospitalet.

Torp took the newspapers and flipped through them. An article in the *Daily News* seemed to be confirming the obituary pusher's thesis that the influenza virus was unusually resilient this year. Many people were ill, some hospitalised, some with quite serious complications that sounded like Bertel's. "We're a little unsure about how long it will last," was the message from a chief physician at the Rigshospitalet. Torp moved on after reading half the article. Maybe he should still just give it a go with the obituaries as long as it lasted. His gaze fell on yet another story in the *Express*'s serial about fraud with private research funds at the University of Copenhagen. Once again, it was with a big picture of a younger Benedikte Koch—the newspaper had found an archive photo, where she was tanned, with long blonde hair, and looked like a happy-go-lucky girl who could easily siphon off a few million which didn't belong to her. *Fraud suspect gone underground*, said the headline. *New documents incriminate university lecturer*, promised the article in its introduction.

Torp looked over at Crabby, who was already writing today's first obituary about a former farmer, *Verner Haakonson, eighty-four, from Bogense.*

"I know you can't reveal your source for the story that's also running in the *Express*."

Crabby looked up and nodded.

"But can you say if it was just one source or several?"

Crabby hesitated.

"And can you say if it was one or more sources that came to you, or if it was you that went to them?"

"Why do you want to know?"

"I'm mostly thinking of the information about Benedikte Koch."

"Why do you want to know?" repeated Crabby. He had gone into a defensive position.

"I can't really say. But it's important. Otherwise, I wouldn't ask."

"Do you really expect me to tell you?"

"Forget it," said Torp hurriedly. "Forget it. Of course you should only tell me if you want to."

Crabby demonstratively turned away from Torp and returned to Verner Haakonson's long life on the farm where he was born in Bogense and the 1,000 kroner that were waiting on the other side.

When Torp had woken up that morning in the allotment house, he had, first of all, tried to get in touch with Karen. Calls were still going directly to the answering machine, text messages weren't being answered, and the messages on Messenger weren't being read—or she had removed the feature that showed it. Torp knew it was possible, without quite knowing how to do it. He had sat alone in the small living room with dry toast, jam, and tea, feeling the cold. It hadn't made any sense to fire up the stove when he had to leave anyway. Moreover, Emma had gone—she must have crept out during the night and wasn't in the office either when, after a long morning spent on public transport, he had finally made it from the allotment into the city.

Then came a text message. Finally, Karen had contacted him. He reached out for his mobile—if they could only meet up; if he could just explain.

Anton here. Can you meet at Café Europa in an hour?

"She has lived in Estonia, but now lives in Russia. She's Russian."

Anton had ordered two cappuccinos and was ready when Torp entered Café Europa exactly one hour later. He sipped the milky Italian coffee, noting that it was already lukewarm, almost cold. Anton put the surveillance picture Torp had sent him of the dark-haired woman from the hospice in Frederiksberg on the table. Beside it, he placed a new picture. It had been taken at passport control at Copenhagen Airport a few hours later and was of the same woman. Even her clothes—a short-sleeved blouse, a thin scarf, and a pair of tight jeans—were the same.

"You were right," said Anton without complaint; that kind of setback wasn't taken personally. "The last woman to attend to Otto Brathenberg and visit Erling Jensen at the hospice just before he died is a forty-two-year-old Russian woman with links to the Russian intelligence service."

"What else do you know?"

Torp could feel his pulse rising.

"I can't reveal everything. It's still being investigated, but it's not only the Danish intelligence service that is involved now."

"Come on, now."

"She entered the country on an urgently issued Schengen visa, probably after a short stay in Paris."

"And what does that mean?"

Anton looked around. There was no one sitting at the nearest tables. Even so, he stuck his face all the way over towards Torp's and lowered his voice to a few decibels over a whisper.

"To get a Schengen visa, she would have needed a number of official documents that you don't just get like that as a Russian."

With an outstretched arm and eye contact with a waiter, Anton ordered two more cappuccinos.

"Among other things, you must have a Russian domestic passport, evidence of a work-related connection, a bank certificate showing your financial situation, and travel insurance, but that isn't the most remarkable thing about her."

"No?"

"No," continued Anton. "Her passport isn't biometric—that is, with fingerprints." He said the last bit so loudly that he startled himself and lowered his voice again. "That is something that has otherwise become standard, even in Russia. The passport was issued just a month ago and was apparently made in a department of the Russian Interior Ministry which we know has issued passports to agents of the GRU, the military intelligence service in Russia."

Torp tried to whistle appreciatively. It only half succeeded, but that was enough for Anton. He smiled proudly, as if he had uncovered it all on his own.

"How do you think they were murdered?"

"We'll probably never find that out," said Anton with a shrug. "Brathenberg perhaps with the neurotoxin Novichok. It's been specially developed by the Russians and used on previous occasions—a few milligrams of it and you die."

"And Erling Jensen?"

This time Anton spread his arms wide; was that so important?

"He was so weak that thirty seconds with a pillow over his head would have been enough."

"Can I write about this?"

Anton shook his head.

"If I now called Police Headquarters and asked if the deaths of Otto Brathenberg and Erling Jensen were being investigated, what would the answer be?"

Anton hushed Torp.

"*You* can't do it under any circumstances—promise me that, Torp. Quite a few people at Headquarters know that the two of us talk together. I'll get my arse kicked, badly, if you call."

"What if someone else were to do it? From a newspaper that has some credibility?"

Torp had sensed an opening.

Anton thought about it for a long time. Two fresh cappuccinos at fifty-eight kroner each, excluding tip, were placed on their small café table. He waited until the waiter had gone with the two used cups.

"If a journalist from a newspaper that has some credibility calls and asks exactly the way you put it—that is, nothing about Russia and military intelligence—then Headquarters will confirm that their deaths are being investigated."

Torp leaned back very pleased.

"That's enough. Plenty for the first story."

"Be my guest. Roger, more?"

Torp sipped his milky coffee. Roger. No more, but it was good enough. He had had an idea.

The *Daily News* had just completed yet another round of cutbacks. Not because the newspaper was losing money; it was actually going fairly well, but the CEO thought that a round of cutbacks that wasn't justified by an acute need for survival was an expression of "due care and diligence." Torp looked up at the façade and the name of the newspaper in the fonts he knew he would never be reconciled with. Was it an indication of him stagnating? Maybe.

Torp recognised the receptionist behind the armoured glass doors and the terror sluice. Some things were as they used to be. He ventured in through the first glass door, which closed behind him before a buzz opened the next. The receptionist recognised him immediately.

"Torp! Are you sure I'm allowed to let you in?" she said, trying a little uncertainly to laugh, but she was clearly happy to see him.

"Charlotte!"

He surprised himself at how happy he was to see her. She reminded him of the old days—newsprint, profits, front-page articles, colleagues, and a belief in the future.

"Don't worry, I haven't been sent on work activation this time."

She smiled—still a little uncertainly.

"If Simon the intern is in the building, could you please just ask him to come down?"

Charlotte pressed a few keys and talked to Simon on her headset. "Yes, he's down here. Right now."

"He sounded a little surprised, but he's coming right away."

"I'll go out on the street again. Tell Simon he'll find me outside."

"Don't go getting him mixed up in anything. Simon's a good boy," remarked Charlotte. She suddenly looked a little sceptical.

"I promise," Torp assured her and slid out through the sluice again, at the same time as Simon came down to reception.

They didn't really know how to greet each other. It turned into a floppy handshake, an unsuccessful slap on Simon's shoulder, and uncertain eye contact from both of them. As the older of the two, Torp knew it was up to him to break the ice. Simon knew that, too.

"You write a lot of good stories, Simon. Nice work," said Torp hesitantly.

"Thanks."

There was a pause which was even more awkward than the situation.

"Emma has got a desk in my freelance office."

Simon nodded. He was well aware of that.

New pause.

"She still has that ring in her nose."

Torp didn't know why he had said that. He just thought he should say something or other. Simon nodded. He knew that, too.

Was that it? That was it, supposed Torp. If it was enough for Simon, then it was also enough for him.

"I have a good story for you that I can't write myself."

Simon looked up, relieved that they were apparently done with the small talk that neither of them liked or needed right now.

"It's important that it appear in the newspaper tomorrow."

Simon was about to protest. He couldn't promise that, and Torp of all people must know that.

"You must promise to get started on it right away. Then it will be in the newspaper for sure," Torp hurried to add. Simon promised.

Super interview with Kirsten Rolighed, wrote the editor of *Around Borgen.* *Remember the video clips for social media with both Frost and Rolighed by tomorrow.* Argh, Torp had forgotten that.

Axel came out of the bay window. He had just talked to Bertel's wife. He was still in intensive care, but his condition was stable, as the saying goes. No one really knew what was wrong with him. He appreciated both the flowers and the card. They could all send sixty-five kroner to Axel via MobilePay.

Torp tried to look involved. Crabby just nodded. He was still working on today's obituaries. Three more had just arrived, which Torp had passed on to him. Crabby would certainly be able to handle that. No problem.

Torp had promised to do those video clips in a moment of weakness. The truth was that he had no experience of cutting and editing recordings like that. He didn't even have any editing software on his computer. That kind of thing cost money. He made a quick decision, copied the interviews onto a USB stick, put it on Emma's empty desk, and wrote an email to her asking if she could do it—in return he would pay her office rent for next month. He knew it would take him a whole day to do what she could handle in a few hours.

His mobile rang. It was Lindskov. No doubt there were problems with his wife's sclerosis again.

"Torp, could you do with six bottles of good red wine?"

"I'm a little busy today," he heard himself say.

"I'm really, really under pressure, Torp. The leader for tomorrow. Now we're cutting Enevoldsen free."

"Jaws comes up to the surface?"

"Exactly," laughed Lindskov.

"It's probably also a little easier now that everyone's saying he's going to lose in the national executive committee tomorrow."

"Are you blaming the daily press for noticing where power is heading?"

"That wouldn't be like me at all," teased Torp.

"It's just words. Three thousand characters, as fast as you can, at the very, very latest nine p.m. this evening. The very latest, Torp. You get twelve bottles. I'm very grateful."

For a brief moment, Torp felt sorry for Palle Enevoldsen. Tomorrow, almost all the leaders and reports would conclude that the man was finished both as party leader and as Prime Minister. It was rarely a pretty sight when the media marched in step. Maybe his time had run out, but one could well have wished him a slightly more pleasant exit after so many years of political work. Why on earth were politicians not better at slipping quietly away by themselves at the right time? Torp knew a little of the answer—vanity, the belief in one's own indispensability, and then the happenstances that could ruin even the best attempt at a respectable farewell. This would be both ugly and nationalistic. Tomorrow's common thread would be the story of a Prime Minister who had passed on a referendum and basically didn't love his country. The first was right enough. And Torp was going to help swing the sword for twelve bottles of red wine, twice the normal rate.

He noticed that Crabby was in the middle of a lengthy phone conversation. He was defending himself; he didn't think he could have done any more. Then he was scolding someone, accusing him of feeding the *Express* with the same documents, and making it impossible for him. Then he apologised and admitted that he probably hadn't been quick enough, but that things had needed to be confirmed first. Then Crabby started whimpering and got red eyes again. Why had it had to be so fast? What had been the hurry? He still didn't understand.

That was how the conversation swung aimlessly back and forth for a quarter of an hour. Sometimes Crabby was on the attack, but for the most part, he was the little one. It dawned on Torp that he had to be talking to the source of his story, and that it was also the *Express*'s source. It was the source of the false story about Benedikte Koch. Torp pretended to be busy with his computer.

"Yes, but how was I supposed to know you couldn't wait a few days? That story wasn't going to go away." Long answer. "That wasn't what you said at the time." Even longer answer. "I can't write a story until I'm sure." Short answer. "I can't see that what the *Express* is saying is true. I have no idea, and neither do you." His eyes were watery. Suddenly he stopped and just looked at his mobile. The source had hung up. Crabby angrily put the phone down and stormed out to the toilet.

"Sorry," he mumbled as he shuffled hurriedly past Torp.

Torp was suddenly alone in the living room office. Bertel was ill, Emma wasn't sitting in the corridor, and Axel was all the way out in the bay window. He glanced down the hallway where Crabby had stormed out. Then he looked at Crabby's mobile lying on his desk less than three metres away from him. How long had he set his mobile to be open before it shut down and required a code to be reopened? Ten seconds? Thirty? A minute? Torp didn't even know how long it took on his own mobile. Maybe half a minute—it was in any case irritatingly short. He turned his head towards the hallway. He could hear Crabby was in the toilet. The water in the sink was running. Axel was sitting in the bay window. Bertel was ill. Emma was away. How long had it been? Twenty seconds, maybe. If it was set to thirty seconds, it was actually too late. If it was a minute, he could easily reach it, provided Crabby stayed in the toilet. The water was still running. This contradicted everything he believed in, everything he had learned. If he was going to do it, it had to be now. In half a minute, it would be too late. Maybe it would be too late in fifteen seconds. It was now, right now, he had the opportunity.

Torp jerked to his feet; in two steps, he was at Crabby's desk, left hand on the mobile. It was still open—index finger on the phone icon, index finger on "Recent." There—at the top—was the number of the person Crabby had just spoken to. The source for the *Express*'s story about Benedikte Koch's non-fraud at the University of Copenhagen. Eight numbers he had to memorise. Quickly, say them out loud, then you remember them better. Now the water was no longer running in the sink in the toilet. Finger on the button so that the mobile went back to the starting point. Two steps away, write the number down. Were the last two digits eight and nine? Sure they were.

"Sorry," said Crabby again.

"You don't have to apologise for anything," replied Torp.

It was eighty-nine. He was almost certain.

Torp worked on his conscience while Crabby quietly returned to his obituaries. It was just a phone number. And if he knew the name of the source but didn't use it for anything—just knew it—then there was nothing wrong with that, surely? Who was he trying to kid? Of course it was wrong. It was something you could be fired for if you did it to a colleague at a newspaper. Could you be fired from a freelance office? Of course you could. Axel Boas would set the tone—*I'm sorry, I hadn't expected that*—and then it would be over. Torp would have reacted in the same way.

He had to know who the number belonged to. Crabby was recovering and was immersed in the obituaries. Maybe they could save his next mortgage payment—maybe also the one after that. The obituaries were really rolling now. They were mostly old people, and they were easy to do obituaries of; there weren't so many considerations to take into account, and the relatives were happy to talk.

Torp took out his mobile phone, went to MobilePay, typed "1" beside "kroner," put his index finger on "Select Recipient," hesitated, and hesitated.

"Fuck it," he mumbled to himself, keying in the number. Eighty-nine. It ended with eighty-nine. That was certain.

Per Frost.

Crabby's source was Per Frost.

CHAPTER 24

Ulrik Torp let Vivi caress him lightly on the cheek. Her hand was even softer than he remembered. She smiled, not invitingly, not seductively—almost in a motherly way. *You have to take care of yourself, Ulrik. You have to take care of yourself,* she repeated over and over again. Of course he would take care of himself. The waves of the North Sea were washing up against them. Torp was standing closest to the water and he was already wet above the ankles. The next wave would reach his knees and thighs. Was it the water he had to be careful of? She caressed him again. *You have to take care of yourself, Ulrik.* He could hear his mobile ringing. It was Karen, but he couldn't find it. It was as if the ringtone was coming from all directions. The next wave hit the beach, and yes, the salt water washed up over his thighs. Even though Vivi was standing less than an arm's length away from him, she wasn't wet, she was just looking deep into his eyes. Where the hell was that phone? He pushed Vivi's hand away. He had to find the phone and talk to Karen. He reached for it but grasped at nothing. Vivi withdrew a little. Now he was no longer wet. She disappeared. There—on the bedside table—lay the mobile phone.

"Karen?"

Ulrik's voice was more than sleepy. He repeated her name. That was better. He stared up at the wooden ceiling of the allotment house and could feel how the unevenness of the night in the worn spring mattress had settled in his back.

"What the hell have you been up to?"

It was Lindskov shouting. Torp moved the mobile a little out in front of him—it wasn't even 7:00 a.m.

"What the hell have you done, Torp?"

His voice was both furious and desperate. It sounded as if the experienced debate editor at the *Daily News* was on the verge of bursting into tears.

Torp was awake enough to know what was going on, but not yet clear enough in his head to come up with the right explanation. In the evening, he had thought about writing an email to Lindskov explaining it all but had given up after several attempts. He had gone to bed in the certainty that Lindskov would react more or less as he was doing now, and that he would have to come up with an explanation before then.

It had actually been very simple the previous evening. Torp had got going with the leader for the twelve bottles of wine. The end of Enevoldsen. Thursday wasn't only the day of the crucial national executive committee meeting of the Liberals, where he would be confronted with Kirsten Rolighed. Thursday was also the day when the contract between the media and their readers was to be fulfilled. The day when Jaws would finally show up after massive foreplay. The leader in the *Daily News* was just a modest, yet indispensable, part of the choreography. And Torp carried out his part of the predictable narrative with a hard-hitting text about how disappointing it had been to watch Palle Enevoldsen since the election victory last year. How he had become synonymous with power, synonymous with his international colleagues, and synonymous with an internationalisation that had very little to do with Denmark. The fact that he had finally turned 180 degrees and was suddenly a supporter of a National Day after pressure from Friends of Denmark and the inner circle of his own party only helped to cement the impression of a politician who had lost all connection, not only to his people and his nation but also to his own integrity. The secret recording from Marienborg, where he in an unguarded moment had voiced his honest opinion about the people behind Friends of Denmark and his own voters, was probably the final drop, but it was the bucket filled with water prior to this drop that had decided it for the *Daily News: Enevoldsen's days are over. New forces must now step up, and Kirsten Rolighed seems like a solid politician in tune with not just the times but also the future. May it happen today.*

It had been extremely easy for Torp to write the leader. There was nothing easier than jumping into a rushing river and letting yourself be dragged along by the current. In the same hours, editorial writers, commentators, bloggers, political analysts, and editors with exactly the same task sat around the media's editorial offices. Not as a result of an overall command. No, Torp knew that this was even more diabolical and impossible to stop. It was like a lot of small brooks and streams that almost of their own accord and at the same time set themselves in motion to eventually flow into each other. This wasn't red against blue; it didn't divide the media and the voters that way. This was Palle Enevoldsen against the rest. Today against tomorrow. A worn face against a fresh one. Seen that way, the choice was simple and obvious. And Torp excused himself by saying that all he did was jump in.

Enevoldsen must go.

The headline was the first thing he wrote. The leader shouldn't reach a conclusion. It should argue for a conclusion. Torp went through the text, corrected typos, put in a few extra commas, in doubt about a single one, and checked in his ancient green spelling dictionary which lay on his shelf. The others had teased him that he must be one of the last people in the country to have it lying around. Of course, some of the spellings had changed, but the grammatical comma had survived a few battles, so whether the book was fifteen or thirty years old was, in principle, irrelevant.

Just like that.

Three thousand predictable characters. Words followed by words.

He read the leader one last time, created a new email, typed *lindskov@ dailynews.dk*, attached the document, stared blankly in front of him, and saw that it was 8:35 p.m. By 9:00 p.m. at the latest, Lindskov had emphasised—at the very, very latest. He was sitting at home with his multiple sclerosis afflicted wife just waiting for the text from Torp, which he with himself as sender would email to a busy sub-editor at the *Daily News*, who was impatiently waiting to be able to close his page so that he could go home and the newspaper could go to print. Torp didn't need to send it yet. He could wait a bit, rewrite bits, maybe soften up some of the sentences a little bit. Argh. He couldn't care less. Only Lindskov would know that Torp had written it, and he would never be able to tell other people unless he wanted to lose the job he had held onto for so long against all odds. *Has Torp written the leader? Torp! That Torp? He got red wine for it, you say?* No one would ever find out that it was Torp who had put the words together that led to the headline *Enevoldsen must go*. He doubted even that Lindskov's wife knew. Nor did Bertel, Axel, Emma, or Crabby know anything. Torp hadn't even told Karen. It was Torp's and Lindskov's completely private secret, and they both had every reason to keep it so.

So why couldn't it just be of no consequence? Torp looked at the computer clock—it showed 8:43 p.m. Lindskov had to have the leader within seventeen minutes.

"How could you do that, Torp?" Lindskov's voice was no longer choked with tears or fury. Now it sounded almost resigned.

"I don't know," mumbled Torp. "Forgive me, Lindskov."

For a brief second, he had considered lying, saying how, for some reason or other, he had written two different texts and had happened to send the wrong one. It was "for some reason or other" that were the key words in that sentence—what reason should that be?

"I couldn't bring myself to do it," he continued. "And it's just words, as you yourself have said."

"Just words? Are you completely off your trolley, Torp?" whimpered Lindskov. "I have the entire senior editorial office on my back right now, and the chairman of the board is demanding an explanation."

"I didn't think boards of directors interfered in editorial matters, or leaders."

"Do bears shit in the woods? Does the pope masturbate?" Lindskov paused briefly for breath before being filled with equal parts self-pity and anger again.

"Sorry, Lindskov. Sorry. What do you want me to say?"

"We are the only newspaper today that is defending Enevoldsen. Are you aware of that, Torp? The only one." He put the stress on *only* to underline the extent of the disaster.

Torp let his mind take a wander back to the evening at 8:43 p.m. When he—without having a plan at all—created a new document and, under the headline *Enevoldsen must stay*, started on 3,000 new characters. About a Prime Minister who had fought for his country and his government. About a Prime Minister who had insisted on unpopular reforms. About a Prime Minister with two election victories behind him, an international network of contacts, and unique political experience. Why has it become suspicious to have lots of political experience, know all the actors, the entire social machinery, and the buttons that can and should be pressed? Why has politics gradually become the only area in an increasingly complicated world where competence and experience are like four-letter words? The words followed each other effortlessly—even the sentences that carefully raised question marks around Kirsten Rolighed—*do we know the alternative well enough?* asked the *Daily News*'s leader rather cryptically. Torp corrected it for typos and commas; at 9:13 p.m., Lindskov called and chased desperately for his text; at 9:14 p.m., he got it and immediately passed it on to the person who was chasing at the other end, who sent it on to another, which got a printing plant twenty-five kilometres away started on printing 50,000 copies of *Enevoldsen must stay*.

Just words.

"It's a vacant viewpoint," said Torp, trying to get himself out of the hole he was in.

"Sometimes there's a fucking reason why a viewpoint is vacant!" shouted Lindskov, his voice cracking as he hung up.

The leader wasn't Torp's only story in the *Daily News* that Thursday morning. He bought a copy on the way to the bus in Brønshøj, and Simon had done his job. *Police investigating the deaths of top politicians*—Simon had been given half of the front page. The rest was the prelude to today's Liberal national executive committee meeting. There was a reference to the leader on page two. So now Erling Jensen has become a top politician, thought Torp to himself as he flipped through the newspaper. Not a word about the Communist Party, not a word about intelligence services or a home help from Russia on her way out of Copenhagen Airport a few hours after the last death. In fact, there wasn't much in the article at all other than pictures of Brathenberg and Jensen, the already known circumstances of their deaths, and then the absolutely crucial quotes from the Copenhagen Police:

So far, the two deaths have been considered natural deaths. Is that still the case?

No. We are investigating both deaths on suspicion of criminal activity.

Is there a connection between the two deaths?

That is, among other things, what we are investigating.

Do you have a motive?

I can't get into that because of the investigation.

Do you have any suspects?

I have no further comment.

Torp could see that the media on the internet were all referring to it and trying to follow up on the story. Maybe it could take some of the pressure off Lindskov and the Enevoldsen-friendly leader that the otherwise experienced debate editor had authored in a fit of daring. He usually dribbled along quite harmlessly far from the boundary line, as several people on the editorial staff remarked with a little astonishment as the rumours around the day's leader, which only a few people usually read, began to circulate.

"The leader in the *Daily News* is one of the most sensible that has been on page two of that newspaper since time immemorial."

Axel Boas was waving the newspaper around when Torp entered the office.

"Rather different than the unworthy accusations that the leader writer has previously fumbled with," he continued.

"Do you think so?" said Torp, trying to maintain a neutral tone.

"Hell, yes. But what an erratic course," exclaimed Axel. "Have you seen that the police think Brathenberg and Jensen may have been murdered?"

Again Axel waved his newspaper, this time so Torp felt he had to take avoiding action so as not to be hit.

"Mind-blowing story," Torp said.

"A little thin, if you ask me."

Axel stopped in mid-thought.

"Just a minute. Didn't you write an obituary about Erling Jensen?"

Torp nodded. "I wrote both obituaries."

"Brathenberg's, too?" Axel looked at Torp in surprise.

"Both. I mean . . . I wrote both obituaries on Erling Jensen." Torp wanted to stop but continued as if he owed an explanation. "That is, some different ones. About Erling. For different media."

Axel nodded absent-mindedly; during Torp's explanation, he had flipped to the central section with Simon's article.

"It's not very specific, but then again the police probably don't give such quotes unless they know more than they're saying."

He was mostly speaking to himself now. Torp's two obituaries had long since faded into the background. Axel turned around and went back to his bay window. In almost the same movement, Emma came into the office. She nodded diffidently to all of them without saying anything and put a USB stick on Torp's desk as she walked by. He had completely forgotten the interviews with Per Frost and Kirsten Rolighed. Torp clicked a few times and sent them to the editor with a "here you are," as if it was the easiest thing in the world to edit an hour-long interview down to five minutes. He watched just the first thirty seconds of each, but then he couldn't take any more. It was like a day-old newspaper, filled with indifferent stuff, precisely because it was from the day before.

"Are you in a bad mood?"

Torp was standing by his old desk in the passage looking down at Emma, who was working on her computer.

"Why should I be in a bad mood?"

"I don't know."

"It was you who asked," she said, looking up at him.

"It's just that you didn't say anything."

"Do I have to say something so it doesn't look like I'm in a bad mood?"

There was a hint of a smile on her face. Just a hint. Torp grabbed the invitation and smiled back.

"Nah, you don't have to. Thanks for the clips of those two. I'll pay your office rent for May."

She shook her head. "No, you won't. It was a favour."

"It was work."

"For me, it was a favour."

Torp turned halfway around, hesitating long enough for Emma to see he wasn't finished.

"It was a favour, Ulrik. Not everything is about money."

"Okay. Thanks." He was standing with his body half turned to depart, half waiting to pull himself together.

"Yes?" Emma discreetly closed the screen on her computer and looked up.

"When we were up in Rågeleje."

"Yes?"

"And knocked on Benedikte Koch's door."

"Yes?"

"And those neighbours came and meddled, and you made them go away." She just looked at him.

"You said we were Jehovah's Witnesses."

Emma shrugged.

"How did you come up with that?"

"We had to say something."

Emma's gaze wavered a bit. Torp's body began to turn completely around to go back to his own desk. This was absolutely none of his business, and it went against all his instincts, both in terms of interfering in the lives of others and in terms of accepting Emma's fragile private sphere. Yet he remained standing there.

"You said there was a Kingdom Hall in Helsinge with meetings on Sundays."

Emma looked down at her desk without saying anything.

"I've checked. There *is* a Kingdom Hall in Helsinge. They *do* have meetings on Sundays."

"That's what I said." She looked at him. Defiantly.

"How did you know?"

Torp decided he wouldn't say more, allowed the pause to be long and embarrassing to force Emma to continue. Almost a minute passed and Emma's chair became more and more uncomfortable to sit on.

"It was just something I said."

New pause. Axel was talking on the phone from inside the bay window. It sounded as if he was speaking to his wife. No, it would probably be a long day; he had a lot to write about and might want to call in at the hotel where the Liberals' national executive meeting was to take place in the afternoon. No, it wasn't cheating; he had a press pass. Yes, all right, he would certainly go into the butcher afterwards.

"You come from up there. You've been to the Kingdom Hall in Helsinge."

Emma folded her arms and looked down, still defiant. She looked like someone who was going to hold her breath until she got her way, thought Torp.

"You've been in the Jehovah's Witnesses."

Now she looked up.

"Have you also left your family?"

"That's not how it is," she replied quietly.

"How is it, then?" Torp tried to soften his voice but sensed that it sounded inquisitorial.

"Do you believe in Judgement Day?"

The counter-question confused Torp. He shook his head slightly.

"Imagine," she continued, "imagine growing up with Judgement Day."

"Maybe I believe in some kind of fate," he replied.

"Imagine that everything you do is just preparation for Judgement Day. That the great apocalypse is just around the corner. That this life isn't the real life."

Emma's eyes were watery, not enough for her to dry them, but enough for it to be just about noticeable. Torp regretted that he had aired his suspicions.

"So if you ask me if I still believe in Judgement Day," said Emma, as if she had already seen that Torp wasn't able to carry out the conversation he himself had forced upon them, "then the answer is yes. All my life I have grown up believing that it will go wrong. I still believe that."

"Judgement Day?"

"Another kind of Judgement Day," she said, smiling a little apologetically. "I don't believe in a happy ending. If I had lived during the Cold War, I would have believed in an atomic holocaust. I think we're going to experience a new Chernobyl. I believe in a new financial crisis. I believe in a devastating virus. I believe in cancer in my breasts, in the collapse of the system, in . . ."

She was waving her arms and looking up at Torp, who stood watching her. She suddenly looked like what she also was—a little girl. The ring in her nose that made it hard to see if she was pretty or defiant. The slender, almost androgynous body. The breasts that might have been there somewhere but were hidden in oversized T-shirts and sweaters. The nails that weren't really bitten, but probably had been once. The ultra-short hair and the jeans filled with holes that looked like fashion holes, but seemed so arbitrary that they might just be what they looked like—holes in a pair of worn jeans. Her big brown eyes could have been pretty and strong in a happy, slightly freckled face. Now they were placed in the completely wrong place and didn't come into their own at all.

"I just don't believe in a happy ending. That's how I've grown up. Okay?"

Torp nodded. He also had some doubts. They looked silently at each other, then Torp turned around. This time he managed to turn all the way around.

"Besides that . . ." she continued, now in a completely different gear and leaving all talk about Jehovah and Judgement Day behind them. "Besides that, I have something important to show you. I just have to be absolutely sure first."

CHAPTER 25

It looked as if there were more present on television than in reality, but it still surprised Ulrik Torp to see hundreds of people—mostly young—with placards, banners, and battle cries, as if it were a football match. Everything was being followed up massively on social media and with one single message: that Palle Enevoldsen was finished as a politician. The organisers were again Friends of Denmark, and the plan was that after a few hours assembled at Rådhuspladsen, the march would go towards the Scandic Hotel by the Lakes, where the Liberals would be coming together in the late afternoon for the national executive committee meeting. Torp watched the assembled masses from a distance. He was to meet Per Frost at the Liberty Memorial in ten minutes for the promised photographic session. So that was why the old anti-Communist, now patriot, had time for a photo shoot in the capital.

"*Off with his head—your Palle's dead!*"

"*Off with his head—your Palle's dead!*"

There was already a heated debate on social media about the battle cry. Torp didn't understand why people could be bothered, even though he understood the criticism. He found the discussion about "your" Palle more interesting. Who were "you"? And why this insistence on "them"

217

and "us"? Torp was impressed by Friends of Denmark's both elegant and cynical use of the language.

"Your Palle." It could almost only be said with disgust in the voice.

Torp recognised Mona Kongsted from some way off, the young blonde parish priest who had come to personify the "Danes' revolt," as she called it. This was her military service for Denmark, she explained every time someone was willing to listen—in the fight for the fatherland and freedom of speech. She was talking to some of the young men in white shirts who seemed to make their presence felt every time a gathering was held, the same types who had pushed the Polo into starting outside Per Frost's house, one of whom also worked for Kirsten Rolighed inside Christiansborg—at least, he had been sitting in the front office. For a brief moment, Torp and Mona Kongsted made eye contact without either of them wanting to. Torp had interviewed her several times, and he knew she didn't like him. Kongsted turned her face away and instead directed her attention at a TV journalist who was approaching with a camera crew. Torp knew everything about how this worked. Both TV stations would be broadcasting flat out all day up to the national executive committee meeting. That would mean eight to ten hours of live TV, with nothing really happening until the last hour. They could easily fill most of the time with small talk in the studio and a lot of stand-ups in front of the Scandic, *where the national executive committee would be gathering in less than seven hours for a fateful meeting.* But despite everything, there were limits to how many times they could do it before viewers realised that it was just a matter of making time go by. Rådhuspladsen offered images, sound, conflict, and development. They could switch back here lots of times.

"We love Denmark. We love Denmark. We love Denmark."

The demonstrators suddenly started shouting their battle cry when they found out that Mona Kongsted was being interviewed live. Torp thought it was an indictment of his own profession—not much better than the ritual demonstrations and flag-burning in the Middle East which stopped the second the TV cameras were switched off.

"Off with his head—your Palle's dead!"

"Off with his head—your Palle's dead!"

"Danes deserve a better Prime Minister than Enevoldsen. The small replacement is going to prevent the Great Replacement."

Kongsted almost managed a smile as she said it. Torp checked Twitter and Facebook—it looked as if there were thousands of people in Rådhuspladsen. TV viewers would probably get the same impression, too. Off camera, some counterprotesters—it must be "their" Palle—were pushing a pair of young white shirts, who pushed back without escalating the incident. It seemed as though the mood was more aggressive than when they had gathered around the Liberty Memorial in the battle for a National Day. Maybe the atmosphere was just better when you were in favour of something, thought Torp. He was tapped on the shoulder. It was Crabby.

"I'm going to do a reportage for *Around Borgen*," he said, in answer to Torp's unspoken question. "She does it really well." Crabby nodded in the direction of Mona Kongsted. He turned a little anxiously towards Torp. "I hope I haven't taken anything from *Around Borgen* that should have gone to you."

"I never do reportage," replied Torp.

Of course he could do a reportage; it was journalism's answer to hammering two nails into a plank. But he couldn't be bothered anymore.

"Your man from Funen has also sent me some obituaries today. I hope that isn't screwing it for you, too."

Torp shook his head. It wasn't. He was also done with the obituaries. Would it all end badly, as Emma had said? Would she have her atheistic Judgement Day? He only wanted to get hold of Karen. He had to meet Per Frost at the Liberty Memorial in three minutes. He could almost see it further down Vesterbrogade. He apologised to Crabby, heard another battle cry that Palle should have his head chopped off, and hurried across Rådhuspladsen. To the right, he could see the first masked anti-fascists gathering at the edge of Ørstedsparken.

Per Frost was waiting at the foot of the Liberty Memorial when Torp, a little late, defied a couple of cars on Vesterbrogade and leapt over onto the traffic island in the middle of the busy road. Two young men in white shirts were standing beside Frost. Torp couldn't see if it was the same two who had helped with pushing the car the other day. They all looked alike, he thought—short-cropped hair, slim, unusually tight trousers, and serious faces. Funnily enough, neither of them apparently had tattoos. Maybe one of them was the one who had also been sitting in Kirsten Rolighed's front office. He was in doubt and therefore didn't know whether to greet him as if he recognised him or just say hello. He settled for a nod to both of them and a handshake to Frost, who was in the middle of a major coughing fit.

"Excuse me," said Frost, appearing a bit strained as he cleared his throat an extra time and hawked several times. He had become slightly red in the face from all the coughing.

"I should be doing the apologising—for being late," replied Torp.

"It's all this city air. It's not good for us," explained Frost, pointing to the cars whizzing past them on both sides while getting control of his coughing.

"Congratulations on the forthcoming change of Prime Minister. Then you'll be getting what you want." Torp nodded back towards the demonstration on Rådhuspladsen.

"*We*, Torp. It's called *we* when we're talking about the Danish people." He smiled and immediately agreed to step over the iron grille around the Liberty Memorial so he could stand right next to it. That would give the best picture.

"Who is actually threatening us?"

Torp positioned himself outside the grille and began taking his pictures. He was curious but also knew from experience that pictures were better if the subject was made to forget the situation.

"*What*, Torp. It's a *what* that threatens us. Always systems and ideologies. If you're looking for the answer in an individual person, then it's the wrong question."

"Goodness me, how I'm being corrected today," remarked Torp, kneeling down with his camera. The light was good and by shooting a little from below, he got the bright blue sky included.

"That's because you're imprecise and only consider the individual human being instead of the whole," replied Frost. He enjoyed lecturing, and in contrast to his anti-Communism tirades in the 1980s, he had an audience today.

"What threatens us?" asked Torp. It was a terrific picture. "Would you mind turning your face slightly to the left?"

Frost obeyed generously and turned his head.

"When you were young, the threat came from within—left-wing radicals using violence, intellectuals with delusions, and politicians with stupidity."

"Chin up a bit. And what about today?"

"The intellectuals are still deluded and the politicians are still stupid. But today the threat comes from outside."

"You mean Muslims?"

Frost shook his head slightly and smiled. "Oh, how you simplify it all."

"Now it's you who says *you*. I thought it was *we*. Head slightly to the right so you cover the sun. Thanks."

"*You*"—Frost spread his arms wide—"and all this big city radical reality. Come to the concrete Denmark, then you'll understand, Torp."

"What will I understand?"

"That the threat to our people and nation comes from outside. It's Muslims, but not only Muslims. Globalisation has made us dependent on factories in China, soya beans in Argentina, and a judge in Luxembourg."

Per Frost had completely forgotten about the photography and took a step towards Torp with his hands by his sides.

"I don't know about you, but I'd rather be dependent on a factory in Holstebro, a farm in South Funen, and a city court judge in Elsinore."

A car sounded its horn at them, or rather at Frost, who waved back.

"A patriot," he exclaimed. "Human rights, liberal democracy, and conventions have been made into a religion."

"And they're not?"

"We could do with less. Can't we agree on that, Torp?"

"A couple more pictures, then we're done. A little to the side. Thanks. And all this is due to Palle Enevoldsen?"

A series of red traffic lights from both H. C. Andersens Boulevard and the Central Station meant that suddenly there were no cars around them for a brief moment.

"This is a happy day for Denmark and Danes because we will get rid of him," stated Per Frost, while obediently posing for the photographer.

"Why?" Torp lowered his mobile phone, which he was using as a camera, and looked at his subject.

"Because now we get an extra chance. I just hope it's not too late."

"Why are you destroying Benedikte Koch?"

Torp tried to convince himself that he regretted his sudden impulse. That he had so abundantly violated Crabby and respect for source protection when he eavesdropped on—no, stole—the telephone number of his source. That he had promised himself not to use his knowledge actively, only as background.

"Why does she have to be smashed?"

It was as if he couldn't stop. As if someone or something had taken control of him. Per Frost would probably think that it was the journalist at the *Express* who had given it away. The old man accepted the attack without flinching. His face was exactly as before: scrutinising, awake, suspicious, on guard.

"I thought we were talking about Denmark. I wasn't the least bit aware that we were talking about Benedikte Koch."

He said it so quietly that the cars that were rolling past them again almost drowned out his voice.

"So you know her?"

"By name—and then that she's been in the newspapers the last few days. It's been hard to overlook."

"Why? It's a simple question."

"And what is it that you keep saying—that there are no simple answers to simple questions?"

"I'll gladly accept a complicated answer."

"I hear you're in a freelance office with the sacked TV journalist Herman Krabbe."

"That wasn't an answer, as you know."

Torp tried to look unaffected. Frost didn't have to matter for Crabby now that he had the obituaries. Were they Torp's attempts to achieve forgiveness? If that were the case, they hadn't succeeded.

"Can you make a living from obituaries?"

Per Frost coughed heavily again as he took a stride forward to step over the iron grille between them. He was clearly finished with being a photo model. The two white shirts seemed more interested in their mobiles and weren't following the conversation, if you could even call it a conversation.

"Benedikte Koch knows Kirsten Rolighed's secret."

The words rushed out of Torp's mouth. He had neither thought through nor planned this at all.

Frost was standing with one leg on each side of the grille around the Liberty Memorial; he stopped in mid-movement and turned his head towards Torp, who could see for the first time that he had scored a bull's-eye on the old man.

"That's why she has to be scandalised. So that no one will believe her."

"I actually thought you were a little smarter than most of the journalist pack."

Frost used both arms to lift his left leg over the grille. The exercise wasn't without difficulty. Now they were again standing next to each other on the traffic island, while the cars drove past on both sides.

"Why don't you even ask what kind of secret Benedikte Koch has about Kirsten Rolighed?"

The two white shirts looked up from their mobiles and sensed that their boss needed help.

"It was you who found her name in the Moscow archives."

Suddenly it all made sense.

The white shirts came between Frost and Torp.

"It was you who told Brathenberg about it, who told it to the Parliamentary Control Committee. Back then, you were on the same side."

"Would that have been so bad?"

"As long as she was far from power, it didn't matter. But Erling Jensen could remember it. Did Brathenberg then contact you to get it confirmed?

Did he tell you that he and Erling Jensen were going to expose Kirsten Rolighed? Did he think you were still on the same side?"

Per Frost said nothing.

"And Erling Jensen's notes from the meetings of the Control Committee. I guess it was one of your faithful disciples who broke into my office, found the bag, and took the papers?"

Torp nodded in the direction of the two white shirts.

"Who did you tell? Your Russian friends?"

"That's it, my friend. It's over now," said one of the young men whom Torp now confidently recognised from Rolighed's front office. Per Frost stood by the iron grille with a bent back in the middle of another coughing fit.

"You forgot the secretary in the first round. You forgot Benedikte Koch."

"Leave now," continued the white shirt.

"You have your hand up Kirsten Rolighed."

Frost straightened up a bit and stared at Torp. The other white shirt stepped right up to him.

"And what about your fortune hidden in a tangle of Russian companies and names? Do they have their hand up you?" asked Torp.

"You're leaving now. Right now," threatened the white shirt without raising his voice.

"Otherwise what? Will I also have my head chopped off?"

Torp turned his head and looked at Per Frost, who hadn't moved.

"Get lost."

The white shirt gave Torp a push in the chest with both hands. It wasn't vigorous, but Torp had his weight on the wrong foot just at the time of the push, so he tumbled out into the road. A car braked sharply, tried to avoid him by driving up on the Liberty Memorial traffic island, grazed Torp with the outer part of the right front bumper, and hit the iron grille around the Memorial with the left. The cars behind all managed to brake; some of them began honking their horns. Per Frost remained standing a few metres from where the car had stopped. Torp got to his feet with difficulty. The man in the car opened the door and shouted angrily as soon as he saw that the idiot in the driving lane hadn't been seriously injured.

Both white shirts and Frost ignored the motorist and instead watched Torp, who had come across to the pavement on the other side in a state of confusion. The cars had started driving again, some tooting, either to acknowledge that everyone was okay, or perhaps to complain about the delay—it was difficult to determine properly. Torp brushed the road dust off his trousers and jacket as best he could. After one last moment of eye contact with Frost, he turned around and stumbled back towards Rådhuspladsen.

"Off with his head—your Palle's dead!"

They were well on their way with chopping off heads, it seemed. The anti-fascists had advanced as far as the stairs down to the Metro in the middle of the square. Friends of Denmark had withdrawn to the entrance of the town hall, and battle-dressed police were standing between the two groups. The numbers on each side were constantly increasing, and the police weren't being very convincing in exercising their authority. Torp saw Crabby standing with a handful of journalists and photographers a good distance away by the pedestrian crossing. Simon from the *Daily News* was there too. Torp made eye contact with him and waved him over.

"Great article today."

"Thanks. And thanks for the tip," replied Simon, almost having to shout.

More police cars and a few police wagons were on their way with sirens blaring. The sight called to Torp's mind a law professor who had once described the whole philosophy behind the law-based society's monopoly on violence and thereby explained why the police never— as in never—could be seen to lose a confrontation. It seemed as if the police had also read the professor, thought Torp when he saw yet another group of combat-clad officers jump out of two wagons that stopped right beside him and Simon.

"What do you think about the leader today?"

"The leader?" Simon looked baffled.

"About Enevoldsen. In your newspaper."

"Have no idea. Never read it. Should I?"

"Nah, forget it. It doesn't matter," Torp shouted back.

"Many people are wondering who could have murdered Brathenberg and Jensen," said Simon, looking at Torp.

They moved a little away from the pedestrian crossing so as not to get too close to the officers who were piling out from two newly arrived wagons wearing helmets, visors, and bulletproof vests. They looked like what they were—the holders of a monopoly on violence that felt itself challenged.

"Some are saying it's the Russians. That sounds a little far out," said Simon, putting Torp to the test. They were now at a good distance from what was happening and could hear each other better.

"They've done it elsewhere—in both Britain and Germany."

"But this is Denmark."

Torp nodded.

"So you've also heard something about Russia?"

"I can't say."

"Aren't you a journalist?"

"Yes."

"Then why can't you say anything?" Simon was again baffled as he looked at Torp, who was clearly uncomfortable. "Is it something to do with source protection?"

Torp nodded.

"Then we do like Deep Throat in Watergate. I say something and you can choose not to protest."

Torp said nothing. Simon became eager.

"Is it the Russians?"

Torp said nothing.

Simon let ten seconds pass. Fifteen seconds.

"Is it GRU, their intelligence service?"

Again ten seconds. Fifteen seconds.

"Does it have anything to do with them over there?" He pointed towards the Friends of Denmark.

Ten seconds. Fifteen seconds.

Now the anti-fascists attacked. They had brought cobblestones and catapults with steel nails and were walking in with military precision from two sides in a V-shaped attack, thus forcing the officers to spread out more than they wanted to. And just as they had done so, another group of frustrated young people ran straight towards the middle. The anti-fascists had been practising this.

"Fuck, they're crazy," exclaimed Simon. Then he turned back towards Torp. "Do the police know all this?"

Ten seconds. Fifteen seconds.

"Thanks, Torp. I have to make a few calls. I'm off."

Simon's happy face was a contrast to the whole scene in Rådhuspladsen. The Friends of Denmark hadn't yet made an attack. They clearly expected the police to handle the task. More wagons came with sirens blaring. At this point, law enforcement fired the first tear gas grenade.

"Good luck with the Cavling Prize," Torp shouted after Simon. He waved back happily and ran off.

CHAPTER 26

What the hell happened to you?"

Axel's spontaneous outburst made Ulrik Torp look down at himself. There was a tear in his right trouser leg, and a bit of blood had left a dark stain on the fabric. He hadn't noticed until now that his clothes were covered in dust after he had been rolling around on the asphalt in front of the Liberty Memorial. His leg hurt; the car hadn't just grazed him.

"Were you for or against Denmark?"

Axel had borrowed Torp's office chair and rolled it over to Crabby's desk, where he and Crabby were sitting together. He was trying to ease the situation but looked both worried and surprised at the sight of his office companion.

"I was probably mostly anti-fascist," said Torp, trying to force a small sarcastic smile. It almost succeeded, and Axel noticed.

"At your age!"

He became serious.

"It's getting crazy down there. We're watching it on TV."

He nodded in the direction of Crabby's large computer screen, where they were following the clash on Rådhuspladsen a few hundred metres from where they were sitting.

Axel got up. "Here, sit down, and I'll get a cloth and a glass of water."

Torp sat down gratefully and watched the fighting, which from the outside was a cacophony of shouts, screams, and arbitrary blows.

"It's impossible to make out who are the anti-fascists and who are the Friends of Denmark," said Crabby, moving to the front of his chair with his face close to the screen.

Torp nodded. "It looks like one big game of ring-a-ring o' roses."

Crabby turned his head quizzically.

"There's no front, no line or area to defend or occupy," said Torp, pointing at the screen. "Everyone's milling around. It's all fragmented."

"That's why it's so hard for the police."

Axel came back with a wet cloth and a glass of water which Torp eagerly emptied in a single gulp. He hadn't noticed that his throat was parched. Through the open windows, they could hear the sirens from police cars, fire engines, and ambulances driving to and from Rådhuspladsen. The monopoly of violence and the welfare state were fighting side by side for dominance. Torp took the wet cloth and wiped it around his face. It felt nice.

"Have you heard from Karen?"

Axel was standing with the empty glass and holding out his hand, ready to take the cloth back when it was no longer being used.

Torp shook his head. For a brief moment, it had slipped his mind, but he could feel in the sigh of despair in his stomach that his body hadn't forgotten.

"If you want to have a chat, like tight-arse to tight-arse, just let me know."

Torp didn't know how he could both show gratitude for the offer and reject it at the same time, so he mumbled a little about if only he could talk to her, then everything would probably be all right again.

"Fuck!"

Crabby's outburst got Axel and Torp to focus on the computer screen. A group of police officers had been hemmed in against the façade of the town hall, just below the balcony. They were part of the original police force at the demonstration and thus not combat-clad. Two of them were lying on the ground, and several hooded men were kicking them in the head indiscriminately. The other officers were trying to come to their aid but were being pushed farther away. The image shook violently, as if the cameraman were being pushed, too.

"Who started all this?"

Crabby was mostly speaking to himself.

"The real question is who's going to stop it," said Axel softly.

The TV channel suddenly changed position to an unprepared live reporter who was standing at a distance from it all in front of the main entrance to Tivoli on the safe side of a combat-clad police chain.

"They mustn't lose. They must never lose," muttered Torp.

The door to the office was flung open, and Emma strode in with her computer under her arm.

"Have you been down on Rådhuspladsen?" said Axel, looking up.

She nodded. "Things are getting lively."

"Getting lively! That's the understatement of the year," he exclaimed. "It's a minor civil war."

"That's a load of shit. But it always looks worse on TV," she declared.

This clearly wasn't the first time she had been close to a violent demonstration.

"You just carry on watching. There's just something I need to be absolutely certain about."

Emma disappeared into her desk in the corridor, sat down immediately, and turned on her computer.

Slowly, slowly, the police began to regain control of Rådhuspladsen. The most peaceful protesters were trying to get away from the tear gas—and were being allowed to do so. The aggressive ones were loaded into police wagons and transported away. The injured officers were being taken away by ambulances with sirens blaring, while even more combat-clad officers were being rolled out.

"Your monopoly of violence wins again," said Crabby, when it was clear that the battle was over.

"It's like the Israeli state. You just have to lose once, then it's all over," commented Torp.

"That at least is a state that takes things seriously," replied Crabby, without wishing to initiate a discussion.

"Okay, I'm ready!" came a shout from the corridor.

Ready for what?

"You can come in now," continued Emma, sounding like the party in hiding in a game of hide-and-seek.

"Come now? What are we coming to?"

Axel, Crabby, and Torp looked at each other but obeyed the order or invitation and went out to Emma in the corridor. She sat triumphantly at her computer, smiling at them.

"I knew it, but I just needed some help."

"Help with what?"

"Fetch some chairs and sit down, and I'll show you something."

Palle Enevoldsen was sitting at his desk in the Prime Minister's Office going through his speech to the party's national executive committee. His special adviser was sitting opposite him biting her lip, anxious about his reaction. Christine was good at these kinds of speeches; she wasn't just into the subject matter but also into him. She knew his rhythm, his penchant for some special phrases and displeasure for others. Christine had been loyally at his side for almost all the years in the Prime Minister's Office, setting a new record in endurance for every day that passed. It was probably a record that would stand for many years. And maybe it would be over in a few days or weeks. They both knew that. If his party's national executive turned their thumbs down in three hours, it would be over for him both as leader and as Prime Minister. Then the expectation would be that in a few days he would announce his departure. And then Christine could become a TV commentator, columnist, or adviser at the heavy end of business and earn double for half the working hours. He didn't begrudge her that and wasn't worried about the book that would almost certainly follow. Her loyalty wasn't blind but fair. What about himself? A single book in a modest edition and a few middleweight board positions. He had no illusions and could just look at his predecessors if he should be in any doubt. A former Prime Minister in his mid-fifties was rarely much sought after, and certainly not if his successor was Kirsten Rolighed. A change of government with the Labour Party's Pernille Hjort in office would ironically open up more opportunities for a gift of grace.

"Third section on page three," said Palle Enevoldsen and read aloud from the papers: *"When one has responsibility for one's own country, one quickly discovers that seemingly simple questions have very complicated answers. How I wish the world was as simple as some people try to make it out to be. Do you think that's wise? At least half of the executive thinks the answers are simple. Now I'm saying that they are the ones who are stupid and don't understand anything—just before they have to support me."*

"The key words in the sentence are *responsibility for one's own country*," Christine pointed out. "*That's* what they have to remember. *Some people* means Kirsten Rolighed."

"Yes, I've worked that bit out," he mumbled.

Christine continued undaunted. "If you think the answers are simple, as Kirsten Rolighed will try to have them believe, then you aren't looking after Denmark's interests. That's your contract with the national executive."

Palle Enevoldsen pushed his glasses down and read on. It was his way of saying okay.

Several of his people had been ringing round in recent days. Out of the eighty committee members, he was sure of twenty-two. Kirsten Rolighed had seventeen in her pocket, they thought. It was all those in between that needed to be massaged. Palle Enevoldsen acknowledged that it was a sin of omission that things had even come this far. Previously, at least seventy of the members would have followed him even if he had nationalised Maersk. But after seven years as Prime Minister, he was showing signs of wear and tear. This was part and parcel of the eternal compromises. People thought that political power was about choosing between good and evil, but that was a big misunderstanding. Political power was the privilege of being able to choose between the least bad of many evils. Only a few on the national executive committee understood that. Especially after many of them had been replaced while he was busy in Brussels, Berlin, and Washington, or wherever the hell the Challenger plane happened to land in an attempt to position a small country in the right place. In reality, that was the only major political task for a prime minister.

His political gut told him it was all over. The feedback from the phone round was more than hesitant. The popularity polls between him and Kirsten Rolighed revealed, if nothing else, that in her short political life she hadn't had to make many choices between evils. And perhaps worst of all, for the first time in his political life, he no longer felt in tune with the times. He convinced himself that he understood the young people but not his own generation. Where had the hatred of the elite and the scepticism towards knowledge come from? He was honestly also at a loss as to what he would spend the next three years in the Prime Minister's Office doing if he was allowed to continue. Mentally, he had prepared himself for it being over. His gut was seldom wrong, even though the *Daily News* had had a welcome but strange leader in the morning edition, which supported him unreservedly.

"The last third must be tightened up. The speech is too long, but the content and tone are as they should be," he said, pushing the papers over to Christine. "Ask Jeanne to put a hold on phone calls for the next hour, if possible. I'll go down and iron a shirt and take a nap."

He went down to the bottom of the huge office and the hidden door, behind which hid a small private room with a couch, a wardrobe, and an ironing board.

If he was going to be defeated, he at least wanted to be well rested and in a freshly ironed white shirt when it happened.

Emma clicked the mouse and started the recording. Crabby, Axel, and Torp had all seen it countless times. Most of Denmark had.

"I can't be bloody bothered to hear more about those idiots in Friends of Denmark. I don't want to waste my time on such a bunch of provincial fascists. They can piss off with their fucking National Day—do they think I'm raving mad?"

Palle Enevoldsen was fuming on the recording against the National Day, which he had later accepted in a vain attempt to quell the revolt against him.

"What are we supposed to be seeing?" said Axel, with a slightly irritated look at Emma.

"Now just watch the rest. And pay particular attention to his eyes."

"*. . . a dog they can just push around? A little fucking puppy? I don't give a damn about those politicians who don't dare to speak out against them. Christ Almighty, what a bunch of sissies.*"

Emma stopped the recording and looked up at them excitedly.

"Can you see it?"

No one answered.

"When you know what to look for, you can hardly believe that you overlooked it."

"Emma, stop this hide-and-seek. What is it we're supposed to see?" Torp sounded, and was, impatient. He didn't have the energy for this.

Emma went into the recording again, clicked a little forward, and froze the picture where Palle Enevoldsen was staring straight into the camera. She pointed at his eyes.

"Look! See what isn't there."

"What isn't there?" Axel was also running out of patience.

"There's no reflection in the iris," said Crabby. His past as a TV journalist with countless hours in an editing room suddenly came to the fore.

"Yes!" Emma clapped her hands. "Exactly! There is no reflection in the iris. And what else?"

"Run it again," continued Crabby eagerly.

Torp and Axel sensed they were outsiders and said nothing. They saw Palle Enevoldsen fuming against Friends of Denmark once more. Crabby was sitting with his face so close to Emma's computer screen that he almost blocked the view for the others.

"The clip lasts almost thirty seconds. He doesn't blink once," said Crabby, mostly speaking to himself.

"Bingo!"

Emma looked up at Torp and Axel, who were still standing like two silent spectators at a performance that they didn't understand. She clicked a few times and again froze a picture of the Prime Minister.

"And look at his hair, the outermost part by his left ear."

Crabby put his head up very close and narrowed his eyes; the others couldn't see anything, but it also didn't seem important.

"It stops a little abruptly. The hairline, right?" He looked uncertainly at Emma. She nodded.

"That's also what I think. You can see it if you compare it with the hair by the right ear."

Crabby studied the hair by Palle Enevoldsen's right ear and nodded.

"It's been compressed from one format to another," added Emma. "Look!" She pointed to the hair by the left ear. "The algorithm has formed artifacts according to a certain pattern. It becomes clear when you fiddle with the contrast."

"I think they have generated it over onto an MPEG-4 video. It simply doesn't have the same artifacts as the original video. But it's bloody well done," said Crabby.

"Do you mind telling us what's going on?" asked Torp, still a little irritated.

"This is deepfake, what we have here," said Crabby, again mostly addressed to Emma.

"What are you talking about?" asked Axel, spreading his arms wide.

"Deepfake," repeated Emma. "It's fake. Enevoldsen never said that."

"Because there is no reflection in his eyes?"

"And because he doesn't blink, and because the hair above his left ear stops abruptly—yes."

"But he says it anyway," objected Axel. "Palle Enevoldsen says what we see in the pictures."

Emma shook her head.

"I've seen similar things," recalled Torp, "but mostly for fun. Where an actor suddenly gets another face or part of another face and just carries on talking."

"It's the same technology." Emma seemed grateful for a moment that one of the two old men at least faintly thought he had heard of the phenomenon.

"How is it done?"

"In principle, with an app and a laptop. But this," she said, pointing at Enevoldsen, who was still frozen on the screen with no reflection in his open eyes, "this is well done. It requires an advanced algorithm and good encoding to make it match as well as it does."

"Who would do such a thing?" Axel stood with his arms down by his sides looking lost.

"As with so much other digital technology, it was the porn industry that made the breakthrough with it," replied Crabby eagerly.

"Have you never seen Scarlett Johansson or Jennifer Aniston in a hot threesome?"

Both Torp and Axel shook their heads. No, they hadn't.

"Loads of famous actors have been put into porn movies using artificial intelligence and algorithms. Until a year or two ago, it was pretty easy to see that it was deepfake. Today, it's almost impossible. Almost," said Crabby.

Emma nodded once more.

"How can you expose it when it's so hard to see?" continued Axel.

"Using artificial intelligence and algorithms," said Emma with a smile. "Isn't it ironic?"

"How did you expose this?" asked Torp, pointing at Enevoldsen.

"Firstly, I noticed that he didn't blink. In principle, you don't need to do that for twenty-five to thirty seconds. But it seemed odd."

"Yes?"

"Then I sent it to some people I know who know about this sort of thing. They ran it through their scripts, which among other things revealed the lack of reflection in the eyes and the hair by the left ear."

"And that's enough to conclude that it's a scam?" Torp sounded and was suspicious.

"It's enough to open up the whole undercarriage. There are quite a few other things that we can't see but that a good algorithm or artificial intelligence will capture right away—for example, the mouth movements, even though that part is extremely well done"

"How extremely?"

Emma thought about it for a long time. "The people who have made this are really good. Those I know are a little better."

"But why?" continued Axel. "Why did you start looking at whether Palle Enevoldsen blinked his eyes?"

"What is it you call it, Torp? A hunch?" she replied with a smile. "I didn't have a hunch about Palle Enevoldsen. Most people had a sense that it was something he thought but didn't dare say in public."

"So what was your . . . hunch?"

"This," said Emma.

She turned back to her computer and clicked a few times, so the Torp video with Vivi kissing him appeared. She ran it to the end and the still image of the unfaithful husband.

"I had a hunch that you couldn't do something like that. It just didn't fit the picture. You, unfaithful? Come on!"

"No reflection in the iris," said Crabby.

"Of course not," continued Emma. "And you don't blink, either," she said to Torp, winking with her right eye. "The big trip in the machine gave the same result. Compression from one format to another creates some specific artifacts that show up as a hint of snow in the image when you adjust the contrast."

"Deepfake," said Axel.

"Deepfake," repeated Emma. "And then I didn't need to have a graduation diploma from the School of Journalism to think that the other posting from monkeybusiness was probably also fake."

"Bloody hell," exclaimed Axel. "What can you believe in these days?"

"In a few years," said Emma, leaning back, "you'll probably be able to do deepfake on live TV which no one will be able to see with the naked eye. With reflection, hairline, and the whole works. That's how fast it's moving."

"And when something actually is true, people can just say that it's deepfake," added Crabby.

"Like the President of the United States," exclaimed Axel.

"Him too, yes."

Crabby sat down on Emma's desk and relaxed his shoulders. All four of them were completely silent for a moment, this time with Torp staring out of the screen just after kissing Vivi on a sunny spring day.

"But who would have an interest in ruining your marriage?" asked Axel, giving Torp a disoriented look.

"They're not interested in my marriage. They just wanted me to become preoccupied with something else. That's why they've also made sure that the clip is spread out all over social media."

"Who? Why?" Axel didn't understand a thing.

"The same people who did the deepfake on Enevoldsen to make Kirsten Rolighed Prime Minister."

Torp turned his face towards Axel. Now the old journalist would surely understand it. There was complete silence between the four of them. The sirens from Rådhuspladsen were still sounding through the open windows, but the intensity was decreasing. The battle was over for the time being.

"You'd better get a move on with making contact with Karen," said Axel, breaking the silence and looking at Torp.

"If she'll believe me," said Torp.

In a way, he was relieved, but also plagued by a guilty conscience. He had come too close to Vivi, enjoyed her company too much. There had been a little flirtation—both at the beach on the west coast and the other day by the Lakes. The touches on the thigh, her caresses on his cheek, her lips against his lips. He had let it happen and also led her to believe that there was something. It wasn't illicit, but neither was it innocent, as with Enevoldsen's outburst. Palle Enevoldsen hadn't said that Friends of Denmark were provincial fascists, but there was a reason why the population—including himself and his special adviser—either believed it or were brought into doubt. When Torp himself was in doubt about what had happened with Vivi, how could he then blame Karen for believing what she saw?

"And what about Enevoldsen?" said Axel, interrupting Torp's thoughts. "He's on the verge of being overthrown by his national executive committee in a few hours. Don't you know his special adviser?"

"You can't just be put through to the country's Prime Minister," said Christine dismissively. "Besides, he's having a nap to be fresh for the national executive committee meeting."

"But it's incredibly important."

"It's incredibly important six times an hour, now into its seventh year. You'll have to do better than that," she said.

"Don't you trust me?"

"Yes," she said. "But you must also trust me."

"Can I tell you, then?"

"I'm sure the Prime Minister has a lot of secrets he doesn't tell me about. But what you want to tell me is guaranteed not to be one of them. Go ahead."

Torp took a deep breath. "The recording of him about Friends of Denmark, which you yourself were in doubt about. The one from Marienborg, where he's wearing the new tie you were talking about."

"Yes?"

"It's a deepfake. It's a scam and a lie. That monkeybusiness person has put it together."

Torp could hear her hesitating on the phone. He let the pause hang and prepared himself to come up with a longer technical explanation before being put through to a sleep deprived Prime Minister.

"I thought as much," came the quiet response from the other end.

"So don't you think you should wake him up and give him the phone?"

"For what?"

"So he—so you—can do something about it."

"And what do you think we should do?"

"Tell people about it. Correct it. Tell the national executive committee, too." Torp was becoming disoriented. What kind of special adviser did the country's Prime Minister have?

"Do you really think they'll believe him?"

"But they'll have to," objected Torp. "Most of the population has seen that clip."

"Exactly."

"And it's a lie."

"But it could actually just as easily be true." The Prime Minister's special adviser took a deep breath. "Do you think the truth is going to make a big difference in this case?"

"What do you mean?"

"Those who like him will perhaps believe it, or at least be in doubt. The rest will either not hear your explanation or refuse to believe it."

"How do you know that?"

"Trust me," sighed Christine. "I know."

"And the national executive meeting?"

"It won't make any difference." The special adviser was about to prepare for landing. "Go and tell your story, Torp. Both the Prime Minister and I will appreciate it, but don't think it will change anything at all."

"So you won't wake him?" He thought it sounded as if she was already packing up the office.

"If it was really extremely important, then I would." She paused. "What about what that monkeybusiness character has put out with you and the woman you're kissing who isn't your wife? Is that also deepfake?"

Of course, she had seen it, too. Torp could hear in her voice that it was no longer the special adviser who was speaking.

"Yes. That's a lie, too."

"So why don't you go and talk to your wife, if you haven't already done so. *That* is extremely important."

CHAPTER 27

Palle Enevoldsen seemed calm and acquiescent when he got out of his ministerial car. With his hands a little pointedly in his pockets, he strolled over to the waiting journalists, who had been placed behind a red ribbon to the right of the entrance to the conference hotel.

"Is this your last day as Prime Minister?"

"We've just had a general election. There are a good three years yet before I call the next one."

"Are you surprised that Kirsten Rolighed is trying to overthrow you?" asked one of the most aggressive commentators, pushing himself to the front.

"There's no one trying to overthrow me, Henrik, although I'm sure you're looking forward to that day. I have asked the national executive committee of my party to express its confidence in me as leader. I expect it to do that in a little while."

"Do you regret calling Friends of Denmark provincial fascists?"

"I have nothing more to say. It was, as always, nice to chat with you all," said Palle Enevoldsen, giving short shrift to the question and continuing calmly up to the entrance, followed by his two bodyguards and his special adviser. He turned his head and cast a single glance at the protesters who had been allowed to gather on the other side of the street at the Tycho Brahe Planetarium and the edge of St. Jørgen's Lake.

The whole scene oozed Danish history in the making. Most observers were taking it for granted that Enevoldsen was finished and that Kirsten Rolighed would become Prime Minister within a few days. The supporting parties had unofficially pledged themselves. A few weeks later, she would then formally become leader of the Liberals at an extraordinary national conference, according to the current analysis. All major newspapers except the *Daily News* had come out with ruthless leaders about Enevoldsen and had, by and large, endorsed Rolighed as the natural alternative.

The faithful assembly of the Friends of Denmark and other inquisitive people behind the police roadblock at the Planetarium didn't seem to have any doubts, either. The battle cries had been left on Rådhuspladsen, but the atmosphere exuded satisfaction, thought Ulrik Torp, when he and Axel Boas arrived at the scene after a tiring walk across the now empty square, which looked like an abandoned music festival with broken bottles and piles of rubbish. Torp's leg really hurt as they walked past the Liberty Memorial and approached the conference hotel and what Axel called their well-deserved gawp wedding.

They were just in time to see Enevoldsen disappear behind the glass doors. Torp made brief eye contact with the special adviser, who sent him a hint of a smile before she too disappeared. He looked over at the gathering of spectators and earlier demonstrators. On the edges, he recognised several of the white-shirted youths. In the middle, he saw Per Frost and Mona Kongsted, the blonde theologian and the Friends' intellectual spokeswoman. They were in a seemingly heated discussion, but much too far away for Torp to hear what it was all about.

The last of the national executive committee members strode up past the journalists, wise enough not to stop and make any comment. Many of them had already said more than enough in anonymous form in recent days, thought Torp. Now they just had to carry out their role. Kirsten Rolighed was one of the last to arrive. By bike!

The Friends of Denmark and also the more ordinary spectators at the Planetarium erupted in applause when they caught sight of her.

"Bloody hell, she's making a number out of it," exclaimed Axel, who didn't try to hide his indignation. Torp, on the other hand, was fascinated by her entrance. Long, light-coloured skirt, tight blouse, youthful white sneakers, casual hair, and a friendly smile—not too broad.

"She looks like a modern prime minister," said Torp.

"She looks like a calculation," was Axel's assessment. "No one can look that casual without it being carefully planned."

Kirsten Rolighed parked her bike in the conference hotel's bike rack and walked confidently towards the journalists and the TV cameras. She coughed heavily a few times and apologised with a hand gesture. She didn't look completely healthy close up.

"Are you now going to be Prime Minister?"

"Honestly, have you spent all day coming up with that question?" she replied, turning her face disarmingly towards the *Express*'s journalist.

"You're also a member of the national executive. How are you going to vote?"

"I'll be voting for the Liberals," she said, stifling a fresh fit of coughing.

"Do you support Palle Enevoldsen?"

"I always support the leader of the Liberals," she declared, disappearing behind the glass doors.

"My God, she's good," said Torp.

"You're too easy," replied Axel, but in a way that showed that he more or less agreed.

She had something about her, Kirsten Rolighed. Something else. Maybe one should just get used to the fact that modern politicians were like that.

Torp caught sight of Anton from Police Headquarters about fifty metres away, down by Gammel Kongevej. He looked as if he was searching for someone. Torp went down towards him, and Anton waved him over as soon as they made eye contact.

"We've been contacted by a journalist from the *Daily News*," he began, not aggressively, as Torp had feared, just plainly stating a fact. "I'm assuming you've had something to do with it."

"Simon. He's a good guy. The same one who wrote today's story about Brathenberg and Jensen."

"He's asking in a very clever way if the Russians are behind their deaths. He must either have a good gut feeling or good sources."

"Maybe a bit of both."

Anton nodded. "That's probably the way it hangs together."

"Does it matter?"

Anton shook his head. "Nah, it's speeding things up a bit, but it's probably not doing any harm, either."

"What do you mean, speeding up?"

"We're going to arrest him over there in a little while." Anton nodded in the direction of the Friends of Denmark at the Planetarium. Torp turned his head. Per Frost and Mona Kongsted were still in a seemingly heated discussion.

"Per Frost?"

Anton nodded.

"What do you have on him?"

"The bikers and immigrant gangs have long since found out about using anonymous talk-time phones." Anton pointed over to Per Frost. "His call list was like an open book."

"Is that enough?"

"Enough for a remand in custody and a search of his home and computers. Who knows." He smiled. "Maybe we'll also find some monkey-business in the middle of all his stuff."

"What about the Russians?"

"The politicians will have to handle that—we'll never get them. So far, we're content with him over there."

"But Kirsten Rolighed will be Prime Minister soon."

"Take it easy, Torp. First, we take Per Frost. So now you know that much." He turned and walked over to his colleagues.

Torp went back to Axel, who was talking to a couple of old colleagues. Now came the time that was so unbearable if you were broadcasting live TV—the hours where absolutely nothing happened, but when you still had to fill the broadcasting time with generalities to "be in on the event," as it was so beautifully called. Torp didn't envy them. As a rule, a tip-off would be received from negotiations that white smoke would come in the course of half an hour or a full hour, but this national executive committee meeting was in another category. This could take anywhere from an hour to well into the night. Nobody knew. The journalists were spending their time on Enevoldsen's political obituary. The assessment was that not even a third of the members of the committee supported him, and that support was waning in time with the prayer rugs being turned.

Torp received a text message. It was Emma. *You'll be getting an email shortly. It's important.* No more.

Torp was distracted by noise over by the Planetarium. Some white shirts were shouting. He could see four police officers standing around Per Frost, one of them with a firm grip on the old man's arm. He was clearly protesting, as were some of the young men around him, while Mona Kongsted was retreating into the background. Per Frost indicated with his free arm that the white shirts should stay calm. Torp watched the four officers and Per Frost on the short trip down to Gammel Kongevej, where he was put in the back seat of a police car and driven away.

Was that it? That was certainly it.

Very few people had paid attention to the incident. He could see Mona Kongsted hurrying away while talking on the phone. Several of the young people from Friends of Denmark tried to follow her, but she angrily waved them away. Torp couldn't figure out what they were up to and who was in control of whom. He wondered if they even knew themselves.

The sound of two bamboo sticks being struck against each other told him an email had arrived. It was Emma. There was a text and a link.

Benedikte Koch said that the only way we could tell her story was to get Kirsten Rolighed to tell it herself. Now it's up to you to postpone Judgement Day.

No more. Torp looked up. Axel was still standing talking to a couple of journalists he knew from the old days. Stand-ups were being made on both TV stations. *"That's a good question, Bjarne. No one knows how long it will last, but according to my sources close to the party leadership, it could very well be a midnight performance."* Several of the journalists were already looking tired at the thought of keeping the story afloat for the next eight hours. Many of the writing journalists were sitting on the paving stones in the process of making yet another update to the internet. He withdrew a little from the whole menagerie and quickly found himself behind the Imperial Cinema, almost alone.

He clicked on Emma's link in the email. Kirsten Rolighed loomed up. She was sitting in her office. Torp recognised the camera angle and the clothes from his interview. She sat calmly and confidently explaining. Torp turned on the sound:

"Dear friends, thirty years ago I made a terrible mistake. I received two hundred fifty thousand American dollars from the KGB, which should have gone to the Danish Communist Party. I used the money to start my own business. It wasn't just un-Danish and illegal. It has also made me vulnerable as a politician in relation to Denmark's enemies today. I would therefore like to announce that I am, of course, withdrawing from politics. My sincerest apologies."

Torp looked over his shoulder. No one noticed him. He pressed "Play" and watched the clip again. And again. Emma, for Christ's sake! She had added a user guide with hashtags and codes to a newly created account on both Twitter and Facebook, to which he could upload the twenty-five-second clip. The profile was called realbusiness in both places. He paced back and forth. This was a breach of all his principles. He watched the clip again, looking for the missing blinks and reflection in the iris but couldn't see anything on the small screen. Who was it Emma knew who could do this sort of thing? It was a lie and a scam. He would never be able to be a part of it. Torp made up his mind, put his mobile in his pocket, and was about to go back to Axel Boas and the other journalists. Per Frost had been arrested; that part of the story would be described by Simon tomorrow in the *Daily News*. What more could he wish for? It wasn't his job to choose who should be Denmark's Prime Minister. What was his job anyway? *Ulrik Torp—everything in journalism.* Obituaries and anonymous leaders for red wine. What illusion was he actually trying to hang onto?

He took out his mobile, made sure no one was standing nearby, and watched the clip again. Kirsten Rolighed would immediately see that it was made based on his interview with her, but that didn't mean he had to have anything to do with it. He imagined that her voice faltered a bit between *dollars* and *KGB* and that right there it was possible to rumble that it was a deepfake. If he posted it and was found out, it would be the biggest journalistic scandal since World War II. His name would be destroyed forever. This had nothing to do with journalism. On the other hand, it was true.

Torp put his smartphone back in his pocket and went back to find Axel. Over his dead body. He wasn't like that.

"Enevoldsen is no doubt already finished," said Axel, worked up by all the excitement, when he saw Torp. "The rumours from inside are that he has gone down to a basement room with Kirsten Rolighed to work out an agreement."

"What is there to make an agreement about?"

Axel nodded towards a group of journalists. "They're the ones with the sources. Not me. But several are saying that Enevoldsen is trying to negotiate an ambassadorial post in exchange for resigning."

"That's a new one," exclaimed Torp.

"Everything is new," sighed Axel.

"What do you mean?"

"This," said Axel, pointing over to the Friends of Denmark at the Planetarium; the atmosphere was aroused—they had also heard about the development at the committee meeting and had apparently forgotten all about Per Frost. "This is a paradigm shift. Do you think they will be satiated by getting their own Prime Minister?" He shook his head. "They'll just get hungrier."

"For what?" Torp was well aware of the answer, but wanted to hear it from Axel.

"More nationalism, more borders, more division, more them and us. Continue for yourself."

Torp was about to come up with some ritual objections but didn't have the energy for it.

"Excuse me," he muttered, turning around. "I just have to do something."

The recording first spread like a contagious virus among the journalists, penetrating the room where the national executive committee was located, down into the basement, where Enevoldsen and Rolighed were trying to find a solution, on to the spin doctors, commentators, and special advisers and out to the white-shirted Friends of Denmark. Thousands of shares, likes, and comments spread Kirsten Rolighed's apology out in the country before both TV channels showed the twenty-five seconds, commented on it, and showed it again, while a small picture in one corner of the screen was showing *live pictures* from the glass doors into the conference hotel. *We are still waiting for an official announcement from Prime Minister Palle Enevoldsen and further explanation from Kirsten Rolighed.*

"What a piece of news," said Axel, standing next to Torp with his hands deeply buried in his pockets.

"You might well say that."

Neither of them said anything for a long time. They watched the anthill of journalists writing, reporting, and excitedly walking around amongst each other, while tossing around adjectives usually only sports journalists were allowed to use.

"Isn't it just mind-boggling?"

A journalist from the *Express* and a commentator approached them.

It certainly was, confirmed Axel.

"Now we just have to hear Kirsten Rolighed say it, finally," added Torp.

"What do you mean?" The political commentator looked at him in surprise. "She *has* just said it."

"Exactly, she has," exclaimed Axel, looking at Torp. There was a hint of a smile on his face, a hint only Torp noticed.

When Prime Minister Palle Enevoldsen came out of the conference hotel a little over an hour later, he held a small impromptu press conference. No, Kirsten Rolighed had taken a back exit and wasn't available for interviews. She had suddenly become ill. No, nothing serious. Yes, he was also surprised by the story, but that was thirty years ago, so she should be given a little peace. Yes, he thought Kirsten Rolighed had made a wise decision by withdrawing from politics. And yes, he had full confidence in all the members of the party's national executive committee—it was made up of talented people who were thinking of both Denmark and the party and in that order.

"I remember what has been said. Not who said it," he assured them. Several of the journalists suppressed a giggle. No, he didn't know anything about an ambassadorial post. No, what had happened in the basement was between him and Rolighed. No, he had no further comments today.

"Now we're going to get on with the political work. The economy is good, unemployment is low—if we think about it, I can't see any threats ahead."

Enevoldsen walked the less than ten metres to the ministerial car together with his special adviser, who briefly made eye contact with Torp, but didn't give any indication of stopping.

There was a general uproar on the square. As had been agreed, the members of the committee didn't come out until after Enevoldsen had left. Several of them seemed shaken, but several assured the waiting crowds that Palle Enevoldsen had always been the right man for the job, and that he had just asked for confirmation of their support, which he had received 100 per cent. So what exactly was the story? The Friends of Denmark and the people around them spread out, many of them looking shell-shocked as they walked away with tired steps and arms down by their sides. The journalists had given up on the idea that Kirsten Rolighed would come out to collect her bike. She was gone and in the course of a few days—maybe weeks, if nothing else happened—would be thoroughly chewed and spat out.

"It worked," said Axel, hitting Torp on the shoulder.

"Yes, this time," replied Torp softly.

"Now I'm going home to my wife. It's been an exciting day, Torp. Like, really exciting."

"Is that good?" He looked doubtfully at Axel.

"It's not right. But it's good." The old journalist winked, turned around, clenched his fist back to Torp in a gesture of victory, and left.

Torp was left all alone, surrounded by a mass of people. It was good, but not right. He still had misgivings but felt the relief in his stomach moving out all over his body when he was interrupted by a text message. It was Lindskov. He just wanted to—discreetly—say thanks for the day's leader backing Enevoldsen. *We are the only newspaper that held firm. The management is very relieved*, he wrote, apologising for his vehement outburst in the morning. Lindskov would probably survive—even the next round of firings. Torp smiled and responded to the text message with a smiley.

A new text. It was probably Lindskov with a return smiley. Some people definitely had to have the last text. It was Emma. *You didn't learn that at the School of Journalism! By the way, I've talked to Karen. Judgement Day cancelled.*

CHAPTER 28

The sun was low in the sky when Ulrik Torp walked up the gravel path in the allotment association. He was limping increasingly with his right leg, the dust from this morning's roll on the asphalt at the Liberty Memorial was still sitting in his clothes, and the dried blood on his trouser leg completed the picture of a person who didn't belong here. He felt it clearly in the glances that followed him all the way up to the house. He nodded greetings in vain several times.

Torp had tried unsuccessfully to contact Karen, but her phone was apparently turned off. Emma also hadn't responded when he texted back to hear how Karen had reacted to her explanation. Would Karen readily believe a woman who called and said that the clip hundreds of thousands of Danes had seen on social media where her husband was kissing another woman was fake? He doubted that he would believe it himself.

There were a few slices of toast bread left in the cupboard from his and Emma's sparse dinner. He spread some jam on them and found one last teabag in the back of a cupboard. It would be enough for two cups, he decided, and sat down heavily in the allotment house's only armchair—a low, old chair with short, thick wooden legs and holes worn in the seat and on the armrests. If he leaned forward a little and stretched his neck, he could just see the national flag fluttering in the wind from the flagpole in the neighbour's garden. The sky was blue, and whatever opinions one might hold, it was a beautiful sight. Why was it so hard to agree? Ulrik was looking for painkillers in the toilet bag that Karen had put—perhaps thrown—in the suitcase. There weren't any. Only now did it dawn on him that he hadn't taken his happy pills since he came to the allotment house. How long was that? Three days. Torp felt neither more nor less happy.

He watched the first part of a TV news broadcast on his mobile. Palle Enevoldsen's political survival—*he is getting going on his eighth political life*, as one commentator put it—was, of course, the top story, sharply pursued by Kirsten Rolighed's thirty-year-old relationship with Russian intelligence agencies, the KGB and GRU. Most people were agreeing that she certainly didn't have it in her, was a lightweight politician, that there had always been something wrong with her, and that the national executive committee had come close to making a catastrophic mistake. A historian with special knowledge of the Danish Communist Party could tell viewers that the 250,000 dollars she admitted to having received solved one of the great mysteries about what had happened in the final years between Moscow and the DCP in Denmark. No one could ferret out Kirsten Rolighed for a comment.

The news that Per Frost had been arrested had long since come out, and incipient speculation about a connection between that and the deaths of Otto Brathenberg and Erling Jensen was beginning to take shape. The *Daily News* in particular seemed very well informed. The Foreign Minister had no comment to make yet on reports of a Russian connection. The key word here, according to the TV station's political analyst, was "yet."

Ulrik got up and squeezed the last dregs out of the teabag in the kitchen and sat down again with difficulty. When he stretched the injured leg all the way out and sat still, it didn't hurt.

He recognised the squeal of the rusty garden gate when it was forced open. He stretched his neck, and his leg immediately protested. At first, he could only see the blue sky; by stretching a little more, he could glimpse the neighbour's flag. Torp defied a sudden coughing fit and recognised the face through the greasy pane. It was Karen. She continued up the paved path in the small garden. Now he could see her in full figure. Now she was approaching the door; she was smiling uncertainly and had a bottle of wine in her hand.

Right now, it was a beautiful day.

ABOUT THE AUTHOR

Niels Krause-Kjær (b. 1963) is a Danish journalist and former press chief for the Conservative People's Party of the Danish Parliament. His political thriller *Solitaire* became the award-winning film *King's Game*, directed by Nikolaj Arcel. *Darklands*, the second volume in the series featuring journalist Ulrik Torp, is also being adapted for film.